D1594139

He Goes, She Goes

Also by Joanna Torrey

Hungry

He Goes, She Goes

joanna torrey

a novel

Crown Publishers
New York

Published by Crown Publishers, New York, New York.
Member of the Crown Publishing Group.

Random House, Inc. New York, Toronto,
London, Sydney, Auckland

www.randomhouse.com

Printed in the United States of America

Design by Elina D. Nudelman

Library of Congress Cataloging-in-Publication Data

Torrey, Joanna.
He goes, she goes / Joanna Torrey.
1. Fathers and daughters—Fiction. 2. Fathers—Death—Fiction. 3. Ballroom dancing—Fiction. 4. Young women—Fiction. I. Title.

PS3570.O738 H4 2001
813'.54—dc21

00-065930

ISBN 0-609-60123-7

10 9 8 7 6 5 4 3 2 1

First Edition

To my mother, Noreen

dying

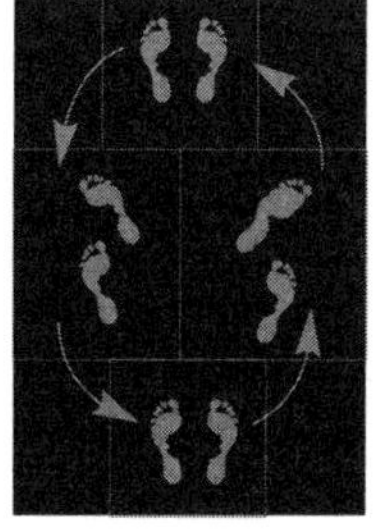

part one

one

My father is going to die today. I'm sitting on the bed next to him, leaning down, my forearm propped against his. Our palms are pressed together in a formal dance position. We stay this way for a weird eternity. If he weren't in a coma, I'd never dare do this. My father refused to dance at his own wedding. And all the years after that. My mother has never forgiven him.

In one of the first home movies my parents ever took, my father is standing inside a bright yellow wading pool with black whales on the sides, holding me above his head by the waist and spinning around. This is the closest we ever came to dancing together. He's wearing bathing trunks the same color as his skin. My arms are stretched out to either side in a reckless attempt at a nosedive, half plane crash, half drunken swan. As he holds me steadily under the stomach, I try to dip and swoon out of his grip, diving toward the camera, blurry with motion. I remember the feeling of that bathing suit—could I have been two? three?—the wet bumps of the blue ribbed cloth, the way it felt clammy against my stomach where his hand pressed.

My sister, Gwen, stands over to the side watching us, jumping up and down, occasion-

ally landing hard with both feet on one side of the wading pool, then the other, so that it melts into the grass, gushing water. In a flurry of motion, she splashes the lens, seizing my father's attention. He puts me down, moving me in a careful circus-act motion that I take full advantage of, stretching my legs and pointing my toes, reaching out my arms until my fingers extend toward my mother's hand, moving like the shadow of a bird just to the right of the camera.

I was not my father's favorite.

He deposits me by the side of the flattened wading pool and picks up Gwen. Hoisting her high around the back of his neck, he grimaces, adjusting first one of her legs, then the other around his neck so that they dangle down his chest. In the flickery movie light, the water and the dark hair on his chest run down as though he's standing behind glass. Gwen's arms circle the crown of his head. Her smile is triumphant, her teeth huge as a cartoon rabbit's.

Some thirty-five years later, here I am touching the white hair where it curls out of his pajama top, wondering how I can feel so angry at someone who's about to die. I grab a tuft and pull gently. His eyelids flicker but don't open. I try to remember the exact color of his eyes. Are they blue-green? More gray-blue? Ocean? Sky? How can I not know for certain? Because I never stared long enough into them? Did he know the color of my eyes? My finger hovers over his eyelid as I fight down panic. What if his eyes are rolled back in his head?

Go ahead. It's time to take liberties before it's too late.

I can't remember ever holding my father's hand before. I can hardly even remember him touching me, not really, at least not after I'd grown up a little. Now the experts call it good touch. I know what bad touch is. What is no touch? My father's hands are big and strong, even now, and filled with veins. They spoiled me, although only at a distance. I've stopped sleeping with men because they've had the wrong hands.

My mother first noticed my father's hands when they met on a fishing trip in Scotland soon after the war. My mother sat in the car the whole time, freezing, playing gin rummy on the backseat and drinking sips of whiskey from a flask and eating horehound drops while her friends waded around in the loch. At some point she wandered off along the bank to find a place to pee and my tall American father was there, almost handsome, standing knee-deep in the water. She noticed how big and red with cold his hands looked holding his fishing pole. She wanted to go right up to those big hands and start rubbing them. She stood watching him for a while. She knew he noticed her because he turned ever so slightly toward her so that she could see his profile. He definitely turned. She knew that much. She would remember that much the rest of her married life.

If she hadn't slipped and fallen down the bank, he would never have dropped his pole that way. He rescued her. She'd wet her pants when she fell, peed a good amount, but she didn't tell him that, just held her skirt in tight around her legs. Together they walked along the riverbank, searching. They found his fishing pole moored in the roots of a tree. He wrote her address on a pound note from his wallet. She didn't know it then, my mother says, but this was the most wild thing he would ever do.

"And the rest is the history of you," she says to me and my sister. "Be careful, because all it takes is a pair of nice hands and a little whiskey."

My boyfriend Jack's hands aren't my father's, but they're nice hands, more indoors than outdoors, with an intelligence around the knuckles and nails. Amazingly, Jack likes to fish, too, although he's happiest sitting on the end of a pier and staring out to sea. I don't think he's ever gone fly-fishing in his life. I take after my mother around fishing. I'd rather sit in the car and drink (although I prefer wine to whiskey), but I admit I've had a secret fantasy that my father and Jack would go fishing together. I see the two of them walking side by side carrying their poles, dressed in beige cotton jackets with stretchy waistbands and saggy pockets full of strange stuff. Talking. Not talking. Passing a thermos of coffee back and forth (of course not a beer). I can still taste the plastic cup, the way the coffee was so sweet when my father gave me a sip from his old metal thermos. Still dark outside, the ocean crashing, the cup so warm, the shivering disappearing. I think about my mother at home with Gwen, their lives bathed in yellow lamplight while I sit in cold blue morning with him. Neither my father nor Jack could talk about baseball, but they could have shared a silence. And in sharing a silence they would share me. Maybe Jack would teach my father to laugh and joke when he didn't catch a fish, instead of looking as though he was lost and would never find his way home.

"I didn't know women actually touched blood worms," Jack said the one time we fished together. I was afraid, but I'd picked one up anyway, curled it onto the hook, penetrating all the layers of the rusty horned thing the way my father had taught me, not letting the stinging matter. I threw the pole behind my shoulder and launched it recklessly out to sea, my father's careful lesson completely forgotten. Jack laughed when I reeled in absolutely nothing after a few minutes, the hook lost, a fragile wisp of sewing thread dangling in the wind.

"I'm trying for an old boot myself," he said.

He'd brought along a box of doughnuts and we ate them all, chewing around the holes and tossing the powdered-sugar circles like life rings off the pier. What would my father have thought of this waste? Sometimes wasting was fun and right.

The hospital bed looks so foreign in his study, the sheets white and crisp in a different way from home sheets, more bleached and synthetic. The head of the bed is tilted up slightly, which gives the illusion that he's about to slide off. I envision those planks they use to pitch dead bodies off the sides of ships.

Picking up his hand again, I cradle it, palm open. A car is coming up the drive. Probably it's Gabriel, the home hospice worker, arriving for his shift. His name is Joe, but we've decided his name should be Gabriel. He first arrived here two weeks ago, on the day we brought my father home from the hospital to die.

I shake myself, trying to pay attention. His palm is smooth and slightly yielding, the hair on the back of his fingers crinkly, with hints of softness. I stroke the paper skin, the small, scaly age spots. These I pick at automatically, trying to smooth them. I want to rub cream into them. Cream, that's all he needs! Turning his hand over, I stroke his palm rhythmically back and forth, then stop, remembering why the action feels so familiar. As kids, Gwen and I played a game we called Tarantula. We took turns paralyzing our hands by stroking each other's wrists and open palms in such a way that our fingers became numb. The numbness was supposed to have something to do with sex.

Holding hands with my father is like holding hands with a new lover at the movies. Together they feel huge and warm, a messy bouquet of fingers. I want urgently to pull away, but don't want to be the one to do it. I long for this intimacy to be already transformed into memory. *(Remember the time I held hands with Daddy for so long right before he died?)*

I'm the one to flex my fingers first, just slightly, and his hand drops to the bed. Quickly, I pick it back up again and cradle it, bring his open palm to my lips. He hated anything that was too emotional, even though once I caught him crying when he was listening to classical music on the radio. He pretended that he was wiping his whole face with his handkerchief. Why would he be sitting in his armchair in the living room and sweating as though he'd just mowed the lawn?

He would hate me kissing his hand this way.

He's lost so much weight. When he could still walk, he moved across the driveway, his neck a stalk propelling each movement forward, eyes fixed on the door knocker, a sickly bird heading for its final nest. I remember the day he put it up when I was little, the shiny brass against the green, the way I worried that the whole door would break, he pounded the nails in so hard, taking them one by one like long metal teeth from between his lips. He only let me use it once. I climbed the ladder halfway up and braced against him. The sound was deep and hollow and grown-up. "I'm coming," my mother called out, and bustled to the front door in her apron and acted surprised, going along with the game. My parents stood on the front porch arguing about whether it was crooked.

When I first heard the sounds of my father climbing into the hospital bed, the light metal of the bed's sides clattering down, then up, his helpless, mewy grunts, I had the sudden strong urge to polish the door knocker. I went into the kitchen and rummaged under the sink looking for Brasso. My mother and Gwen were afraid he would fall out of the bed like a kid. I knew he wouldn't.

My father always believed in single beds, narrow, monkish, tucked-in sheets, the bed for sleeping, holding the dreams of a man who had pushed everything away. Once as a kid I tried climbing into bed with him, creeping into his room and tiptoeing over quietly, bare toes cold and clenching the floor, breathing shallow. Just as I arrived at this perfect bedside, was pulling at the sheet to untuck it, already feeling the warmth inside, his eyes popped open. "Alice!" he barked. I gasped as he sat bolt upright, the sheets pulling out, his legs swinging over the side. No more soft breathing, his strong eyebrows pulled together in a frown, the tiny secret whistling inside his nose abruptly stopped. I kept standing there, staring at the creased places on the sheets in the middle where he'd lain, suddenly smooth as a skating rink at the edges, as though he'd been lying very still all night, thinking. I wondered if my mother could fit in next to him. I'd never seen them together in bed, my mother in the next room with all the softer things, the blankets piled at the foot, the quilts. "We don't sleep together because of our thermostats," she told us, and laughed. What did that mean, thermostats? "Your father burns like a furnace," she said when I asked her. She was like a refrigerator, always cold, her feet and her hands and the tip of her nose. She liked to keep the light on at night and read herself to sleep. The light bothered him.

But do you go into his room? I wanted to know. When do you go into his room?

"That's for me to know," she said, "Nosy Parker," pinching my nose.

Despite all this, I still wanted to climb up, to lie down beside him, to pull up the covers, to snuggle. My father guided me back to bed, walking slightly behind me, one big hand resting on my shoulder. He tucked me in, but we didn't snuggle. You didn't snuggle with Daddy.

May I snuggle now?

Gwen pokes her head around the study door and says in a loud stage whisper, "Alice, he's here, let's go." She doesn't even glance at Daddy. She's wearing big yellow dishwashing gloves. Gwen has been dying to escape all day, go for a drive, go for a drink. I think she's convinced herself that he isn't really dying. I figure my mother's already making Gabriel a cup of tea. My mother is English. Over the years Gwen and I have adopted her automatic response to any problem. This is to put the kettle on to boil and reach for the teapot. My father drank only coffee. My mother would mock him for his instant, stirring it and stirring it until she'd created a frothy head. "Your Nescafé," she'd say sarcastically, heavy on the French accent, handing it to him by the saucer's edge with exaggerated care as though she might drop it.

My mother and Gabriel walk into the study together without knocking. Her husband after all. She goes straight over to the windows and briskly pushes back both curtains, looks up and down the street like she's checking for traffic. Proximity to Gabriel has given her the status of efficient nurse.

Reluctantly, I let go of my father's hand and lay it gently back down on the bed. Of course, he doesn't notice when I get up and walk backward toward the window so that I'm standing out of the way, perched on the sill. I'm not ready yet, I want to tell them, I need more time.

Time for what?

Gabriel takes my place next to the bed and folds down the blanket, then the sheet. As usual he has on faded blue jeans and a matching, tucked-in work shirt with the collar neatly cut off. This is his uniform. He always smells faintly of patchouli, as though the oil has embedded itself in the pores of his skin and clothes and become his own smell. He wears a frayed woven cotton band tied around one wrist. His blond hair is pulled back in a ponytail. Gwen cuts hair for a living, and I see her studying him sometimes with a familiar hunger in her eyes. No more haircuts for my father. For the past ten years he allowed her to cut his hair, sitting in the kitchen or in the backyard with a tea towel draped across his shoulders, although he never took off his shirt. I have to admit I was jealous. He even let her shave his neck with those little electric clippers. She'd pull his ears forward and stoop low, breathing right on his neck, almost crossing her eyes in concentration, as though he were just another customer. I'd watch sometimes, but always at a distance.

I can hear Gwen in the kitchen, still clattering dishes, the water running. She can't stand being around our father like this. She makes a big show of being busy whenever there's something important and scary that has to be done for him. "Do I look like a nurse?" she asks. We've all stopped trying to persuade her that she'll regret this one day.

Gwen was never scared of our father. She's a year older than I am. From the day she was born, my mother says, she clambered fearlessly onto his lap. She did this until she was too big to fit. She picked up his hand and played with his fingers, braiding them and then shaking his wrist to untangle them again. Sometimes she called him Pop, as though she was a kid on a TV show about the rural South and he was a farmer wearing overalls who would call his daughter Pumpkin or Sam. When she threw up at night, she would call for him, not my mother, and he would hold his big hand on her forehead and look over her shoulder into the toilet at her vomit. She didn't seem to mind that he saw the ugliness in her.

I tried to imitate the way she was around him, but it never worked. "Daddy-o," I said to him once, playing around after I'd seen a television show. He looked up at me with no expression at all, as if he was hiding how silly he thought I was. I felt my face and neck burst into hives.

When Gwen and I were thirteen and fourteen, we climbed a mountain with our father. At the summit she threw her arms around his neck and said, "We made it!" as though we were *National Geographic* explorers. He put his arms awkwardly around her bulky jacket and tucked his head into her collar. I crowded up behind her, wanting to take my turn on the tail of hers, to squeeze through the open door before it slammed shut. He raised his head and stared off at the mountains and put his binoculars to his eyes and spent a long time adjusting them.

Finally he handed me the binoculars. "Look over there," he said, pointing. I put them up to my eyes and deliberately didn't look far ahead to the mountains, but only at the inside of the binoculars, the edges of the round holes and the narrow, fuzzy lenses. I made some high, crowing noises as though I was amazed and pleased at the great view, but really I was looking at nothing.

I remember wanting us all to take our clothes off, strip out of the bulky layers, my jacket and sweater and outer shirt, down to my flat new bra and little-girl underpants. So much so that I began to unzip my jacket. I wanted to stand there feeling the cold air on my body, the hairs everywhere standing up in the wind. I longed for my father to open his jacket and rip open his shirt, to see his white skin and to watch him shiver and cradle his arms together, then seek out his daughters for warmth.

I imagined the scouting party finding us huddled this way, frozen and covered in a coating of ice, our lips blue and open in conversation.

Late-afternoon sun shines through the curtains of my father's study, making our task surreal. My mother is on one side of Gabriel, I'm on the other. We flank him, assistants of the Archangel, learning our drug detail.

"Alice, come on!" Gwen's voice from the other room sounds high, manic. I don't answer. Outside the sky is wintry, with pale streaks of blue. I'm thinking about lighting a fire next door in the living room. Years ago my father taught me how to drag safety matches one after another against the brick fireplace until it was covered in long white scratches like sunburned skin. The matches kept breaking. He crouched behind me and put his arms around me. He placed his hand over mine, his finger pressed along my finger onto the head of the match. I saw our fingers going up in flames, fused and charred. He insisted I keep going, not give up, until I cried and then finally there was a fire.

Gabriel rolls my father over and pulls down the blanket, then the pajama bottoms, as though he's about to spank him. His skin there is startling, white and smooth, the expanse of a young girl's forehead. I want to reach out, to stroke his skin, to feel its lack of heat, make sure that he's still alive. My mother leans over him. The expression on her face is interested. She's not cold, I tell myself, only detached because she must be. Next to my father's ghostly skin, Gabriel's hands look suddenly huge and masculine and tanned, as though he works for the phone company, laying cable.

"Gently, gently," he instructs, taking the yellow morphine egg and hiding it up inside the broken cave of my father's body. He does this with a delicate, appreciative look on his face, staring into the distance. He makes a faint murmuring sound of satisfaction. I reach out and touch his forearm, certain that he has indicated with his eyes that I should do this. I can feel the pincer movements of the bones and ligaments in his arm. Gabriel gestures for my mother to do the same. She moves forward, blushing. She's always said that blushing ruined her life, and her mother's before that, and that it was my turn, and she's sorry, and now here she is at the end of her husband's life, still blushing.

The day I came home crying because the whole class snickered at me for turning so red, she grabbed my head in both of her arms in an elbow lock and brought it to her breasts and just held it there and squeezed it tight, as though gathering all the offending blood she could in one place. I imagined her cutting open the top of my head and letting out the blood that had ruined everything for both of us. Dancing, she told me, was the first time she could move in public and not blush.

I place my hand on top of my mother's and together, our hands layered this way, as though I'm leading her in a waltz, we lower them to settle on my father's skin, so pale it burns.

Gwen is standing at the door to my father's study, afraid to come in. She has her jacket on, the collar turned up as though it's cold, her hands shoved in the pockets. Gabriel gestures for her to come closer. Tentatively, as if approaching a drugged tiger, she moves toward the bed. My mother is standing a little aside, her arms crossed in front of her chest. She's still wearing her apron and has her timer tied around her waist. All our lives, the timer has gone off at odd moments. The minute steak? The spin-dry cycle? The grim reaper?

Gwen strokes his forehead and then the sides of his face, making a sound that's part hum, part coo. "Daddy?" she says, so girlish and hopeful. Then she goes to stand near Gabriel, leaning into him unnecessarily close, her hair falling over her face.

Deathbed romance. The words form in my head like poisoned chocolates. Gwen always does this. Even here, even now, I feel so secondary.

Gabriel has turned the bedclothes down so that my father's upper body is showing. His arms are no longer trapped inside the covers, his tangled chest hair still growing out of his pajamas in a viney fur. The stubble on his chin is shadowy and rough, with unfamiliar glints of soldierly gray. His face looks handsome, chiseled. His breathing is raw and rasping, eyes lidded, half open, the color just barely there.

Bracing his flopping neck with one hand, I fix my mother's special pillows under his head. His whole life, he denied himself sweet oblivion, and now here he is at the end, a goose-down king.

He begins hiccuping in a grotesque, almost comical way. My father would never make sounds like this. Gwen covers her ears, then turns and leaves the room. I wonder if Gabriel's thoughts have left with her, but he's looking down at my father, his eyes soft. Moving up close, I lean into Gabriel, breathing in his scent. At the same time, I reach past him and pick up my father's hand. He begins to bark, a sudden harsh seal's cough. Gabriel pulls the sheet even lower, almost to his knees.

Two nights before, my father propped himself up in bed and we took pictures. We joked about "red devil's camera eye." His neck was a narrow stalk, but for a dying man the color around his cheeks and chest-V was still strangely ruddy. Each day one of us remarks on this good high color that looks so normal, even though the shape of his head is smaller, simultaneously younger and older, his smile newly impish and sometimes frightened, eyes welling with tears.

We beckoned Gabriel to join the pictures. He smoothed his ponytail back and stuffed his shirt deep into his jeans, pushed in tentatively next to me. I placed my arm around his shoulder and pulled him in, the way you do for pictures.

"Smile," said Gwen, then she paused, lowering the camera.

Even through the eye of the camera, this embrace had not gone unnoticed. I loosened my grip slightly around Gabriel and let my hand slip down to his waist, unseen. I hooked one finger in the loop of his jeans, rested my other hand on my father's shoulder, the way they used to in old-fashioned portraits. Deliberately, she raised the camera again and took the pictures quickly, one, then another, and then it was over. Gabriel glided away as though he had sensed the controversy. His faint patchouli lingered on my hand all that day, a smell as pungently alive as I imagined peat moss would be. I kept sniffing my fingers.

Following Gabriel's instructions, we each place a hand on my father's body, then, bolder, another, anywhere: an arm, his forehead, a foot, his toes sticking up. I choose his legs, the big hard calves I can feel through the blankets like solid rubber balls. I squeeze them once, then again, harder, wanting him to sit up and yell out in pain. Gwen used to wake up in the middle of the night with leg cramps that rose like trapped animals burrowing under her skin. I want to give him those youthful, blood-filled cramps. Good strong pain will bring him back. But he just lies there, breathing roughly in and out.

I used to come home from school every afternoon when I was thirteen and put records on and dance in this room. The old stereo is still here in his study, gathering dust. He rarely listened to music, only the news, but here he could keep an eye on it. According to our mother, before they got married, he used to love music. They'd go to band concerts and sit on the grass with their legs stretched out and she'd lean against his shoulder and he'd conduct with his big feet sticking up at the edge of the blanket. They had a good time, even though she wanted to be drinking wine or brandy, something, and they only drank root beer. But still, they had a good time.

I turned the music way up when my father wasn't home. First

I pushed back the desk, then his recliner, until I'd made a clearing in the middle. My mother didn't mind. Sometimes she came in and stood there watching me, swaying to the music with her apron on, eyes closed. I wanted her to go away. I'd hold the album cover out in front of me with both hands and look at it as I danced. It was a pale, high-cloud blue, with a picture on the front of a man in a billowy shirt leaning against a blue Mustang. My hips moved in circles around and around, front, side, back, side. I stared into the singer's eyes and mouthed the words. *Everybody needs somebody to love.*

One afternoon, as I danced, I grew very warm. My sweater was already hanging on the back of his chair. I unbuttoned my shirt, letting it flap open. My slip clung to my stomach, where inside the music unfurled. This feeling was too big and warm, filling my body. Underneath the music, the study was so still and quiet it seemed to shrink and grow darker and browner. I closed my eyes, threw my head back, and cupped my hands at the back of my head, elbows straight out so that my newly sprouted breasts stretched with an aching, tugging feeling. I sucked in air and let it out in a rush. My hips circled and circled. All that was impossible seemed possible. Dancing could make you feel this.

I didn't hear the front door opening, my father placing his hat on the front-hall table. Later I would imagine him standing there for a moment and flipping through the mail, raising his head in the direction of his study and frowning, walking deliberately down the hall toward me. I'd turned the stereo up as high as it could go. It was never supposed to be raised above a certain level, marked on the console with a piece of masking tape. I was breathing hard, enjoying the light sweat under my arms and along my upper lip. The change in the air, the way it filled with electricity before a thunderstorm, made me look up. He was standing in the doorway in his overcoat, still holding his briefcase, watching me. I had no idea what he was thinking.

Wheeling to face the stereo, my back to him, I clutched both sides of my shirt to my chest, willing the music to stop. My heart was pounding as though he'd found me naked. I turned the volume down below the marker. "Hi, Daddy," I said, not looking back at him. "I was just dancing."

He kept standing there as I fumbled with my clothes. His eyes burned through my shirt and my slip and straight into my back. I managed to do up a few buttons on my shirt. I wanted to grab him by both hands, draw him into his study still wearing his dark raincoat, and make him dance with me right there. I wanted him to be a different father.

He turned away. His tread was heavy on the stairs, as though he was trudging along with an army that had been given orders to move on.

I started dancing again, but the warm, possible thing inside me had curled right back up, the way a worm folds up when you touch its middle with a stick.

His breath stops abruptly on the inhale. The silence is so complete, I can tell we're all holding our breath along with him. We look at Gabriel for some kind of sign, but he's leaning into my father's chest, listening. We all just stand there. His calves under my hand are still hard and springy. I remember them at the beach, blue-white and shockingly a man's legs when he rolled up his pants. I squeeze them, once, twice, three times, as though this will start his heart pumping again. Gwen is crying, making little snuffly noises and wiping her nose on the sleeve of her jacket. My mother is looking down at him with a puzzled look on her face, as though she's waiting for the answer to a question. She's not touching him. She's holding her timer in one hand, muffling it completely as if it might go off by mistake and wake him.

Finally, reluctantly, I let out my breath. How can he not breathe out? His breathing in had sounded almost hopeful, like the beginning of something. I'm worried he didn't get to the end. I have the urge to crawl onto the hospital bed, to lie on top of him, to cover his dry lips with mine and just breathe.

Gabriel is the first to move. I'm waiting for him to do something theatrically tender, close my father's eyelids, which are already closed (I'll never now see the true color of his eyes again), or pull up the sheet. But Gabriel simply pats my mother on the back, squeezes her shoulder. Then he walks toward the door with his head bent, his hands clasped behind him. I wonder if they're trained to walk away like this, like priests, after someone has died.

Gwen follows him out of the study, her hands in her pockets again, the collar of her jacket turned up. She looks back over her shoulder at me, not at our father, her eyes red. She shrugs, then points at our mother as though to say, *You* take care of her.

I question my mother with my eyebrows, whether I should leave or stay. It seems wrong to speak. I want them to have had the kind of marriage where she needs to say good-bye alone. She shakes her head, no.

My mother and I join hands over him. For just a moment, a turn pattern flutters through my head. I have the urge to spin her and spin her, make my mother laugh. As though we've done this in our thoughts, our arms float back down to the bed.

I put my hand on his forehead. His skin already radiates coolness. I bend and rest my forehead on his chest, a blush rising in me at this romantic gesture. My mother places her hand on the back of my head. I press deeper into his chest so that his protruding breastbone pushes at my mouth and nose, and inhale deeply. His skin smells like bread dough. She pushes down harder. What does she want?

"I don't know if he was ever happy," she says from behind me, stroking my hair.

two

Gwen backs out of the driveway, turns the wheel violently, and steps on the gas. The tires squeal. We haven't put on seat belts. I remember the way my father would study Gwen's face when she asked to borrow the car, unafraid to chart the map of his own blood there. I would watch them sideways, wanting him to turn to me. For some reason he trusted her, but I looked too much like my mother. He thought my mother drove way too fast and didn't pay attention. She thought seat belts belonged in airplanes.

I turn back, expecting to see him still standing there at the front door, frowning, his newspaper down at his side, his hand shading his forehead. He always did this, as though he was looking out to sea, reading the fishing conditions for the next morning. I lean back far enough in the seat that Gwen can't see, and wave at the empty doorway.

Although I think Gwen wanted him to come out with us, Gabriel has promised to sit with my mother for a while. He has paperwork to complete, forms for her to sign. Our father has been dead for just two hours. Gwen can no longer sit still. I'm worried about letting her go off in the car alone.

Without consulting me, she drives to Mario's, a restaurant just outside town. She pulls into the parking lot and stops with a jerk so that we both lunge forward toward the windshield. How can she be hungry? I know we're both thirsty. I keep thinking of my mother sitting at home in the living room, still holding her timer, although when we left she was already busy in the kitchen, putting the kettle on to boil. "Let's have a nice cup of tea!" I heard her say to Gabriel as we left. Death has never before come, and here it has arrived, so familiar after all. The domestic wheels click through the house and grief settles sideways, finding places to slide into.

Mario buys us our first carafe of watery Bardolino. He doesn't know that we grew up nearby. Just thinks we're sisters who show up once in a while and order food as an excuse to drink house wine. My father didn't like going out to restaurants.

They chill the red wine here, so it tastes like grape juice and it's easy to gulp one small, straight-sided glass after another, in between pieces of bread. My father never once drank wine in his whole life, not even in church. What that means about his body, and why it is that he's now dead while we're sitting here drawing on our place mats with the house crayons, I don't know.

We pick at our food. Gwen is play-acting the Italian princess, letting Mario kiss her hand, lounging in the red booth and throwing her hair back, kissing her fingers into the air with fake ecstasy at the soupy fettucine Alfredo and garlic powdered/margarined/reconstituted parsleyed garlic bread. "Bellissimo!" she says. She doesn't tell him that Daddy's dead.

There's a tiny raised dance floor between the tables. I want to be wearing a lacy dress and dancing with my mob-boss father, who has put aside big decisions in order to dance with his daughter. I've always wanted to have the kind of father you see on TV who takes his daughter on his lap and comforts her about the scrapes and the rapes. The kind who comes out into the hall and tells the boy not to try any funny business, to get her home on time.

Mario slides into the booth next to Gwen and puts an arm around her. She leans her face into the shoulder of his black satin vest and laughs at something he's whispering. He picks up her fork, expertly wraps a few strands of fettucine, and holds it to her mouth. She shakes her head in protest and then finally opens and swallows and says, "Mmmm," rolling her black-rimmed eyes at me. She's given her hair a new set of highlights. They make her look young and patchy, like a molting leopard cub. Mario keeps glancing down at her breasts.

When we've finished picking at our food, downing two carafes of wine between us, Gwen asks that the fettucine and a sodden piece of tiramisu, layered and gray as a chunk of cement wall, be wrapped. I can't imagine these leftovers in the same house where my father has lost his appetite, then his life.

Gwen hangs behind at the door and talks with Mario while I wait in the car. They're both waving their hands, Gwen more Italian than he is. She hands him her card. She's probably offering him a free haircut. She does that. Gives away her professional services when she has no idea how else to tame a situation. Come in for a free haircut! Most people do. Hopefully she's not agreeing to go out with him. Going out with married men is our shared habit of the past.

I lean over into the driver's seat and press the horn. The parking lot is almost empty. Gwen doesn't look my way, but Mario does. I beckon, and then he says something to Gwen, who turns back to me, nods in my direction, then raises the cluster of doggy bags and shakes them at me in a silent rustle. "I'm coming," she mouths. Even her mouthing is slurred.

When she gets into the car she's holding a big ragged corner of the paper tablecloth that she's torn off, covered in our scribbles. She folds it into a smaller and smaller square, pressing the creases against her knee, until the tablecloth is the size of a cigarette pack, then reaches across my lap and puts it in the glove compartment. I catch a whiff of wine and crayons.

"A memento?" I ask. We'd worn the crayons down and had to keep peeling the paper back, our scribbling and cross-hatching so thick it tore through to the linen cloth underneath.

"You know I'm superstitious," she says, not looking at me. She turns on the overhead light and puts lipstick on, coming so close to the rearview mirror that her lips fog the glass. She pulls out of the parking lot too fast.

There's a new women's bar in town, and this is where Gwen drives us next. "For a nightcap," she says. I've never heard her use this word before. It sounds like something our mother would say.

Gwen goes straight to the bar and orders a Scotch. She doesn't drink Scotch. She doesn't sleep with women. I wonder why we're here. I want to go home. I imagine our father still sitting there at his desk when we get back, studying one of his fishing flies through the dentist's magnifying headpiece he found at a flea market. He'll look up at us with one enormous, all-seeing eye, and then down again, an almost imperceptible disapproving look on his face. Everything will be just the way it was.

If Jack were here he'd be making Gwen and me talk about it. He'd sit us down at the bar with our drinks and raise his voice over the lousy country ballad on the jukebox. He'd conduct one of his impromptu encounter groups, embarrassing us. Although I'm glad he's not here, I do miss him. He'd pull off my shoe and rub my arch and massage my pressure points until I started to cry.

I hang back, not yet ordering a drink, trying to make up my mind whether to leave. I could call a taxi, or take the bus home. Where's home? I keep trying to imagine where my father's body is. I picture him at the local funeral parlor, lying lonely and pale and cold. Covered. In a drawer? His big hands frozen into a final shape.

A woman young enough to be Gwen's daughter is standing at the bar next to her. She's wearing a man's ribbed undershirt tucked into baggy pants cinched with a leather belt. Her hair is cut short on one side and practically shaved on the other, giving it the shape of one of those old-fashioned bathing caps adorned with a layered rubber gardenia. Maybe it's one of my sister's razor specials.

Gwen started cutting my hair when we were in junior high school. I'd undress down to my underpants and she'd drape a professional plastic cape around my shoulders. The smell of plastic still reminds me of those basement shearings. She would start off slowly, tenderly, bending each of my ears forward as though searching for bees behind flower petals. The air felt gradually cooler as my hair grew shorter and thinner, my scalp more exposed. I would watch her in the mirror as she leaned in close, her expression intense.

She taught herself how to cut hair by studying a library book. She sent for a hair-cutting gadget along with a cape and an instructional video through a mail-order catalog for beauticians. The gadget was a doubled-edged razor blade tucked inside a pink plastic comb. The blade gleamed through the teeth. From the top of the part she scraped the gadget down in a repetitive combing motion. Out came clumps of hair piled in the teeth like grass in a mower. Briskly, she pulled the clumps off with her fingers and fluttered them down to the floor, always behind me so I couldn't see. She would shake her own thick hair back when it fell into her eyes.

"I think that's short enough," I'd say, gesturing helplessly up by my neck. "Relax, I know what I'm doing," she'd say, batting away my hand.

Afterward she would sweep, the broom propped in readiness against the wall. "Let me do it," I'd say, eager to see the damage myself, maybe even keep the hair. Gwen, the good nurse, had already whisked it away. Six weeks later, like clockwork, she would fix me with a look at breakfast, her eyes rising to study my bangs. My stomach would lurch and settle uneasily. When she was through with me, I always looked as though I'd had brain surgery.

Once I took a double piece of bubble gum from my mouth. It was chewed thin and slick as a balloon. I hid it between my fingers and stood behind Gwen as she sat in an armchair, reading. Plunging the gum into her shoulder-length hair, I smeared it in. At first Gwen didn't react. Continuing to read, she reached behind her head slowly, humming, and fingered the sticky clump. She let it hang there all through dinner, deliberately turning her head so our parents couldn't see. Later that night, she stood in front of the bathroom mirror, cutting her hair in meticulous sections, evening it out until it fell in a short blunt cut to her chin. She left the door open so I could watch. She'd already chopped her hair off once when she was a kid.

For years my father read to us, allowing us at the same time to rub my mother's cold cream into his bald spot. Gwen and I perched on opposite arms of his chair and took turns stroking the tiny dry patches that had formed from too much sun. Sometimes we'd get cream in his wisps of hair by mistake, and we'd look at each other over his head, trying not to laugh. When his reading slowed, his words slurred as he started to fall asleep, and we would make our rubbing more vigorous, trying to keep him awake. The top of his head was one of the only places on his body I remember being allowed to touch. He always marked his place in the book the same way, one finger centered on a word. We chose the books we knew he liked, the ones about courageous animals or children getting lost in the jungle. If his finger drifted to cover a word, we knew he was asleep. One of the reasons we liked reading so much was we weren't afraid of him this way. Gwen got so used to playing with his hair, it was a natural next step to begin cutting it a few years later.

From across the bar, I watch Gwen and the woman talking. Gwen is in full-throttle flirting mode, pressing a bottle of beer between her breasts. Turning, they both wave at me as though I'm moving away on a train. Arms touching, they go to the pool table. I'm jealous of the giddy tension that radiates off Gwen. An image hovers and recedes, of my mother tossing her hair back, touching a melting ice cube to my father's dry lips. I want to be at Mario's, still guzzling house wine.

I think again about calling Jack. He'll be up working late. He won't notice that the curtains are wide open so that the flat black night is right there crowding at his desk. The way I'm picturing him, he's hunched over his computer, staring into it, hardly blinking. His ability to focus so completely is one of the things I admire about him. But tonight I can't risk such a gamble. I get halfway to the pay phone, then turn around and return to my bar stool.

Inexplicably, the only thing that remains clear and brilliantly focused right now is the studio where I took dance classes for a while. In my mind, an overhead spotlight shines, illuminating Carlos, my dance teacher. His slicked, black hair gleams. He's wearing a bright red silk shirt. He's holding out his hand, beckoning me.

Overnight my life in New York has become someone else's. I can hardly even remember how Jack looks or smells or the sound of his voice. I have no idea if I will have a job when I return. Office floaters can so easily float right out of the picture. I know my father could never understand why I chose this ghostly job. A bank swallowed up his life. As kids Gwen and I never figured out what it was he actually did, except that it involved a briefcase full of papers covered in neat writing, and tiny notebooks filled with columns of numbers, and the occasional early-morning phone call from home, and that it gave him headaches for which he wouldn't even take a whole aspirin. "Mr. Half-a-Bayer," my mother would call him, and give him this funny look with her head to the side, one eyebrow raised.

Sometimes now I work for men who could be my father. Men who are cool and steady and quiet, and whose fingertips ripple over the keys of their calculators as though they're playing the piano. I walk to my assigned desk each morning, carrying my pens and Visine and private Kleenex supply and bottle of water in a shoe box under my arm as though I'm a cabdriver. I work for a day or a week or a month, then I move on. Sometimes I tried to imagine what my father was doing at that exact moment in his office: sipping coffee, taking orders, sharpening pencils, picking up the phone, staring out the window. Did my father ever daydream? We never saw his office. "Not for kids," he said. Gwen and I wondered if he had a framed picture of us and our mother on his desk, separate ones, or maybe a group shot of us all smiling. We wondered if his office even existed.

"Everyone needs an anchor," my father said to me recently. I figured out later that he was probably already sick. Impossible to explain to him that I needed this kind of free-fall life, daily anonymity with a bungee cord attached.

Thea, my neighbor next door, keeps offering me a job in the catering company she operates out of her apartment. For the past couple of years when one of her regular prep cooks has called in sick, I've run next door at the last minute and helped her wash thirty heads of Bibb lettuce or hack up a hundred raw chicken breasts. I've even assembled a black-and-white outfit and helped serve at a couple of big weddings. But floating at the edge of all those rites of passage depresses me.

Sometimes, at my request, Thea will pay me in belly-dancing lessons, not cash. Belly dancing never panned out for her as a career, so now she just throws it into a catering package once in a while for a bachelor or retirement party. I like the clattery sound of finger cymbals and her collection of bras hand-embroidered with beads and sequins and matching trains of diaphanous silk. She shows me how to tuck and drape them into an elaborate skirt, first around her own fleshy, tanned midriff, then my paler, less undulating one. She says I don't really have the belly for it. She straps the little brass cymbals to my thumbs and middle fingers and explains how to move fingers and wrists to coax out the delicate sound. She's given me a set to practice with.

Afterward we sit around and talk. She always has elegant nibbles in her fridge, cold sake and seaweed rolls. She'll complain about her boyfriends, generally small men with tragic, bloodshot eyes rimmed with eggplant-colored circles who stand out in our hall half the night knocking low and continuously on her door, muttering in hoarse, urgent whispers. Once I found a pile of shredded cigarettes outside her door, as though a rite of exorcism had taken place.

"Why don't you and Jack move in together?" she said one night when I came over to tell her that my father was dying, and would she feed my cat, Herbert, for a while. "You should move in together, and come and work for me, start a real life," she said. We sat together at her kitchen table, swigging warm Chardonnay straight from the bottle. I was helping her arrange baby's breath and rosemary in bud vases for a wedding the next day.

"This has to be a secret witch's curse," I said, twisting the stems together in a maypole.

"Bad sex?" she said. And laughed and laughed. Her laugh is exactly the same as my mother's.

Gwen and the pool shark are finally playing pool. I order a vodka gimlet, imagining the wine and vodka making a terrifying science experiment inside my body. The bartender reaches for a stubby, uninspired juice glass.

"Don't you have a martini glass?" I ask. It seems important tonight, on the night my father has died, to have the right glass.

She disappears into the back room and returns with a modest V-shaped one covered in dust. Baptizing it vigorously in the sink, she holds it up for my inspection.

"Perfect," I say.

Piling up the ice cubes with sarcastic ritual, she fills the glass with ice cubes and water and sets it on the bar to chill. She swoops down with the bottle, then up again, pumping out the perfect amount of vodka, barely splashing. I try to pick up the glass and the drink spills over the side. Leaning down, my neck feeling taut and breakable, I pucker my lips forward and take one whispering sip, then another. "Cheers," I whisper, my mouth hovering at the edge of the pool. It's the drink Gwen and I usually choose because it's supposed to be undetectable on the breath. My father never tasted vodka, never knew its sweet medicinal subterfuge.

Gwen is practically lying on the pool table to shoot. The woman stands behind her, bending over the length of her body, just barely to one side, showing her how to hold the cue. Gwen pokes at the wrong-colored ball and shrieks as it leaps into the air and bounces down in a series of hollow jumps. She's already drunk.

The other woman is a very good player. Her movements are fluid and deadly calm under the bright green triangle of lighting. Pale and without lipstick, her lips blend into the planes of her cheekbones. I think about Gabriel, of leaning my head into his shoulder, of running my hand up the inside seam of his jeans.

After one gimlet, my tongue is bumpy from the lime juice. The bartender deliberately overpours the second one, straining the spill into one of the stubby glasses. Tucking it under the bar as though it's lodged right alongside a gun, she winks at me.

"You two live in the neighborhood?"

"Our mother and father do."

Their game over, Gwen and the woman are sitting on separate arms of the same chair, talking with the sincere rapture of serious drinkers, passing a beer back and forth. My sister is feeding her the leftovers from one of the doggy bags with a plastic fork. Gwen comes up behind me at the bar and snakes both arms around my neck and plants a wet kiss right on my nape. Her cold, yeasty mouth gives me goose bumps up and down my arms. Her breath smells of beer and tomato sauce.

"I'm going to call Mom," she says, waving at the pay phone in the back. "Alice, talk to Minnesota Slim here." Gwen places the woman right in front of me, her hands on her hips, as though she's presenting me with a gift, and turns away, giggling. I want to ask her what she's going to say to our mother, but decide to keep quiet. Gwen has always been the family expert in brinkmanship. For a while she was obsessed with trying to trick our mother into blushing because it seemed to animate our father. The obvious way to do this, she thought, was to talk about sex during dinner. She would start by clearing her throat and edging her body closer to the dining table, her hard, pointed breasts almost resting on the rim of her plate across from me, her hands folded innocently under her chin. She was wired differently and didn't really understand the blushing curse. She seemed to take after our father, lit by a small internal lamp with an unwavering yellow-green flame.

"These girls found a used sanitary napkin in gym class," Gwen pronounced once at dinner. She looked brightly at each of us, around the circle a few times, finally stopping at my mother. My parents kept their eyes lowered, kept chewing. I put my fork down.

"Someone had a miscarriage," Gwen continued lightly, mashing a potato puff on the back of hers. My mother arranged her knife and fork so they were neatly parallel on either side of her plate. The air in the room was still and chilled, as if it were suspended inside the refrigerator. I wanted this to turn into a fight; for my mother and father to stand up and yell at Gwen; for someone to throw a plate on the floor, to screech back in the chair and make lots of noise.

"Would you like seconds, dear?" My mother looked straight ahead to where my father sat at the end of the table. She picked up a serving fork and held it poised over the bowl of boiled potatoes as though she planned to stab one. Her cheeks were faintly pink. My father leaned back, running his tongue over his teeth.

"No thank you," he said. "It was delicious, dear."

The word *miscarriage* hung in the air like a black balloon. I wanted to reach up and burst it with both hands. I could see the gray metal walls of the gym stalls, shreds of skin and blood dripping from the bench. Why hadn't Gwen told me this when we were alone? She looked at me triumphantly.

My father pushed his chair back with a loud scrape, dabbing his lips with his napkin. "I think I'll have dessert in the living room," he said. This meant my mother would bring it to him on a tray with a spoon and he would sit and eat it while listening to the radio, the tray balanced across his armchair as though he were a baby in a high chair.

I cleared his plate, first plucking his napkin off and folding it neatly into thirds, even though it was covered in roast beef blood. I wanted to put it this way into the sideboard, undiscovered and shocking, but my mother would know I had done it. Instead I touched it to my mouth, tickling my lips with the crusty dried blood.

Gwen was still sitting in the dining room. She leaned back, her hands folded on the tablecloth in front of her. In the living room I could hear my parents murmuring in the low, halting way they had. I sat down across from her.

"Who had the miscarriage?" I asked.

"No one you know," she said. "A senior."

While I was out of the dining room, Gwen had retrieved the ancient photograph album from the sideboard and was sitting there, flipping through the brittle pages. We would both study these dingy pictures for hours. I especially liked the ones of my father and his younger brother, the one who was killed in a car accident a long time ago. The subject of my father's brother was off limits. There were only two pictures in the album, showing the two boys fishing together, standing in the middle of the stream wearing hip boots, holding a prize trout high in the air. Each clutched at the same line as they stared, sullen and sepia-faced, into the camera. How strange, I always thought, to see my father with no shirt on, the two brothers, at nine and ten, with identical bony, inward-caving chests and khaki pants tucked into waders, the stream frothing creamy around their knees. I liked to imagine that I had stood behind the camera myself, entering the forbidden landscape of my father's past.

My mother would lean over Gwen's shoulder as she looked at the album, pressing her breasts into the back of her head, pointing out her favorite pictures with her finger damp and swollen from cooking and washing dishes. "That's Rafe." She pointed to one of the photographs of herself in her WAAF uniform. She was standing next to the wing of a plane with an officer, and they were both wearing caps and she had on a trench coat that was blowing open and back. The collar was turned up and she was wearing dark lipstick that made her mouth look like a bow. She was smiling, looking up at him so that the dimple in her chin and her cheek showed. He looked down at her as though he was in love with her. She says she never took any of them seriously, any men seriously, they were such fools over her. They both looked like old-time movie stars. It was hard for us to accept that this was our mother.

I liked to imagine what happened immediately after that picture was taken, as though it were a movie. The smiles fading, she would turn and embrace him around his belted raincoat. She would kiss him, his mustache tasting of tart citrus aftershave. They would walk hand in hand away from the airplane, Rafe patting the wing with one neatly manicured hand. He would place the other hand around my mother's waist. She told us once that he had wanted to marry her (even though he was already married), but that things had been different during the war. What you looked for in a man wasn't necessarily the same, she would say. He was such a wonderful dancer, but not husband material. Definitely not husband material.

They would go back to her room, and she would be wearing a black slip under her uniform, and she'd smoke a cigarette without a filter, leaving a dark lipstick print, and later he would take her dancing and they would drink champagne.

"I hear your father's sick, Alice," the lady pool shark says. Her forehead's puckered. She tucks the long side of her hair behind all those earrings. "I'm so sorry."

"Actually, he's dead," I say. "Didn't Gwen tell you?"

She looks at me mournfully, as though she's already heard all the terrible things there are to know about me.

"How is your sister doing?" The way she says this makes me think she thinks Gwen shouldn't be out playing pool. I figure it's none of her business.

"Gwen loved him as much as I did, more maybe," I say. Why is it that talking about love always sounds so fake?

When Gwen comes back, she squeezes between us like a kid between her parents. "We should go," she says. She gives me a big beery smack on my mouth and then turns and does the same to the pool shark. I wipe the kiss off with a bar napkin, leaving my lipstick smeared across it. The woman does the same with the back of her hand, only without the lipstick, when she thinks my sister isn't looking. I pay our bill and leave a big tip. I don't bother counting what's left.

"Mom wants us to stop on the way home and buy a bottle of wine," says Gwen. "We can stop at that place near the highway. It's open until eleven." Completely ignoring the pool shark, she pushes the door of the bar open with her shoulder and walks out without looking back, as though she's leaving a body behind her on the saloon floor.

three

We both smell baking bread at the same time. No matter what time the yeast calls, my mother answers. The bready warmth stops our laughter short.

Tiptoeing into the kitchen, we crash into either side of the door, getting stuck. I press my fingers hard against the crotch of my jeans. "Shush," Gwen keeps saying, then, "Hush, you lush!" We pinch our noses, giggling. The bottle of red wine stays safely wedged under her arm. I'm not as drunk as Gwen, but pretending in order to keep up the giddy laughter. Our guilt has disappeared somewhere back in the bar.

My mother is standing at the kitchen sink still wearing her apron. Gabriel is sitting at the table. Her back is turned toward him, as though they're in the silent stage of fighting. Her hair looks grayer than normal, a matted cushion of flat, wild curls. One of her best china bread-and-butter plates glows on a place mat in front of him, a special bone-handled bread knife alongside. A teapot bundled in a knitted tea cozy sits in the middle of the table as though it's the exact hour for high tea. Next to these things, so perfect and ordinary, is a pint of brandy. I feel Gwen stiffen. My mother always kept a bottle in the bottom of her bureau, buried beneath sweaters. Gwen and I came upon it one day while exploring. We twisted off the cap and each took a swig, gagging at the raw, syrupy taste. This was what she used on occasion to make "hard sauce," the brandy-laced icing-sugar confection that she missed so much from her English childhood. Unable to serve it to our teetotaler father, she'd make up a small bowl and then eat it all by herself in one afternoon, standing in the kitchen looking out the window, then washing away the evidence, hiding the brandy back in its drawer. How many pints had she gone through over the years?

I sometimes wonder if she thinks about the time she met my father. Whether she ever wishes that it had never happened, that walk out to the woods to pee. Her tipsy head, her horehound breath, his big hands which looked so good to her that day. And then there were those perfect letters he wrote afterward. "Good husband material shouldn't be first on the list," she always said to us, as though she was giving us a stock tip.

Suddenly alert, Gwen is searching up and down the kitchen counter for a glass. As though to distract her, Gabriel stands, unfolding his long, thin body, spreading both of his hands toward us, palms up, a gesture both religious and jazzy. Without thinking, I grab his right hand. Gwen takes the left and reluctantly takes my free one, and we stand that way in a circle, looking down at the pattern on the linoleum. Gabriel's hand is warm and dry and encompassing. Gwen's is hot and soft, strangely moist. I have the urge to circle slowly, swinging hands. I try to hold my breath so he won't smell the liquor. My cheeks pulse in the heat.

"What kind of bread are you making, Ma?" Gwen slurs. "I'll die if it's not cinnamon raisin." She snorts. Our father's favorite bread, although he usually picked out most of the raisins and circled his plate as though he disapproved of how many there were in a particular slice. She moves in on Gabriel like a serpent, her arms winding around his neck, tucking her face into his chest.

He drops my hand and stands there with both arms around her, patting her on the back.

I turn toward my mother. We used to bake bread together. Whenever she was in a bad mood, I knew what she needed to do.

"Shall I help you turn out the loaves?" I ask. I know she won't let me. My mother bakes bread as though it comes from some place deep inside her. She understands its language, the rising and punching down and kneading. Growing up, we used to clamor for store-bought bread, the kind that tore as soon as you touched the middle with a knife and peanut butter, bread that, she said, would line our young stomachs with thrilling, terrifying mucus. She prides herself on never having purchased a commercial loaf since she's been married, although we know this is a lie.

Gwen and Gabriel move into the living room and sit side by side on the sofa as if they're now married. He's rubbing the backs of her hands as though she's just come in out of the cold. They sit there holding hands and staring straight ahead, looking strangely content. She's always been good at getting there first.

My mother comes up behind me where I'm standing in the doorway to the living room, watching them. Her hands are stuck in oven mitts, which she places on either side of my waist, and she presses her forehead against my back. "I can't believe he's really gone," she says. "I keep thinking he's going to walk in." I'm trying not to open my mouth too wide, although I know alcohol escapes from your pores no matter what. Probably she can't smell it because of the brandy in her tea.

My mother's breath is hot and sorrowful in my ear. I want to tell her I'm sorry that Gwen and I are drunk. I'm sorry her husband is gone. Maybe I'm sorry he was ever her husband. I want to replace the gimlets with ice water in my veins; to be able to rise, tall and cool, to this occasion. My mother's perfume is sweet and celebratory. We've been so careful of smells around the house until now that this feels like a party. She hugs me tightly from behind and then makes a low, dog-growl sound deep in her throat.

Gabriel's ponytail looks golden in the lamplight. He flips it on and off his shoulder. He's saying something to Gwen. She leans in toward him, her eyes bleary and worshipful, her mouth hanging slightly open. Even from across the room I can see that her lipstick is smeared. It doesn't seem fair that she's been flirting with the woman in the bar, and now has absorbed Gabriel in one hard swallow.

She runs an expert, appraising hand through his hair front to back. Then she looks over at me. We stare steadily at each other, waiting to see who will turn away first, another ancient ritual. "Problem?" she asks. We learned early the power of passing boys on to each other like day-old rolls.

Eddie was our very first sharing crime. He was tall with wide, bony shoulders and a hint of a stoop. He had huge dangling hands that seemed to carry him forward, grasping air. When he kissed, he held the backs of our heads in exactly the same way, kneading gently as though palming a basketball. Gwen and I had laughed about the high-pitched smoke alarm sound he made when he kissed, saying we should disconnect his battery. We discussed the way his erection looked like a tent pole stuck in the middle of his corduroy pants. Gwen showed me how to give a blow job, demonstrating on a red Christmas candle covered in Saran Wrap.

Then came the married ones. My father never knew we'd gone out with married men. My first was a banker I'd met at a bar during my first year of college. Every Friday night we did exactly the same thing. He picked me up after ballet class, his necktie pulled open, the sleeves of his raincoat pushed up to his elbows. He liked me to throw a sweater over my leotard and stay that way, a drunken ballerina. We always went to the same bar and usually ended up not eating dinner. Lots of drinks, and baskets full of peanuts, splitting the shells between our teeth. By the time we left, my breath would feel metallic and flammable. Sometimes we stopped at a coffee shop for a late snack, although usually we went straight back to my apartment and fucked. We always did it the same way, minor variations on the missionary position. He always left by three. I'd never seen a picture of his wife, but knew she had long dark hair and was trying to get pregnant.

I can't remember now what we talked about every Friday night for five hours. The waitress smiled at us when we came in and seemed pleased. We had our regular table, one in the corner with a mirror on each side, so that both of us could watch ourselves talk. I liked his salt-and-pepper sideburns and the dark-rimmed eyes that made him look like a sad dog. He tipped well.

"I'm dating a banker," I remember telling my mother. The only thing she said was, "Does he take you out dancing?" Somehow it always came back to this. To the relived pleasure of what music once made her feel; of moving in a man's arms as though she had the rest of her life to circle her way to the end of a song.

Gwen went out with married men, too, for a while, but now she acts all outraged and self-righteous when I bring this up, as though it never happened.

"Remember Alan Mason?" Gwen and Gabriel look so small sitting below me on the sofa. I deliberately don't include him. She doesn't even look up at me. Alan had been one of the better ones, tall and rangy and careless. He'd told both of us that he loved us on different Sunday mornings, months apart. I was sure that he meant it at the time.

"I can't believe you're still thinking about that," she says.

My mother's standing in the doorway. "Let's have a glass of wine," she says. The bottle appears from the folds of her apron and she holds it up. "Let's drink to your father." I want to remind her that he thought drinking was evil; that this is no way to remember him. He would walk out of the room if he were here.

Gwen and Gabriel get up from the sofa and stretch and we all follow my mother obediently into the kitchen. We stand around the table watching her struggle with a corkscrew, a sleek black and silver construction that looks as though it belongs on the cockpit of a speedboat. When did she buy it? She sticks the bottle of wine between her knees, wedging her skirt down into her crotch. She doesn't know that this is how kids open wine bottles, first-time drinkers who don't own fancy corkscrews and need the pressure of their young bodies to defy gravity.

Neither Gwen nor Gabriel nor I move to take the bottle from her and help. Even though her husband has just died, and it's past midnight, I think we all know she needs to pull this cork out alone.

When my mother used to drink at other people's parties, she would get two high spots of color in her cheeks, as though she'd opened the oven one too many times to check the roast. Gwen, my father, and I used to keep vigil over these spots, staring right at her cheekbones. She liked having that kind of good time, the kind that two or three glasses of red wine can give you. Instantly giddy, possibly harmless, serving the Brussels sprouts suddenly a sexy act. Why wouldn't she wish for that once in a while under her own roof?

The cork bursts out with a loud, satisfying pop. My mother just misses her own chin with her fist and laughs. She smells the cork and wrinkles her nose but doesn't say anything, then solemnly places it next to the base of the wine bottle, where it promptly rolls onto the floor. I feel embarrassed at how much I want it to be a really good bottle of wine, blood-of-Christ caliber. It seems only right. Sacrilege shouldn't happen over rotgut. Gwen goes to the sink and fills one of the wine goblets with tap water, sets it back down on the table, and strokes the rim with her forefinger, producing a thin wailing sound.

My mother starts polishing the wineglasses, rubbing them on the hem of her skirt, showing the tops of her stockings and the tabs of a black garter. Is this what she normally wears? With a quick, coy glance over at Gabriel, she takes a tea towel from the kitchen counter drawer, holds each glass up to the overhead light to check for smudges, and continues to polish.

"Ma, I think they're clean enough," says Gwen.

"I've never used these glasses in my life," my mother says. "I want them to shine."

One day years ago, after my parents had an argument, she went out and bought a set of eight fat wine goblets that swallow up your nose in a goldfish bowl of liquid. Statement glasses. They take up an entire shelf in her china cabinet, gleaming and obscene. We used to stand and stare in at these sultry objects, winking as the sun hit their curves. My father would turn his head away when he passed. They never discussed her purchase or the fact that they remained empty.

She looks so pretty. Her cheeks are pink and her lips are reddish and full, as if she's been biting them, not because of nerves, but because she remembers that this is the way her mother told her to prepare for a party. The heady excitement of losing her husband has left her young and beautiful again. The tragic fairy tale is picking up and galloping toward the end of the road in the next kingdom, where the wine flows and there is dancing.

My mother still looks like Ava Gardner. As a kid I remember seeing *The Barefoot Contessa* and thinking I was watching my mother. They shared the same devil-eyed beauty and raw longing. When I saw *Night of the Iguana,* I wondered whether my mother would have been happier with two handsome young men without shirts on, making music with maracas just behind her, ready to lure her down to the beach to dance.

Sometimes she went out to the garage and smoked cigarettes. She would tell us years later that she allowed herself one a day, not for health reasons, but because it was so hard for her to get out and buy them. Once I found a crumpled pack inside a flower pot turned upside down. Dirt had fallen inside the cellophane and there were smudged fingerprints on the outside, as though she'd been gardening and had kept them in her apron pocket, reached in once in a while to touch the pack and make sure they were still there. Gwen and I both wanted to catch her smoking, and would hide behind the garage where there was a small dirt-caked window, hoping that we would see the flare of a match, our mother's ghostly face behind it, the ecstatic plume of smoke. We wondered if she also kept a bottle out there, tucked in with the seed starter and the pesticides. These were her solitary cocktail parties out in the garage with the ghosts of her ex-boyfriends.

We knew about drinking only from watching our friends' parents drink, the glasses and ice and syrupy brown or clear liquids before dinner, the flushed cheeks.

The only time I remember seeing her cheeks as pink as they are now is when she danced. Only then, it seemed, was there a certainty to her steps that spanned the continents. In bread and in dancing she had her own special language, and it was not my father's. Her bread had too many seeds, her music too many notes. Her lilting voice when she spoke on the phone to her one brother back in England had the cadence of music sung to a deaf man, too loud and enunciated. Even with him she struggled to be heard.

As a teenager, she'd practiced dancing in the kitchen to World War II dance music, the radio at her elbow, and a sinkful of dirty supper dishes ahead of her. "Turn it off," is all she remembers hearing for years. Later she would sneak out to meet men who could afford to take her dancing.

Decades later, our mother would start in the kitchen and move into the hall and then the living room, where my father sat reading. Her waltz step grew larger, more violent. She seemed to grow taller. One-two-three, one-two-three, she counted, whirling around. My father looked up from his reading and back down again. She whirled around and around in front of his chair. The dishcloth flew off her shoulder and landed with a damp slap on his newspaper. Looking up, not smiling, he threw it back at her, aiming for her shoulder, but it landed around her neck, whipping her in the face. She threw her head back and laughed, whirled faster.

"Cut it out," he said. She ignored him and kept dancing. Gwen and I sat on the sofa watching her, not saying anything, wanting to join in, but scared at the same time. "Cut it out," he repeated, still without raising his voice. He folded the newspaper back on itself and shook it, the way my mother always punished sheets just out of the dryer.

"Rafe was a glider, so elegant," she said. She closed her eyes and looked up at the ceiling, as though she was remembering the way this old boyfriend smelled behind his ears. My mother had dark eyelashes and a beautiful long neck. We worried at this point that she would fall over. She seemed to find her equilibrium somewhere up there in the light fixture.

Secretly we liked hearing her dancing stories. There was a guilty pleasure in the way they brought us into a private circle that excluded our father. Not that she invited us to dance, or that we really understood. We stood right there on the sidelines, but she never grabbed one of us as her partner. We just knew how much he didn't belong. If there was an open door there, he refused to walk through, refused even to stand at the entrance and enjoy the spectacle of her. Our mother taunted him with this.

When she twirled in front of us, the smell of food rose from under her skirts, the baked potatoes she was cooking, or the meat loaf. We could see her in the blue gauzy dress she described, with the boat neck and the tiny pearls lining the cuffs. We saw her hands in bright red nail polish holding a martini. Sometimes she pretended to be standing at a cocktail party, a cigarette in one hand, a drink in the other. She cocked her head so that her ear touched her shoulder, looking up at an invisible man whom we could actually see, the dark hair and the even darker eyebrows crossing his forehead, and she laughed with what my father called her fake laugh. "Your father wouldn't know what to do with a drink if it was put in his hand," she said. "Or thrown in his face," she added dreamily.

Once when my father was away on a business trip, my mother danced in the backyard. She balanced the stereo speakers in the open kitchen window and turned the volume up. She danced barefoot in a wide skirt, holding a cigarette in one hand, whirling round and around until the pattern on the hem was a blurred band of white. She wanted the neighbors to see. She'd put on bright red matching finger- and toenail polish as though she were going to a party. We could see her underwear.

That night she stood in front of the open fridge. "Too bad, nothing for dinner," she said, and laughed. She began pulling everything out and stacking cartons and bowls on the floor behind her. "Find every piece of cheese you can," she said, and we launched into a frenzied treasure hunt, crawling around the floor, unwrapping wax paper packages and peeking under lids. We found an unopened brick of Swiss, an old leathery piece of Monterey Jack, two inches of Velveeta in a box, crumbly, vomit-smelling Parmesan from a jar that we had to hit against the counter to loosen.

Gaily, she dumped every cheese into a pot on the stove along with a stick of butter, throwing the wrappers on the floor. Gwen ran into my father's study and put on my mother's favorite Herb Alpert record. We hopped around the obstacle course created by the ketchup and relish and Hawaiian Punch and my father's Metamucil until we were all breathless. We wondered where this sudden sharp joy had come from, although we didn't really care. The air was alive with our naughtiness.

We ate our bowls of melted butter and cheese in front of the television, normally forbidden. Whenever I eat lobster with drawn butter now, I remember the thrilling richness of that meal.

"This would give your father terrible indigestion," my mother said, and this thought seemed to change her mood. Gwen and I returned to the kitchen with her and started jigging up and down again around her, trying to recapture it. But she was wearily picking up the bowls from the floor and peering under their shower-cap lids and sniffing and frowning, as though she'd discovered the end of the world inside her own refrigerator and didn't know what to do about it.

My father was born without the dancing gene. When he fished, it was like watching a ballet, but the minute he heard music, you could see him freeze up and shrink inside, get all stiff. My mother waited until her wedding day to get upset about this. You'd think if dancing was so important to her, she would have added it to her laundry list of essentials: Good Provider, Mows the Lawn, Cuts a Rug, etc. Over and over again, she's told us the story. How she stood there in her wedding gown, the train hooked over her elbow, holding out her arms to him. He didn't move, he just stared at her. The music swirled around them menacingly like smoke. The wedding guests stopped in their tracks and looked over. My parents' faces hardened like clay, my mother's in disappointment, my father's in shame and defiance.

Why hadn't he gone out and taken dance lessons?

If only she'd laughed then, and gone to him and said, "My love," taken his hand and led him out onto the dance floor. She wanted him to be instantly suave, debonair—a dancer.

That same afternoon he refused to drink a glass of champagne. As soon as the toast was over, he turned and hurried away, his head bent with purpose. At the door, he stopped and turned back, as if listening to a voice inside his head.

"I didn't go after him," my mother told us. "I turned around and went up to the first man I saw, who was your uncle Edward, and I said, 'Dance with a newly married woman,' and because he was my brother, and because it was my wedding, he couldn't say no."

He was a terrible dancer. He stepped on my mother's white satin shoes, leaving black smudge marks all over the toes, marks that never really came out. He turned her around so clumsily that she was dizzy and sick by the time the dance was over. She had to find a place to sit down and drink a glass of water. After the water she drank a glass of champagne that Uncle Edward brought to her, gulped it right down, the first (and practically the last) drink of her married life, little did she know.

She wanted to cry. But she didn't.

Already she felt guilty, not yet knowing why. She'd figure it out later. She turned to look back over her shoulder, wondering where he'd gone. She both wanted him to come back and find her, and didn't want him to. It all seemed to have turned around so suddenly, upside down, her life on its head, and she wasn't sure what she had just done.

Her brother stood over her, worried. He thought he'd injured her foot, sprained it, maybe even broken it with his clumsy tromping. Where was her husband? he wanted to know.

"I married two left feet," she told him, her voice sharp, shutting him up. She wished she hadn't given up smoking.

Her brother laughed uneasily, stooped to rub at the toes of her shoes with his handkerchief, which he'd touched to the tip of his tongue, making the black stain far worse.

*"To my husband," my mother says, raising her wine-*glass. She acts like she's been giving toasts her whole life. Gwen and Gabriel and I raise our glasses and clink hers. We stay that way, our glasses huddled. "He worked very hard," she continues in a conversational tone. We lower our glasses, settling in for a ramble. I'm worried because my mother isn't crying. All those years and years of tears, frozen inside her like insects in amber.

She stops abruptly and gulps her wine, draining her glass and holding it out for more. Gwen pours. Setting down the bottle, she says, "That's all you're going to say?"

"Don't rush me," says my mother. She holds her glass up to the light, appearing to study the sediment.

"I guess we're all still in shock," I say.

"Loss has many stages," says Gabriel. He fingers his ponytail. "This is just the first."

"The drinking stage?" says Gwen, and smirks. We all laugh uneasily.

"To a man who gave what he could," I say. These are the small, sensible words that come out, not in the least what I intended to say.

The wine is terrible. I notice that Gabriel isn't drinking. I look at Gwen and we roll our eyes together at her choice, a lowly house red. On leaving the home of our teetotaling father, we made our own discoveries. I prefer a bottomless cabernet, the first mouthful like a tongue poking into ancient crushed velvet, sexy and dry. I don't mind the expense. Is my sister assuaging her guilt by buying such a cheap bottle?

At the head of the table, my mother is standing, swaying slightly, regal and pleased, fingering the stem of her glass, luxuriously pondering.

"To my husband," she says again, and raises her glass toward the ceiling in a triumphant gesture.

She doesn't yet seem to realize that she is now alone.

four

Now my father will never meet Jack. I will always wonder whether he worried about Gwen and me, why we weren't married, or if he wanted us to be; why we rarely brought men home to meet him. Why we were both so secretive. Over the years, I would practice introductions in my head. My father standing in the hall, his right hand thrust out to meet a man who was in love with me. In my dream, I never managed to give the man a voice or a face.

This is what really happened once. I thought my parents should meet Michael from my ballet class. Of course, they didn't know I was sleeping with him. I wanted my parents to be like other parents. I told Michael my parents wanted to meet him, even though they hadn't asked.

One Sunday when I stayed home from church, he came over as soon as Gwen and my parents had left for church. We went down to the basement and practiced that week's ballet combination and then kissed. Pretty soon we fucked, lying on the floor on top of a lot of clothes that we took out of the dryer, piled into a comfortable mound. Then he left.

My parents and Gwen came home from church. Michael came back twenty minutes later as I'd instructed, and we all had lunch. He kept looking at me across the table, poking my sore calf muscle with his toe. Even though he seemed nervous, I knew he wanted to laugh. I felt sorry for my father. I could tell he didn't know what to say. He was sweating inside his good Sunday jacket. He didn't know how to ask a young man about ballet, so he left it all to my mother. Of course, she loved it. She asked him all kinds of embarrassing questions, like what boys wore under their tights and whether his father minded that he took ballet. Michael flirted with her. My mother got all blotchy on her chest right above where the V of her dress started. I wondered if she reminded him of Madame, who also liked to show off her breasts.

I'd made tuna and egg sandwiches on toasted English muffins, with sliced cucumbers on the side. My father cut the seeded centers carefully out of each separate cucumber slice using his knife and fork. All through lunch, I saw my father eyeing my mother. I didn't let Michael stay for dessert, just got up after the sandwich part was over and announced, "Michael has to go." He didn't stay for my mother's sherry trifle without the sherry.

*I'm sitting at the little telephone table in the down-*stairs front hall with my hand on the receiver. I don't pick it up. With a journalist's insatiable desire to thrash the bushes, Jack's first question will be: What was the last thing you said to him? I can imagine him on the other end, rumpled, eager to analyze, the phone braced between his shoulder and ear, doing too many things, taking notes. Am I going to be his next article idea? How can I explain to a man who talks even in his sleep that the final conversation I had with my father was completely silent; that I'd lured him into an illicit stand-still dance while he was in the final stages of a coma?

Jack can always tell when I've been drinking. He thinks my voice lowers by at least an octave and I become Southern in my intonation and syntax. Sexy. He thinks I'm depressed. He thinks everyone's depressed. He's always trying to send me to his psychopharmacologist. If I call Jack to tell him my father has just died, he'll seize upon my melancholy, deciding it's the perfect opportunity to pressure me to try medication. But the drinks are wearing off, and I'm not in the mood. It's too late for so many things.

The person I really want to call is Thea. She'll have some brisk response and will ask practical questions like, Who's doing the food for the funeral? She's willing to travel, she'll tell me. She'll give my mother a deal. If I were there, she'd sit me down in her kitchen that smells of cooking and sandalwood, and she'd pour me a huge glass of wine and sit there with me until I'd drained it. Then she'd put on some weird belly-dancing music and put me to work.

I leave my mother sitting at the kitchen table with Gwen and Gabriel. As I disappear down the basement stairs, a match scratches, a curl of cigarette smoke follows me halfway down. My mother's crumpled pack, promoted at last from garage to house.

I pull on the worn string hanging from the ceiling bulb. Suddenly illuminated, the old Ping-Pong table in the main room of the basement is stacked with my father's shirts, thin layers of fifties pastels, green, pink, blue.

My mother started going through his clothes when he moved from his bedroom to the study downstairs. She said, Take whatever you want, it's high time we cleared out his closets. "She can't even wait for him to die," said Gwen. I reminded her that keeping busy was our mother's way of maintaining control. I chose his rumpled Pendleton fishing shirt and old pajamas. He always insisted on drawstrings, no snaps. These are thin and see-through as gauze, the collar and button-placket rimmed in threadbare black cord. Gwen took a sweater vest and a brown corduroy jacket with elbow patches, a few pairs of wool socks, his army hat.

The basement still reeks of mothballs, the old-fashioned kind that you secretly want to eat. I turn off the light. In the dark, I move into the laundry room with its trapped warmth and comforting detergent smell. Something is crumpled on the dryer. Even in the dark, I recognize my father's jacket, the one he always stuffed with Tums and Doublemint gum in one pocket when he went fishing, his handkerchief in the other. I check the pockets and pull out some lint, rub it between my fingers as though it will reveal some final truth about him. I ball up the jacket and, after a moment's hesitation, bury my face in it. The jacket smells of skin and hair, like the inside of his hatband. I put it on and zip it to my chin. I don't want her to wash it.

Standing in front of the long mirror on the back of the laundry room door, I swing the door back and forth. The back-porch light coming through the high basement window is just enough to make my eyes glint maniacally silver. This was the room I always escaped to. Gwen used to sit here on the hot dryer, banging her legs against the front with her heels, making fun of me while I practiced ballet. She would mimic my arm and leg movements with leering, monkeylike antics to the rhythm of the metal fasteners on her jeans hitting the inside of the dryer.

We never knew why our mother had installed the mirror, a dime-store variety that made everyone look unflatteringly elongated and gaunt. One day, in search of my ballet tights, I barged in on her. Held in the arms of an invisible partner, her head tilted up and slightly back, she was mid–waltz step, humming her own music, left arm cradled across her apron, right arm crooked and raised above her head. She was laughing and moving her mouth, chatting animatedly but emitting no words, gazing up at her ghostly partner, who towered a good six inches above where my father would be if they danced together. She'd danced before in front of us, but never with such dreamy intensity. I felt as though I'd caught her naked.

I started backing out, tiptoeing, but she opened her eyes, straightened up, moved right over to the dryer, and in one fluid motion, yanked open the door, started tumbling out the clothes.

"Don't stop," I said. "You looked nice."

"It's a waste of time," she said. "Here." She tossed me my balled-up pink tights, still damp. "They'll finish drying on you."

*That was the year I was thirteen and fell hard for bal-*let: the shoes, the tights, the sway-backed stance, the rosin chalk in the corner, the competitiveness, the fear. My mother pushed me hard, then turned her back on me as though she really wasn't interested. She helped pay for my classes and tights out of her household fund; I paid the balance with my allowance and baby-sitting money. Gwen shunned ballet, announcing that she had three left feet, then sat around and waited for me to fail. I practiced jumps, holding on to her shoulders, a bony, begrudging barre. My father acted like I was stripping at a nightclub.

"But why?" I pestered my mother when she warned me against parading around the house in my beloved leotard. "Because it makes him sad and mad," she said. This solemn conundrum was supposed to be enough.

It didn't take me long to figure out that I didn't do ballet like a girl. The things I liked weren't the mincing steps, the timid bourrées, the grasshoppery entrechats. I liked the height and the distance. The jumps and leaps. The first time I left the ground, the excitement centered in my gut, a feeling I would come to name as sex. A simultaneous shrinking and expanding in my stomach, a feeling of bigness, of wanting to take a shit and at the same time being empty and flat on the inside. I landed soft and on target, like a paratrooper. I saw the flicker in Madame's eyes and knew I was good.

On my first day in class, she paired me with Michael, the only boy in class. I was the only girl who could jump almost as high as a man. I felt a melting sense of stopped time and a perfect soaring inside my body. My grand jetés across the room covered mountain ranges. At the end of that first class, Michael placed one hand on my shoulder and squeezed. Then he turned and walked away. All that day I was haunted by the memory of the gleaming plums of his buttocks in black tights mocking me.

After my first year, Madame summoned me to her office and waved me to sit down across her scarred wooden desk. I stared straight ahead, trying not to focus on her cleavage, freckled as a smooth brown egg where it rose out of her leotard. Later I would find out that the bottom drawer contained a pint bottle of Wild Turkey and a shot glass, the reason for her mood swings, the warm, smoky breath as she came up to one or another of us during class and took the hand that wasn't holding the barre, forming it into the shape of a beautiful bird.

"Darling," she began. "It's high time you went on pointe." Madame's chest seemed to heave, although it was actually the sea storm of my own breathing. Her breath was strong that day. It rushed across the desk like a blowtorch. I knew with the instinct of a future drinker that the lesson would be sideways and through the ribs. She must have taken a fresh shot before calling me in.

Lighting a cigarette, she rose and walked across the room. She dangled the cigarette from her lip as she adjusted her skirt around her stomach with both hands, retied the neat bow at her waist, and smoothed the skirt down over her thighs. I was so used to my "on toe" mantra that for a moment I didn't react to this unfamiliar word. "Point?"

"If you question, you're not ready," she said in her fake French accent. "You must be serious," she continued, pulling back the curtain and gazing out the window, squinting through the smoke. I had no idea what she was talking about. I opted to say nothing, having already before experienced her wrath at the wrong response. She had beautiful calves, molded and strong as a statue's, and a strange floating English accent when she wasn't speaking French, like my mother's for a moment, then descending into something both more growly and more musical.

"Lower class, the North," my mother had said the first time she met her. They eyed each other warily, two British parlor cats circling, pretty and unblinking. Instinctively, I didn't trust the situation, neither wanting Madame to praise me nor my mother to offer up maternal pride. Maybe my mother, wife of the teetotaling father, smelled the whiskey.

"Oh, yes, yes, yes, yes, I am," I interrupted, half kneeling. I would have inched on my stomach across the dusty floor and sniveled in the hem of her long silky ballet skirt for permission to go on toe.

"Perhaps you are ready," she said in a fake musing tone. She looked down the length of her nose at me as though "pointe" had been my own impertinent suggestion. "Alors, let me kiss you, then." I stood, straight and deserving, as she came toward me. She air-kissed me on one side of my face, then the other. I wasn't expecting the second kiss, and our faces collided in the middle. "The French way, darling, please," she said. She pulled me to her breasts and then held me, just millimeters away, as though a force field kept our chests apart. I wanted to mash my chest against hers, feel these famous freckled breasts that Michael seemed to love against my small, high ones.

I came in once and found them standing very close, as though he was deliberately looking down the front of her leotard. I wondered if they'd been kissing. They didn't quite jump apart, but there was a startled movement in the air as though a leap had just occurred and was as suddenly frozen. Madame looked flushed. I already felt possessive. Michael turned gracefully with his whole body, and I saw his penis outlined in his tights against her aqua skirt. I wanted to cup it in my hand. He was standing half behind a screen wearing only a strange strappy contraption around his penis and buttocks. Madame knelt in front of him and started wrapping cloth around his waist and between his legs.

Backing out, mumbling, I knew I wanted to be the one pinning the costume around his thigh. Madame had already placed us together in the back row. I wondered if she thought of me as another boy, or whether she saw us as a man and a girl. When I was standing next to him in class, I chose his white freckled shoulder near mine to spot in the mirror, and then sometimes without meaning to, my eyes would return to the bulge in his tights. "Look up, eyes up!" Madame would yell, stamping her stick.

I was on my own. Full scholarship, and still no rides to class, no assistance sewing pink elastic to my ballet slippers, no questions asked or answered. Sometimes Gwen would come and watch the last half of class, standing in the doorway, her mouth hidden behind her hand. I could never tell whether she was smirking or not. At home she raised her arms over her head, a broken umbrella, and lurched around shouting, "Oui, Michael, oui!"

My mother recognized my calling and bristled. She was the dancer. She was the one who had mesmerized an entire dance hall with the precociousness of her waltz at fourteen, whose partners had lined up for her regal teenage nod. The way she tilted her chin in the air to demonstrate, held her arms up and out, waiting, as though she was only pretending to cooperate and would change her mind any minute, I could tell exactly how the men must have felt. We argued about keeping time to music. My mother would come up behind me and beat on my shoulder with her fingers smelling of onions.

Each year as I got better at ballet, I waited for her to become interested. I wanted her to come by while I was standing at the bus stop, wind down the window, and tell me to jump in. She talked about ballet indifferently, as though it was medicine I was taking. She said it would give me grace and strength. She wished her mother had made her do it. (Why didn't she make Gwen do it?) When my sister imitated me, my mother would go to her, laugh and shake her head, put her arms around Gwen's shoulder and nuzzle her neck inside her collar.

Erotic dreams of Michael were inextricably linked to dancing. Sex and "toe" were acts that must exist on the same soul-wrenching plane. To bourrée to God, or to the arms of Michael, waiting for me across the classroom, maybe one day a stage! Sometimes he walked with me on the way to my bus, but not often. Usually he waited for Madame, disappearing into her office after class with his beat-up ballet bag, shutting the door behind him. I would linger, pretending that I'd injured my toe, rubbing it and studying it, only managing to unfurl layers of dirt buried beneath my skin. Finally I'd leave, staring at the door as though my X-ray vision could penetrate its secrets, sometimes stopping to listen and hearing nothing but silence behind the closed door. I imagined Madame lying on the sofa in her office, her breasts sticking out of her pulled-down leotard, beckoning me with one of her delicate fingers faintly stained with nicotine.

That first Sunday morning, Michael came to our house as soon as my parents and sister had left for church. I was allowed to stay home if I prepared lunch for the others. I'd told Michael he had to leave by quarter to twelve, no exceptions. He drove up in his old black car and sat idling in front of the house to let me know he was there, then gunned the engine and drove around the corner to the next block to park. He came up to the back door and tapped on the glass with his car keys. He wore his black leather jacket and a piece of his coppery hair flopped down over his eye.

We drank cups of my father's instant coffee while I sat next to him at the kitchen table, dipping cookies into the coffee before each bite, the way my father did. When Michael reached out to stroke my face, he let his fingers linger on my chin and touch my lips. His fingers smelled of car oil, which seemed strange for a ballet dancer. I turned on the radio and we listened to classical music. I took him down to the basement and we practiced in front of my mother's dancing mirror. He lifted me high over his head and then brought me down into his face, nuzzling my crotch outside my tights until I could no longer stay in a split, his arms trembling so hard I was scared he was going to drop me.

He set me on the washing machine. He kept kissing my breasts. I imagined my father walking in.

I continued to watch in swoony horror as the girls in the advanced class gingerly pulled shreds of lamb's wool from their bleeding knobby feet after class, wincing as though an animal had died on the fence between their toes. This, I knew, was when my life would truly begin, the quick hop up onto a pink satin box, a bending and scrunching of my entire being, a Chinese maiming of my toes, a telescoping of all meaning into the exquisite bent arch, the toe shoes with the pink shine of naked burned skin.

Going on toe was crash and burn with beautiful French pastries on my feet. I'd dreamed of trading up my battered ballet slippers for this exotic, perfect footwear. One day Madame told Michael to lift each of us across the room as we did grand jetés. Each girl looked more awkward than the next, feet flapping stiff and large as ducks, unable to even think about pointing in the panic of being suddenly airborne. I was last in line and had a chance to study the aerodynamics. The girls who looked up and focused on the corner of the room where Madame stood like a mother bird sternly entreating her young to fly were less wobbly. Looking down was clearly fatal to flight.

One after another of us just missed careening into the mirror on the other side. Michael's upper arms grew pink with the effort, and his muscles stood out like the flesh-colored bas relief maps we studied in school. He kept shooting looks over at Madame. He swore every time he reached our corner again. "Shit," he said, and then, "Fuck." I felt that these comments were addressed to me. I knew how much he liked me, but his patience could wear thin. And he didn't like me in the same way he liked Madame, the way he stared at her with soft eyes and a little smile, his freckles seeming to jump off his face.

The blood rose up from the pit of my stomach and into my face. Ballerinas were supposed to be white, floury, delicate looking, the inside of a buttermilk biscuit. My hair would never grow long enough to wear in a bun like theirs. I scraped it and pulled it back, greased it with my father's Vitalis. I bought a blue bandeau at a ladies' hair-products store. One of the stage mothers came up to me after class. She touched the band with her finger and said, "That's a wool ski band, honey. No wonder you're so red."

I looked toward Madame in the corner, and then past her, over her shoulder, out the window at the weird grain silo, the dripping half-metal/half-wood water tower that had been the perfect spotting tool for shiné turns in the past three years. The pointed roof brought my eyes just high enough to the horizon, but not so high that Madame said, "Stuck up," the way she did when she thought one of us was putting on airs.

I actually felt the vomit collect and sit in the base of my throat. Michael and I pliéd together. He wore a ripped T-shirt and torn tights that showed bare coins of his flesh. He placed both hands around my waist and I watched the tips of his fingers meet in the mirror over my belly button. He breathed on my neck, and I felt everything harden inside my leotard. I bunched my stomach muscles, and at the same time kept my arms soft and rounded, imagining Madame's hands in front in that way she had, like holding sugar out to a hungry animal and then walking backward and away, teasing. I looked out to the tip of the water tower and thought of a nipple, and Michael's pink tongue hovering near it.

My legs stretched out in a perfect split and together we soared across the room. I could feel Michael's feet and legs thumping hard into the ground with my weight, but still delicate enough, and that look in Madame's eye, the one that admired me, the one I'd hardly ever seen before.

"So," she said when we landed, and that was all. I slipped down out of Michael's arms, sliding hard over his forearm. He stooped under me to let me go as though I were a bag of breakable groceries, including eggs. I tumbled off his arm and strutted away. My heart was beating so fast I thought I would actually throw up. I walked right out of the room and into the hall and leaned against the wall and tucked my head down between my shoulders the way you're supposed to when you're going to faint.

Michael followed after me, doing a goose step, too. He leaned down and kissed the middle of my part right above the ski band. His lips were hot. I could feel where they separated, the shape burning right into the skin in the middle of my head.

"Bella," he said, even though he wasn't Italian. He was red-haired and freckled, but it made my whole body flush.

When I got home, I had no one to describe this to. Gwen wasn't back from school. My mother was ironing in the basement and watching a soap opera with heavy-lidded eyes as though she'd been crying all afternoon. She'd colored her hair, and the blond looked molten and out of control, like bars of hot gold bouillon. Life had been a war that day.

Soon after that, Michael stopped showing up for class. Madame began to drink more and came to class a couple of times with her bra poking out of her leotard. I went home one day and took my toe shoes from their slim pink box with the soaring stick figures dancing. I cut off the ribbons. Then I placed them side by side in the kitchen sink and poured my father's India ink over the toes. It took a while for the black stain to creep up the beautiful strawberry satin boxes. By the time I'd changed my mind and thrown them into the shower like two drunken fish, it was too late. I still have them, a crazy parched sunset on the toes, orange and tragic-looking. On toe, in the basement, on the sofa, hope was pink and it was treacherous. The next month I enrolled in jazz.

five

Upstairs they're crashing around like they're having a barn dance. Chairs moving, feet shuffling, whirring snatches of music, someone dementedly twirling the radio dial. I'm reluctant to go upstairs and investigate. I want food and music and dancing and love, the things my father barely tasted. But surely not this way.

I wander into my father's workroom, a model of tidy hoarding. A wall of hanging tools, myriad cubbyholes filled with screws and nails and pieces of wire. Of all the rooms in the house, this one was strictly off-limits, usually locked.

Through the floor, I hear murmuring voices, the sound of Gwen laughing, followed by my mother talking, then Gabriel's graceful lower register. I have the quick fantasy that I will conceive a child with Gabriel this very night, create a hopeful new location for my father's lonely soul to fly into. The child will be a brilliant soft-spoken genius, half Dalai Lama, half dyslexic cowboy-poet. I can see how the lines in my father's face would have changed as he looked down on his first grandchild. I see him smile and tear up. From that moment on, life would have been different.

I open a few battered shoe boxes, stacked and pushed to the back of the workbench. Why did

he keep all these keys and coins and pairs of old glasses? At the back of the shelf is his square metal tackle box with a picture on the lid of a hooked sea bass, arched and faded. The smell inside is sharp and salty, the tang of feathers fragrant with mildew, bringing him instantly back. He's standing right here next to me, tying, tying, his big fingers moving with eerie delicacy. He liked to name his flies. Royal Coachman, or Queen Dancer, after my mother. Alice Minnow, he might have called one. Or Precious Alice.

Under a tangle of fishing flies is a long brown envelope folded in half lengthwise, the crease sharp and discolored with old grime. I can see the flat tips of my father's fingers smoothing and smoothing the crease. The mucilage on the inside is dark and shiny and mottled as the inside of a shell. My heart starts beating mysteriously fast. (Why, when my body must know that it's far too late for revelation?)

With my fingertips, I coax a small photograph with crinkle-cut edges out of a glassine envelope. I'm afraid that when it meets the harsh basement light it will crumble in my hands. In the photo, a crowd of people are dancing. I recognize my mother. I recognize her wedding dress. The long sleeves and the band of flowers around her hair. Gwen and I have seen these in the album a million times. Which is why I know immediately that I've never seen this photograph before. Here, finally, a chapter I know nothing about.

Moving directly under the bare lightbulb, I hold the photograph up high. My mother is in the center of a crowd of dancers, her head turned, looking up at her partner, her eyes big and dark and laughing. Her mouth with that bright red lipstick she always wore in old pictures is wide open.

Her partner is not my father. Her partner is not Uncle Edward. He's tall and has slicked-back hair. Even in this old matte finish, you can see his forehead gleam bone-white below a swath of black hair. The train of her dress swirls around their feet, and they're laughing.

In a panic, I rummage in my father's toolbox and find his magnifying glass in its old leather case. Scanning the faces as they swim up at me, I tick off the strangers. I'm trying to find my father among all the dancers. Where is he? Why isn't he watching?

Up close, I notice that my mother's left elbow is held properly high, her arm pressed elegantly, correctly, along her partner's. I remember the way it is, dancing with a stranger, the way you don't fit together right away, sometimes for a very long time. They fit.

I can just make out Uncle Edward's round, bewildered face behind the dancers, lower down, as though he's standing at the edge of the dance floor watching his sister dance for the very first time.

I want to take this picture and the glass and go right upstairs. I want to see my mother's face when I ask her who she's dancing with here, at her wedding. Where was my father, right then, that moment? I want to know why he kept the photo. I want to accuse her.

Lying at the bottom of the box is a folded piece of yellowish lined paper that I recognize. It's my eighth-grade masterpiece of verse entitled "The Fisherman," in which I'd written about a late-season angler who ended up being swept out to sea by "life's primordial pounding surf." I still remember the grand, swelling feeling I had while writing this, of discovering that life was about disappointment and loss and deep, cool nothingness, rather than everything safe and large. What could the poem have possibly meant to him?

I'm sitting cross-legged on the floor, facing a jumble of old stuff underneath his workbench. Obviously my mother's sorting mania has not yet found its way down here. With a start, I recognize the back of our old television. How can they not have thrown it out long ago? Gwen and I used to creep in before he came home from work and stare at it, stored away, facing the wall, punishment for our whining panic to hurry home to our favorite game show. We would touch the sternly coiled cord and the acoustic holes in the back, as though we could absorb all that we were missing through our fingertips. Settling down, side by side, we'd sit here talking and staring at it, our thoughts intent on the life we'd have if only we could possess what was inside.

I turn the old television around so that it's facing me. The screen is covered with dust. I rub this away with my hand, not wanting to dirty his jacket, then twirl the channel knob on the front experimentally, the old-fashioned clicking familiar in the silence. Once, I came downstairs and changed the channels on this same television for a good few minutes before my parents realized I was sleepwalking. Only when I got up from my knees and in my long nightgown went straight out the front door, banging the screen, leaving the heavy door wide open, and started walking down the block did they know. I don't remember falling. I do remember my father pulling his handkerchief from his endlessly deep pocket and neatly folding a corner over his forefinger. He wiped my tears, then, moistening the handkerchief with his tongue, knelt in front of me and dabbed at the blood on my knee. His spit drying on my leg made the skin there feel tight. Back in my bedroom, when I bent my head down close to my knee, I could smell his spit. I sometimes sleepwalk when I'm staying over with men I don't know well enough, and they usually get offended, thinking this means I don't want to be there, which is often the case. So far this has never happened with Jack.

Picking up one of my father's old fishing flies, I stroke the feathers, then gently ease the hook just barely under the surface of my thumb and raise my hand, palm down into the air.

Precious Alice.

The best time I ever had with him was when we went fishing, just the two of us. When he caught the fish, the rod bent down in a curve just the way it's supposed to. There was tension in all parts of him. I was only twelve years old, but not too young to feel him wound tight and ready to take on much more than the world had given him, right then, right there, that fish. The muscles in his body fought to get out; they jumped out of his shirt. I watched this more than the rod, more than the sea. His mouth stretched wide in a grimace as he looked at the tip bending low, bobbing. He fought with his teeth clenched, his feet planted. How big could the fish be?

In the middle of his fight, my father turned. I saw the tight joy in his face, shared for that second with me. Looking back once at his line, vibrating and shooting off a fine spray, he turned and looked at me again. A twelve-year-old girl's first double take from a man. With the click of a shutter, once, twice, it opened up a lifetime of desire.

I've replayed the scene again and again since then. Rewinding it to the beginning, my private home movie. The reason I was alone with him in the first place: Gwen at home with the flu; at the last minute my father still wanting to go. Climbing into the car feeling nervous and sick myself, hardly daring to look at his impassive profile under his fishing hat.

Before he cast out the reel, the way he pulled back and watched the hook and the tangled, sandy bloodworm floating in slow motion over his shoulder toward the dunes, his feet in rubber waders planted, and his eye following the arc; the long, whirring sound of the line unreeling across the world.

Suddenly there was a fish on the beach, flopping and silver in the setting sun.

I hurried to gather the smallest, driest pieces of driftwood I could find. Hurrying this way, I felt panic when my eyes didn't immediately light on the next piece. He would change his mind and decide we should go home. The father I knew would decide to go home. I'd never seen him this way. After the fight with the fish, his body seemed to melt inside his clothes. He acted as though he were alone on the beach. I longed for his attention again, but was afraid that without the wild aliveness of the fish, there would only be me, only disappointment.

While he tended the fire, I dragged two logs of charred wood and brought the ends together so they formed a low V-shaped bench. I sat on one side and watched as he cleaned the fish with his knife, slitting the belly and pulling out the guts with a sharp yank. The gulls dipped and cawed, preparing to dive. The guts lay in a mound next to us, leaking watery blood. While he cleaned his hands with sand, I dug a hole and buried the guts, smoothing the sand until there was nothing there. Carefully, he laid the fish on a piece of tinfoil he'd molded into a frying pan, then built a fire.

Usually his fires were so modest, smoky and ungenerous, the kind you could only make from wet wood. Like my mother, I've always liked birch log fires, dry, crackly, burning fast and bright. He felt most comfortable with a slightly greenish fire. But not that evening. He laid the makeshift pan onto the glowing flames, balancing it on three sticks that formed a trivet, holding our supper safely above.

Sticks in our hands, we sat and stared at the fire. The air was full to bursting with our silence. My mind darted wildly for things to say, picking something, then flinging it away, the way he'd flung pieces of seaweed too wet for the fire back into the ocean. I stretched my legs out in front of me and started flexing my feet, then stopped abruptly, worried that he would remember how much I loved to dance.

I was peeling the bark from my stick down to the tender pale center, trying to think of what my mother would have said, the way she would toss her dark hair and say something amusing that would make him laugh, or at least look up.

"Is this the biggest fish you ever caught?" I asked. I cringed at how young and silly this sounded.

He kept prodding the fire. I leaned down and shifted the tinfoil, holding it carefully by each pointed corner. Finally he said, "There was another one, much bigger than this one. A giant carp. My brother helped me bring it in."

I waited for more of the story, but that's where he stopped.

This always happened when my father talked about his childhood. He would start and then stop abruptly, sometimes in the middle of a sentence, as though a voice in his head was commanding him. Gwen and I would sit there expectantly, waiting for more. Sometimes Gwen, who wasn't so afraid of him, would say something encouraging like, "Go on, Daddy . . ." or "Then what happened . . ." as though she were turning the pages of a storybook. He would say gruffly, "The past is the past," or "Nothing that's already happened will get us through the day," and he'd pull out his handkerchief, or jingle the change in his pocket and get up and walk away. Or if he was sitting at the dining-room table, he'd pick up the carving knife and fork and poke at the roast and say something to my mother about work, or about a neighbor or the bills.

This time was different. We were alone, and the surf was pounding nearby, and a fish that he'd caught, that I'd helped him catch just by being there, was sizzling on the fire, and everything was heightened and bright and expectant the way it sometimes is in a dream. I knew absolutely, positively, that he was feeling the same way I was—how could he not be?—which made me brave enough to ask him what I did.

"Do you miss fishing with your brother?" The minute the question was out, I wanted to pull it back. My brain fizzled as though an electric shock were running zigzag, ear to ear. I picked up my stick and began digging in the sand, trying to distract him. Never, never ask about your uncle, my mother always told us. If he wants to talk about him, he will. "But he never even mentions his name," Gwen complained. And my mother would say something bland and soothing like, "All in good time. You can't rush him."

My father leaned forward and adjusted the tinfoil again, moving it away from my stick. "You'll get sand in the fish," he said. Then after another long pause, "Yes, I miss him."

I stopped breathing, waiting for him to go on. He was staring into the fire, very still now. Fishy-smelling smoke rose between us in a plume. "He was taken away too early." The words that came out were halting, jerky. "God wasn't fair on this one."

I had never before heard him talk about God. I wanted him to stop. I wanted to be able to be alone to think about what he'd said.

From the side pocket of his fishing bag he pulled a tiny blue Morton's salt shaker and held it out to me, looking pleased. I knew I should set the table, but couldn't think what to do. Smoothing the sand in front of us, I created two place mats with opposite swirling motions of both hands. He set the fish in its foil between us. We ate it with plastic forks, also from his fishing bag. I wondered if he'd packed them for this occasion, hoping that together we would catch and cook a fish, or whether the forks and the salt had been waiting in there for years, maybe since he was a boy.

The fish was more delicious than anything I'd ever tasted. With a combing motion of my fork, I pulled the flesh from the bones, then sprinkled a little salt on each bite as my father was doing. The backbone soon showed. I was ready now for him to tell me more about my uncle. I waited expectantly, taking small neat bites and chewing quietly so I wouldn't miss anything. But finally, the only thing he said was, "Do you have many bones?"

"Yes," I said, "I do." The words "I do" sat in the air between us, growing larger and more ridiculous. My father had asked me about fish bones. He hadn't asked me to marry him. My father wouldn't even look at me. He was staring down at the backbone of the fish, at the head with the charred eye still wide open and silvery on the blackened tinfoil. He looked as though he might cry. What would I do if my father cried? But his expression was more angry than sad. I wanted to tell him that I loved him, but the words wouldn't form. I wondered if he'd ever told his brother he loved him. Sometimes in my room I would practice saying "I love you," the way they did so casually in some families or in the movies. These strange precious words would be tossed over a shoulder as though they were nothing. In my mind I would run back and gather them up, dust them off, put them carefully in my pocket and save them. There wasn't an unlimited supply of these words in the world, I knew that for certain.

Maybe this is what my father was leading up to. This is what I hoped for, waited for, as I sat on the driftwood log and the sky became darker, the embers turned a glowing orange, hot and cool at the same time. I felt mad at his brother for dying. Maybe if he were alive, we'd all be fishing and laughing, and my mother wouldn't be so mad all the time.

The waves were suddenly right next to us, I felt the salty crash of each one, and I shivered. I knew we had to kick out the fire and go home, but I wanted to keep sitting there, waiting for the words I knew were trapped inside him.

The barn dance noises above me have been replaced by the complete, loaded silence of kids getting into the candy. I refold the poem and stick it along with the photograph in the pocket of my father's jacket, and head upstairs. On the way to the kitchen I pass the study, where the hospital bed is stripped and neatly sandwiched in two.

The kitchen table is covered with bottles and glasses. The overflowing ashtray looks disconcertingly at home. The poker game has just ended.

In the middle of the kitchen, Gwen is standing over Gabriel, cutting his hair. He's sitting on an old stool with no shirt on, his bare feet big and defiantly white, tucked into the rungs and turned inward like a kid's. This is the same stool where my father sat so recently while Gabriel helped him shave for the last time. Gwen has cut off Gabriel's ponytail. He doesn't look like an angel anymore. I'm not sure whether an archangel wears a ponytail, but in my mind I've already, on a number of occasions, slashed the Old Testament leather cord and watched his beautiful hair come tumbling down. Now it's too late.

"I didn't know you were still here," I say to Gabriel, trying to make this sound neither accusatory nor curious. I cock my head appraisingly. "It's a good cut."

We all laugh. What's a little death compared to sex and hair? Gwen looks at me with an unreadable look. I wonder if she wants me to go away.

I'm thinking of another impromptu haircut.

Gwen was six years old and getting all the attention. I was being punished for smearing icing from her birthday cake, using my forefinger as a spatula around the sides. Her most prized present was a doll with beautiful human hair, golden and wavy. My mother had played with her for days, had kept her in the bottom drawer of her bureau and sat in bed with comb and brush each night, fixing and refixing the doll's hair, in a ribbon, in braids, flowing loose. This was when my parents still shared a bed. I imagined my father turning away, punching his pillow and falling into a disapproving doze as my mother sat up into the night, admiring the doll's hair.

Thinking her safe, Gwen had left the doll along with her other presents in our shared room. Alone, hearing the noises of the party with some neighborhood kids continue happily without me, I tiptoed out of our bedroom and into my parents' room. I rummaged in my mother's top dresser drawer until I found her curved nail scissors. Sitting in the middle of my bed, I cut the doll's hair to the roots. By the time I'd finished, it was so brutally short that the rows of dark, frightening pores on the scalp showed. The doll looked startled, her blink too wide, as though I'd also pinned back her eyelids. Back in our room, I tucked the mutilated doll under the covers of Gwen's bed. I draped the sheet around her head so that the once-glamorous face looked sweetly plain, like that of a nurse or a nun. I turned out the lights and pretended to sleep, pretending, too, that what I'd done had been done in the dark, without me.

The next day, I was confined to my room for the whole day. My mother stayed home from church. At lunchtime my father came in with a tray holding a sandwich and a glass of chocolate milk. He sat down on the edge of the bed and waited.

"Eat your sandwich," he said. I wasn't hungry. I didn't know if he was going to wait until I'd taken a bite, so I picked up the sandwich and touched it to my lips, the peanut-butter smell almost making me gag. I put it down again. I wanted to apologize for cutting the doll's hair, tell him that I hadn't meant to do it, but this would have been a lie. Scissors don't lie.

He told me that my mother had found Gwen standing on a chair in front of the bathroom mirror that morning, cutting her own hair. My mother had taken her to the neighbor's to try to get it straightened out. That's where they were right now. I wanted to laugh, but I knew it would probably make him mad. Maybe he wanted to laugh, too. He sat there until I'd eaten half the sandwich. It was almost like he was telling me a story, but without using any words. I wondered if he had ever done anything like that to his brother, maybe stolen his bike, or broken his fishing pole in two.

For years now when she's angry, Gwen has cut her own hair, often savagely and without grace, turning her scissors on herself, then, like some voodoo ritual, on me. Now Gwen is at the final stage of shaping Gabriel's sides, a stage I know intimately. He has a look on his face I also recognize. Hope frozen into something wary and defeated. The hair on the floor is spread around his feet like the spun gold of a fairy tale. Gwen's face is swollen from crying and wine, but she looks stone sober now, with intent to commit further hair crimes. Without thinking, I reach up to touch my own hair, to see if it's still there.

Shorn, Gabriel is so ordinary. I remember my fantasy of earlier this evening, down in my father's workroom. Too late for this, too. I smell sex high in my nose where it prickles. What have they done without me?

I can tell Gabriel wants to stop playing hair salon and put his shirt back on. Now that his hair is short, his ears show bright red.

"Where's Mom?" I ask. With her scissors, Gwen gestures in the direction of the living room. With my hands still in the pockets of the jacket, I walk stealthily in. She's asleep on the sofa, still in her apron, her skirt pushed up, both hands wedged between her knees, lightly snoring. Her timer has finally stopped ticking. I cover her with a sofa blanket, pulling it to her chin, and pat her head, which is lightly sweating, as though she's been dancing for hours. All that wine. My mother, sixteen years old and passed out.

Gwen has disappeared with her tools, and Gabriel is alone when I return to the kitchen. "Why did you let her?" I ask, standing close and running my fingers through his hair, front to back, the way my sister would. I imagine her weighing the ropy heft of his ponytail, tugging it as they fucked, deciding it had to go, her greedy scissors, her hungry mouth. I stoop and pick up the intact ponytail, slip it into the jacket pocket. He doesn't notice. Mimicking me, he runs a hand through his mown hair, and smiles. "She said she thought all this dying would be easier to handle if I had short hair."

"And is it?" I ask.

He reaches over and places his open hand on top of my hair. "You have a beautiful head," he says, ignoring my question.

I nuzzle his hand. "She's dangerous with scissors," I say.

Gwen's sudden return is telegraphed by the wide-eyed look on Gabriel's face. Maybe he's scared of her, too. For just a second when she comes up behind me I think she's going to stab me with her scissors. I spin around.

"That's Daddy's jacket," she says. She's standing in front of me, her hands on her hips. "Why are you wearing Daddy's jacket?" As she says this, she starts unzipping it, trying to peel it back and off my shoulders.

I hold it closed with both hands. My grip gets stronger as hers tightens.

"I don't know. I'd just like to have it," I say.

"Why should you?"

I don't want to explain that it reminds me of the one fishing trip we took without her, one of the only times my father and I were ever really close.

At the sound of ripping material, Gabriel moves to stand between us. I can smell the sweat from his armpits, nutty and fragrant, as he raises one hand toward me, the other toward Gwen.

We both let go immediately, his refereeing action waking us out of a trance. With some difficulty, I rezip the jacket to the neck, following the newly crooked track.

"Do you get involved in a lot of these Daddy's girl arguments?" Gwen says. Her voice is throaty and mocking. I know she's trying hard not to cry.

Gabriel laughs uneasily and backs away, reaching for his shirt.

I help my mother upstairs and into her nightgown. She droops and mumbles, never really waking up. I crawl into my old single bed without getting undressed, still wearing the torn jacket and my jeans. Gwen's bed stays empty. I listen, waiting. Why is it that, as usual, she's the one downstairs being comforted? Finally I hear Gabriel's truck drive away. I have no idea how much time has gone by. Time has completely changed since my father died only a few hours ago. I imagine him sitting next to Gabriel in the pickup truck, rolling down the window and taking in the night air. I imagine myself sitting between the two of them, spreading my arms across the backseat in both directions, cupping their shoulders, just as the sky turns pink. My father's first and only joyride.

Gwen climbs the stairs noisily and pushes open the bedroom door. Although I keep my eyes closed and am facing the wall, I can still feel her standing right next to my bed. I don't move. With a tug, she pulls back the covers and slides in next to me, all legs and giggles. Automatically, I shift to make room for her. Her breath is hot on the back of my neck. This is the way we used to lie together when one of us had a nightmare and our mother or father had already returned to bed. Her drowsy, even breathing and heavy arm slung across my chest always allowed me to sink into the most sweet, protected sleep. Right now my heart is beating wildly in my chest, the way your body signals you to stop and think. Along with the sex, I smell patchouli and wine.

"Was it worth it?" I ask. I mutter this under my breath, but she hears me anyway. The air becomes very still.

"What did you say?"

"I asked you whether it was worth it."

"I don't know what you're talking about."

Fucking him, I want to say. Instead I whisper, "You slept with him."

She sits up and swivels off the side of the bed in one violent motion, yanking the covers half off, reminding me of the way she'd pulled her car out of the driveway earlier this evening.

"Of course I didn't. Daddy just died."

I remain facing the wall, pull the covers up tight around my neck.

After a while, I turn and face the room. She's getting undressed, standing deliberately in the stark moonlight. I know she knows I'm watching by the way she unhooks her bra so self-consciously, as though I'm a man and care. She pulls on a T-shirt.

"Why would that make a difference?" I finally ask.

She walks to the window and breathes on it, draws on the mist with one finger. "I don't know about *you,* but my father's never died before," she says. Impatiently, she swipes at the window with her hand, then climbs into her own bed and faces the wall.

Propping myself up on one elbow, I lean toward the still-damp window, trying to make out what she's written, but it's already illegible.

"He was mine, too," I say to her back.

I turn toward the wall again and hunch into myself, the mirror image of my sister. Her steady, slightly hoarse breathing tells me when it's safe to reach under my pillow for Gabriel's ponytail. I fall asleep that way.

six

We're preparing to leave. Gwen back to her panicked customers with their needy hair and dark roots. Me back to New York and Jack and Herbert and my floating life, which appears to have floated away from me. Without consulting us, my mother is dividing up our father, using her set of brightly colored plastic measuring cups, joined together by a ring. She doesn't ask us if we want him, just hands him to us. ("No thank you, Mom, no leftovers for me.") We're standing around the kitchen table in day three of our darkish outfits, assembled at the last minute, each of us wearing some piece of clothing that belongs to the other, reluctant to give up our communal mourning togs.

Each day this week we've become more ragtag, less mournful. Today my mother has borrowed my blue cashmere turtleneck, the sleeves pushed up youthfully. When I stand close behind her I notice that it already smells of her: bread, onions, thyme, and lavender soap. I mentally add the new smells: cigarettes, perfume (the heavy kind my father never liked), and a sharp new scent, a little sinister. My mother still smells faintly of last night's alcohol.

She levels each cup of ash with the flat of a

knife in the meticulous way she has when she makes bread, the excess spraying down in a thin fan, then dumps each cup into a plastic container. "Make sure the number on the lid matches the number on the bowl," she says, handing one to each of us without looking up, and wiping her hands on her apron. "It's a system."

At the same time, as though we're in a musical, Gwen and I lift the containers over our heads and peer at the bottom, where faintly, against the grayish ash, you can make out a stamped number. We shake them gently. Samba with your daddy.

*The morning after our father died, the morning fol*lowing Gabriel's haircut, we wake up looking across at each other from our respective single beds on opposite sides of the room. Without blinking or moving, we stay that way, animals staring each other down. Gwen's mascara has etched deep circles under her eyes in the night, giving her the look of a grieving courtesan. From across the room I watch a single huge tear drip down from the inner corner of her eye and slide across her nose. She catches it with her tongue before it lands on the sheets.

"Problem?" I ask, knowing I'm mimicking her sour question of the night before. Last night was one of those hazy bad dreams that is certain to reassert itself late in the day. I suggest to my body that it get up and go and hug my sister, but it refuses. "Are you okay?" I ask, softening, as always.

"I'm fine," she says. She turns over on her back and stares up at the ceiling, swipes hard under her eyes with both forefingers, and sniffs. "Our first day without a father. What shall we do?" She struggles to sit up, crossing her arms under her breasts, bunching up her T-shirt.

"We could try being nice to each other."

"Nice." She sits up and hunches over, pressing her pillow into her belly. She doesn't look at me. "What the fuck is nice?"

My mother walks in with a tea tray. Without saying a word,

she places it at the foot of my bed and sits down next to it, removes the cozy, opens the lid, and stirs the pot. I sit up, too, suddenly in a panic to drink tea, the only possible thing that can wash away my hangover, my sadness, his absence. I don't actually have a hangover, but find myself, as always, symbiotically attuned with Gwen. We shared our very first hangover, and here we still are, fuzzy-headed and thick-tongued together. I remember how Gwen always described being hungover as feeling like she'd gone out into the world still wearing her pajamas by mistake. Today I'm wearing the kind with feet and there's no way to climb out.

The three of us gulp our first cups without saying anything. Gwen and I hold our empties out for more. My mother pours milk, rests the strainer on the rim of one cup, pours tea, then moves on to the next cup, barely dribbling, an age-old art, perfect to fill in that which is most essential to avoid. I remember holding out our wineglasses last night. All liquid comfort.

"How are you feeling?" I ask my mother.

"Fine, darling," she says. Her eyes are red-rimmed, but she's put on lipstick, deep scarlet, a little Bette Davis in the application. I want to get up and hug her, but I can't move.

"Are you going to be all right here?" I picture her walking through the house from room to room when she's finally alone, listening to ticking clocks and the downstairs bathroom faucet whose dripping my father never quite fixed. I think of her with her wineglass raised to the ceiling.

"Stan said he'd come over if I needed anything," she says. I try to bring to mind the neighbor, taller and thinner than our father was, with a white pencil mustache. We know him from mowing the lawn a million years ago across the street. Then she says, "Why isn't Jack here?"

"Why? Do you need him to fix the sink?" I know I sound critical, ungracious.

"You don't have to be so hard on me. Or your father."

"He's not around to know. But I'm sorry."

"Darling." It's my mother who gets up and sets her teacup down carefully as though there's an earthquake going on, comes to the head of the bed and gives me a hug.

"Gabriel is awfully nice." Her "awfully" is arch, pearls mixed with bread pudding. She pulls away, looking me in the face. "I think your father really liked him. You know how he didn't feel comfortable with too many people. It's sad we won't be seeing Gabriel anymore."

Behind us, still in bed, Gwen drawls, "Don't be so sure."

"Why? Do you have a big date at the Motel 6?" Again, the words come out, fast, splintery, before I can stop them.

"Girls. Girls!" My father's staccato warning falls from my mother's lips as though he's left it to her in his will.

With preternatural speed, Gwen is standing over me, her T-shirt a mass of wrinkles where she's been clutching it. For the second time in twenty-four hours, she seems ready to inflict bodily harm.

"Ten things to a bench," I say, the private childhood mantra that for years has been shorthand between us to back off and cool down.

Before I'd even started ballet, my mother took the two of us to a modern-dance class offered at a local school. The visiting teacher, an over-the-hill Isadora Duncan in white tights and leotard with gauze streamers tied to both wrists, had placed a wooden bench in the middle of the classroom and instructed each of us to "do ten things to the bench." We stood around whispering, a room full of baffled young girls. Standing apart from everyone, Gwen stared at the bench with stony determination.

One girl flapped her arms as though they were wings, tapping the air above the bench with an imaginary wand. I approached tentatively and patted it gently several times, soothing an aging dog. Moving this activity to the underside of the bench, I finished with a few kindly pats on the splintering rear end. The class giggled and I blushed, glancing over at Gwen for encouragement. She wasn't watching.

She went last. I looked down at the floor, afraid. When I heard a soft thudding sound, I looked up to see her kicking a leg of the bench with her bare foot. A girl behind me started counting softly. Soon the whole class was chanting, getting louder with each number. She kicked harder each time. On the ninth kick, the bench toppled sideways. Gwen stood over it as though it were a fallen body, one foot planted on the belly. Even from the corner, I could see that her big toe was bleeding.

Isadora edged in toward her sideways, as though she was afraid Gwen was going to kick her next. She grabbed her by the wrist and pulled her in tight to her side, shielding her from the rest of us. Gwen was laughing. As far as I know, this was her first and last dance class.

Never before have I so needed this flimsy talisman. I think of Gabriel standing between us, his bare arms outstretched. I grab Gwen's hand and kiss the back. "Ten things to a bench," I say again. She snatches her hand away and stomps out of the room. My mother and I finish a third cup of tea, silent except for our modest slurping.

We're standing around the kitchen table clutching the Tupperware containers holding the remains of my father. My mother's is the biggest, the family-size one that usually holds mashed potatoes or spaghetti with meat sauce. She cradles it in both arms, pressing it against the stomach of her apron. When the phone rings, too loud, as though the ring has been turned way up, she jumps and the container slips out of her arms and falls to the floor. It turns sideways and rolls with the steadiness of a drum into a corner of the kitchen. We all gasp and reach toward it, as though we can actually prevent the inevitable. The lid tips off and a swath of ash dumps elegantly onto the linoleum.

I'm afraid of my father's ashes. Last night we brought them home from the funeral parlor in a square white corsage box.

They spent the night in my mother's linen cupboard. I imagined them nestled in a crush of thin green paper, the color of fern. In the middle of the night, I got up and opened the cupboard, stared up at the box, closed the door, then opened it again, marveling at her choice of this temporary storage place. She'd won their war over the linen cupboard, constructing it with neat shelves and an automatic light. Here he was, leaning up against a pile of nicely folded towels, off-white and robin's-egg blue—a box of otherworldly bath salts.

I carried the box into the bathroom, locked the door, sat on the closed toilet, resting it on my lap. I jiggled it on my knees, holding the top down. *Ride a cockhorse to Banbury Cross, to see a fine lady upon a white horse.* I expected chunks of charred bone, iridescent ash, a cold morning-after campfire, a small, trapped face staring up from it. Instead there was fine, white sand, a little crumbly. I sifted it through my fingers, collected it under my nails, held up a handful and let it cascade down into the box, the dust drifting onto the mauve bathroom carpet. I remembered sifting sand on top of my father's bare feet, aiming for the flash of blue-white skin when he changed from shoes to waders, the way he pulled his feet away sharply, his toes retreating.

With dusty fingers, I touched his things still left in the bathroom, a shaving brush, a splayed toothbrush, a washcloth, spreading him around.

What to do next? Have a conversation with sand? Build a castle? I leaned down close and whispered hello. I took a pinch of him, then hesitated, my hand suspended. It seemed too sad to return him to the box. Instead I stuffed this bit into the pocket of my jeans. I weighed the box on the scale. All of my father—how could he be reduced to so little?

*Out in the hall, my mother's voice is saying her muf*fled greeting on the answering machine, her intonation cheerily oblivious to what has already changed in her life. From a distance I hear Jack speaking in his interviewing voice, soft and low and beautifully ingratiating. "Alice," he says, "are you there, Alice? It's Jack."

I should run and grab the phone and let him know what time my train will arrive, how I'm feeling, what I'd like for dinner (he'll want to know, one of the wonderful, comforting things about Jack), but I just stand there. My mother is kneeling in the corner, sweeping her husband's ashes back into the bowl with both hands. "Remember how your father hated sugar crunching on the floor?" She sits back on her heels and laughs and laughs, as though she can't stop—as though she doesn't want to stop.

dancing

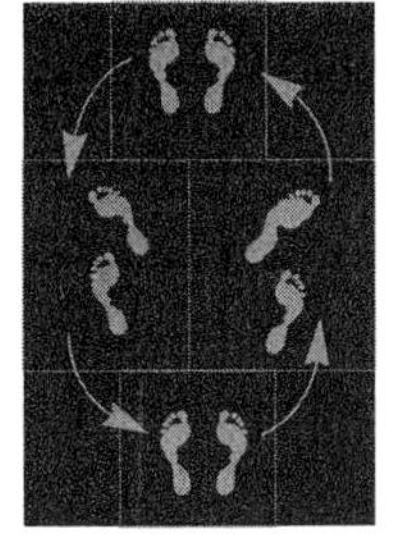

part two

seven

I arrive back in New York late that afternoon to find Jack asleep at his desk. Cross-examination is his bread and butter, and I immediately regret not having gone to my place first. It's my cat Herbert's profound, slightly cross-eyed silence I'm most eager for.

Jack's hunched over his computer in his worn striped bathrobe. He often has a hard time falling asleep, but once he's gone, it's like waking the dead. This scares me. I touch his hair, kiss the back of his neck, snuffle in his ear, stare at his computer screen. When I left he was just starting research on a story about a new drug on the market. Knowing him, he's been conducting his own drug trials. The cursor blinks under the heading "Side Effects."

I think about climbing out of my clothes and sliding naked into his bed, but decide that this requires too much optimistic energy. I stand behind him for what feels like a long time, still wearing my father's jacket.

Finally Jack stirs and stretches, sits up straight, tips his head back against my stomach.

"You're back," he says, and yawns. He reaches behind with both arms and hugs the back of my knees. It's not as though I was a Daddy's girl, but this isn't enough. "My Trazedone prescription ran out," Jack continues, still yawning. "I couldn't fall asleep until four this morning, so I've been bleary all day." Wake-up conversations with Jack generally revolve around such analysis of his drug/sleep ratio. Even so, his tomato sauce is brilliant, and he coaxes a laugh out of me even when there isn't one there. "Sorry about your dad," he says, pulling me into his side, one arm around my waist. I lean my head against his. With his free hand he lightly touches the mouse, and the screen jumps to life.

I drag him out for an early-evening breakfast at our favorite corner coffee shop, choosing a booth at the back. I love restaurant booths, the sweet boxing ring of them, cordoned-off hopes and conversations—all kinds of communication might occur. There's safety in sliding across the cracked vinyl seat, the familiar lifting over the deep, Scotch-taped tear. Jack automatically folds a double-thickness of napkin and hands it to me to sit on. I often think of his face with this perfect coffee-shop art framed directly behind it, two broken-necked ducks hanging from the arm of a hunter, a shotgun raised into a surreal turquoise sky. His hand curves around the white cup, his index finger snaking through the handle in an almost feminine way, his thumb cradling the lip. He drinks coffee the way my father used to (his only vice), sucking it down like a small, urgent engine. I always appreciate a man with comforting coffee breath.

"This doesn't seem very real," I say. I'm cutting my toast into "fingers" the way my mother used to prepare them for dipping into the yolk of a soft-boiled egg.

"Death's like that," Jack tells me.

My heart is suddenly thudding very fast in a peculiarly balanced mix of anger and caffeine. "You're the big expert, I guess." I'm looking down into my coffee cup so hard, I'm cross-eyed. Jack's parents both died a few years apart when he was still a teenager. He's had a long time to fine-tune this wisdom.

"I'm not being competitive, I'm being empathic," he says.

"Stop sounding like a shrink." My mug comes down a little

too hard, sloshing coffee onto my hand and the table. Jack wanted to be a therapist before he got sidetracked by what I like to call his "drug journalism." He's an easy mark, except that he's basically so good at it. He even knows how to look at his watch while pretending not to.

"Death and deadlines," I say as he dabs at me with a paper napkin. "Or is it the other way around?"

I'm really not a drama queen, but I make Jack run after me. I look back in time to see him shrug at our regular waitress, drop a clump of bills on top of the check with this loving, exasperated look on his face. I almost turn back and hurl myself at him.

Later that night, I'm roaming my apartment with Herbert tucked under one arm, heavy and sagging, the ashes perched on my open palm. They don't tell you in the interior design magazines how and where to showcase a loved one's remains. I'm reluctant to transfer him from my Tupperware container into a tasteful urn. The kitchen is the obvious place. But how to guard against one of Jack's unannounced baking binges (most recently, authentic raised doughnuts)? I'm remembering the way my father ate toast. Buttering it so neatly and evenly, spooning jam from the jar and spreading it with the very tip of his knife so carefully. Where did that care come from? Maybe I should put him in a jam jar, a really good one.

I stop in front of my tallest bookcase. Herbert takes this as a sign to unload. With a little push off from me, he leaps up and lands clumsily near the edge, but quickly recovers and starts busily cleaning himself. Reaching high, I shove the bag containing the Tupperware up next to him. Herbert has always loved a plastic bag, fresh in from the world. "Herbert, Dad. Dad, Herbert," I say. Herbert turns and starts licking the bag steadily.

For close to a week, I don't get out of bed except to buy coffee and the paper, which I stack neatly by my side and don't read. I spend an entire afternoon searching for the only message I remember my father ever leaving on my answering machine, but of course I can't find it.

My supervisor calls and leaves a message. When you're a floater, your status is that of part-time ghost, so it's easy to disappear. If you're there, you work and they pay you. If you're not, you simply edge off the radar screen. She doesn't quite say, "Your job is in jeopardy," but I can read between the lines. She has the kind of cheery voice that develops after years of making insincere phone calls, filled with the hills and valleys of faking it. "We miss you," she says. I don't return her call, see myself slipping lower and lower on the ladder until I'm doing the dead man's float facedown in the harbor.

Thea has obviously figured out that there's trouble next door. She's knocked on my door every morning since I've been back, wearing her big, colorful cooking caftan covered in stains. It's not as though she hasn't done this before, borrow emergency rosemary or thyme from my urban kitchen garden, a couple of window boxes that render my fire escape a complete hazard. But now she's trying to make the jobs she gives me sound really urgent, so I know that Jack must have put her up to this. "You have to help me assemble a hundred chicken pot pies for a lunch tomorrow!" And "Please, please, beef boogie for two hundred. I'm frantic!" As though her business hasn't been tootling along just fine without me. Some mornings I find myself over there in my bathrobe wielding a knife, somehow surprised that she'll let me, or julienning a barrelful of zucchinis with a special machine and listening to her rant and rave about a guy the night before who didn't make her come. Or complaining about the way her clients are around food, children with too much allowance and not enough taste. I have the urge to bring my father's ashes over to her in his Tupperware, knowing how Thea would get such a kick out of the leftovers metaphor.

One Saturday, two weeks after my return, I wake up to find Jack sitting on the edge of my bed staring at me. He's fully dressed. This is unusual to the point of alarming, this early on a weekend morning. The first couple of mornings after I got back he tried to cajole me out of bed by burrowing his way up between the sheets. I pushed him away, annoyed by his persistent, pointed tongue. The once-sumptuous caramel mingling of our morning coffee breath, and his complicated dissection of all the major national papers, once a source of bemused pride, only repelled me. At the door he kept looking back at me, a puppy eager for its next instruction. "Go away," I said. "Please go away." He took this as an invitation to come back and start phase two of his tough love program: dramatically pulling the sheets down to my feet, leaving me exposed and writhing on the wrinkled sea of contour sheet.

"You're depressed," he says. "You need medication. I've made an appointment for you with my shrink."

"Shrink?" I struggle to sit up. I'm freezing. My sleeveless nightgown has twisted so that my breasts jut from the armpits. He gestures at them, as though their cockeyed disarray only underscores his point. I surreptitiously adjust them, remembering the parable about the naked women in the road who deal with their shame by covering their eyes, not their genitals.

"Think of it as a vehicle, not the ultimate answer," says Jack, sounding like a pull quote from one of his beloved magazine sidebars. He puts his arms around me. I recoil, but then move closer, trying to relax by smelling the front of his shirt. I can only think of the way the buttons on so many of my dust rags, once his shirts, have scratched up my furniture.

So I go.

Jack's psychiatrist answers the door wearing Birkenstocks and thin ribbed black socks, which make me want to bolt. It's hard to do this when someone has opened his front door to you and is thrusting out a hand, establishing meaningful split-second

Jungian eye contact, and ushering you in, gracious and welcoming, even though he's charging you. I'm trapped. I reprimand myself for allowing so much negative mythology to attach to back-sloping shoes and bankers' socks. Who cares? The man is supposed to be a serotonin-receptor genius, the Leonardo of psychopharmacologists.

But Jack never mentioned the guy's decor. Safari stuff on the walls, masks and tusks and spears, jammed close together. The chairs are low-slung, made of rattan, their festive give making me sit back and spread my legs and crook my elbow behind my head as if I'm on the beach in Mexico. At a hundred seventy-five dollars an hour, I don't approve of this casual lounging.

After all that, I don't get what I want. I thought getting medication was so easy. With this guy it's like an interview for the Peace Corps. He keeps saying things like, "Tell me about a time that gave you joy." I leave with a sheaf of pages from his prescription pad, hoping he's tucked an actual prescription for drugs in with all the instructions for thyroid and hypoglycemia tests and positive life recipes. "Eat six to eight little meals a day," he says. "You'll notice fewer mood swings if you graze the way cattle do." I twist the tiny cream pages into an angry party favor and throw them into the trash can on the corner.

The next psychiatrist (I find his name on the bulletin board at a health-food store) prescribes exercise for my depression. He has a big belly and a handsome tanned face and peeling arms as though he's just stepped off a plane from the islands. His office smells faintly of cigar smoke. This seems vaguely unethical. Before even having a cup of coffee in the morning, I'm supposed to ride a stationary bike for twenty-two minutes and then again at night for twenty-eight, fifty minutes equaling a therapeutic dose of antidepressant medication in terms of its release of serotonin in the brain. I'm not sure what the cutesy time increments mean. He's doing research on this.

"Don't, whatever you do, offer this woman medication," the look on my face must say to doctors. "I'm not really depressed."

When he shakes hands with me at the door of his office, he hands me his scribbled phone numbers (office, home, beeper, cellular) on a page from a prescription pad, with this sardonic, sexy look on his face. The more phone numbers they give you, the less they really want you to call. The quantity of numbers alone is designed to soothe. "Runner's high is not a myth," he says, as though he's telling me that there is a God, but really thinking about fucking or eating medium-rare lamb chops.

The psychopharmacologist who finally gives me drugs (I get her name from a subway advertisement inquiring, "Do you suffer from depression?" and offering same-day appointments) wears a flowing black garment with sleeves that billow behind as she ushers me toward an oversized striped armchair. She rubs her hands together in rapacious delight, the witch in Hansel and Gretel.

"So tell me about yourself," she says, leaning toward me from her puffy, expensive armchair with the flattened seat. Her eyes keep darting down to look at her gold bracelet watch, then over toward the cordless phone on the table next to her. The receiver has a huge curved cradle growing out of its back, stained with desert-hued makeup. She wears outside-the-lines lipstick, which makes me think of my mother's recently acquired Bette Davis mouth.

"I guess I'm pretty depressed," I say. "My father's just died. I'm having trouble going to work. I don't want my boyfriend to touch me. Everything feels blah to me. I can't wake up. I'm crying all the time. I think I'd like to try some medication."

The phone rings and she jumps.

"Ah, my service," the doctor says, looking pleased. Her hand darts out. "What is it? I'm in session." Her voice is stern, strangely eager.

"Okay, put him through." She looks up and winks, stretching out her watch hand to me. "Tonight at eight is fine, sweetie." She hangs up. "Do you ever have suicidal thoughts?"

"Sometimes. But I'd never, ever do that," I add quickly.

"Is there anything else you think I should know?" She smiles again, widely.

The credits of my life fast-forward before my eyes. The producer has quit. The director is doubling as the gaffer. "I don't think so," I trail off. Abruptly the doctor gets up and, standing on tiptoe, dives into a double-doored closet. This fifty-minute hour is clocking in at barely ten.

"My pet drug," she says, handing me three boxes of Paxil samples along with a blue ballpoint pen imprinted with the word *Effexor* and a pad of Prozac stationery. I imagine the drug company salesman pulling out a chair for her at the Four Seasons.

She disappears for a minute, then returns proffering a plastic urine sample-size cup holding an elf's sip of water. "Take one of these every morning and call me in three weeks," she says.

I leave, clutching the colorful packets to my chest. We're face-to-face for a moment as I brush past her out the door, and our breasts graze. She offers me a last enormous smile. She has lipstick on her front teeth.

"Be well," she says.

eight

"If they can design these drugs so you can take weekend vacations away, why can't they design them to not interfere with sex at all, or to make it better?" I ask Jack. "I bet they already know how to do it."

He looks wise and withholding, as though he knows the research inside and out, and wants to save me. "You can't feel better and have good sex, too," he says.

I take Paxil for three weeks, then Dr. Lipstick switches me to Zoloft. Each drug makes me feel like I'm wearing a bigger, baggier hand-knit sweater, with the stitches closing in around the neck. I never believe in the fine print about side effects, but in this case it's true. I'm having heart palpitations and my beloved morning Colombian tastes like old metal fillings. I'm obsessively watching my reaction to random males, worrying about instant repressed libido despite my own reminders that it takes at least two weeks for the drug to reach system saturation. On one of the rare days that Jack's working dressed, I spend the morning staring at him intently as he sits in front of his computer. I notice the way his arms disappear into his T-shirt. I study his shoulders and then his crotch. *Did I feel more attracted to him two weeks ago?* I question my receptors. I envision us having antidepressant sex-weekends where we both go off our medication simultaneously so that we can plan to have high-functioning, multi-orgasmic romping for an entire weekend, then resume popping our SSRIs on grim Sunday night before the made-for-TV movie.

I talk to Gwen and my mother several times, but they sound far away, eerily, inappropriately polite. Our conversations are lifted rote from a bereavement manual.

"How are you coping?"

"I'm okay. How are you?"

"As well as can be expected."

"Are you taking care of yourself?"

"Call if you need anything. Anything at all."

"Remember what they say about time."

Shut up!

"Be well," I find myself closing these conversations, echoing Dr. Lipstick's soothing psycho-pablum. None of this seems to reconcile with the recent memory of Gabriel's naked torso, my mother's winey body odor, Gwen's mutating seductions, my father's last, rasping breath.

My new memory has become prickly and selective. I can hear music, but I can't hear Jack talking. I can remember my father dying, but I can no longer picture him sitting on the side of my bed, hearing my prayers. For some inexplicable reason, waking and sleeping, my former dance teacher, Carlos, hovers above me, beckoning like some swivel-hipped siren. The whole world has gone gray, except for his bright red silk shirt and his outstretched hand. In my dreams, I dance so beautifully that people stand on the sidelines and weep. More than once, I wake up feeling as though I've discovered the answer.

Finally, with drug number two leaching inexorably from my system, I pick up the phone and call Latin-Is-for-Lovers Dance Studio, and make an appointment for their Beginners' Mambo Special for two. (Mambo. Tango. Chemo.)

That night, in dark, final tones, Jack, the professional depressive, my prospective partner in dance therapy, announces, "I have no shoes."

"What about the ones you wore to your brother's wedding?" I ask. Now that I've made a decision to pursue rehabilitative dance, I'm all perky dance mistress.

I head into his bedroom and start rummaging in his closet on my hands and knees and come up with a pair of worn hiking boots, a pair of bent, smelly running shoes, and his L. L. Bean moccasins with the squished accordion backs, before pouncing on his only dress shoes, circa high-school prom night. This closet is the primary domestic roadblock to our moving in together.

I skate one hand over the leather soles, worn thin as shoe box cardboard. "Not Gene Kelly's, but they'll do."

Jack groans and sits on the edge of the bed, his head in his hands. "Shit," he says. "They're too small." He sounds hopeful. I grab his hand and pull him up and we shuffle around in a modified Hustle with a whisper of TV hip-hop and a soupçon of Woodstock.

"Do we have to? Let's do this later," he says, trying to break away, looking panicked.

"Yes, we have to." I nod vigorously. Trying to find a Latin beat on his old clock radio, I hold on to both of his wrists with my other hand. I find the Spanish station and tune it in, not letting go, even though he's straining to get away. It's now or never to begin the dancing cure.

I push and pull him around the perimeter of the Black Watch plaid bed skirt, a gift from his mother, in a quick-quick-slow rhythm that I dredge up from some cerebral compartment that houses the Frug and the Hula Hoop. Moving Jack's hips with both hands, I finally get him to start a tiny sideways action. The minute we're in synch, it becomes clear that we've been dancing to a Goya commercial. I flop down on the bed feeling instantly hopeless.

We arrange to meet at Latin-Is-for-Lovers one evening. The

waiting room looks like a doctor's office. When Jack arrives, we sit side by side against the wall on folding auditorium chairs. Even though I've been here before, I still feel like it's the first time. He takes my hand and holds it in his lap with both of his, as though any minute now a nurse will come out with the results of our first-trimester ultrasound. Our palms become damp. We stare up at a small television hanging from the ceiling from which tango music emanates faintly. Here and there a foot taps, self-consciously on time. Dressed in swirling magenta, a slender woman on the video arches back over her partner's arm, her gleaming black bun pointing toward the floor. I'm already worried about the tacky ballroom gowns you obviously have to wear for these competitions, the weird off-the-shoulder bias cuts, the feather boas swimming at the hems.

Carlos, with his slicked-back black hair and haughty beaked nose, sweeps into the waiting room holding a clipboard. After all my red silk shirt fantasies, I'm startled to see him again in the flesh, so small and busy. He looks over at me and raises one eyebrow. What does he remember? I wonder. He can't possibly know how wonderfully we've danced together in my dreams.

"Hi, beginners, I'm Carlos," he says.

Everyone in the waiting room stands up at once. My mouth is sticky. I wish I'd had a drink to loosen up the rhythm section of my brain.

We follow him through one tiny adjoining classroom after another, stepping over sills and squeezing through narrow doorways, a fairy-tale maze. A man behind me bumps his head and yelps.

Once we reach the classroom, I'm eager to stand by myself. In my mind I'm already excelling in Advanced Couples Performance Practice, preferably without Jack. But he sticks right by me, keeps reaching out and touching parts of me—shoulder, back, waist—as though we've just been reunited after separate years abroad. Our eyes keep meeting in the mirror that lines the front of the classroom; his face is pale, his eyes their most dark and beseeching. He's wearing khakis that bag slightly at the knees and his best-man shoes and Good Humor man shirt, white with wide, stiff sleeves as though it's been starched and steam-pressed at the ice cream plant, his version of the Latin Dance King. Next to Carlos, Jack looks as wide and ungraceful as a refrigerator. I find a stingy welling of love. He rubs his hands down the sides of his pants and shrugs at me, starts doing the twist with an invisible hand towel at his hips, something that usually makes me laugh. The sympathy well instantly dries. I turn away, pretending I don't know him.

We arrange ourselves in one long straggling line in front of the mirror, a chorus of men and women trying to find grace and meaning.

"Boys on one side, girls on the other," Carlos says, clapping his hands sharply a few times, bringing back with a rush ballet class with Madame when I was a teenager, her passionate bloodshot eyes and mysterious, not yet identifiable whiskey breath, the way she would come close and clap her slender white hands with their bright red palms less than an inch from my nose until she'd made me cry.

We take a long time negotiating Carlos's instructions, shuffling back and forth from one side of the room to the other. Someone careens hard into the mirror and we all giggle. Carlos places both hands on his hips in mock disgust.

"You can be a girl if you want," he says. I realize he's addressing Jack, who has somehow found his way over to the wrong side.

Please don't humiliate him, I silently beg. But Jack is looking around, lifting the collar of his Good Humor shirt like a gangster, sidling back to the male side of the room amidst appreciative laughter. He does a little soft-shoe, ending *ta-da!* on one foot. "This isn't a tap class," I want to shout. His face no longer has its cadaverous shine.

I have the sudden sense of him being just fine without me.

Carlos stands between the two lines like an army general, looking us sternly up and down. Then he holds his hand out to me. "We begin with basic," he says.

Well into the dancing cure, Jack completely loses interest, while I can think of nothing else. Turn patterns have turned my head. Quick-quick-slow is the only beat that quickens my heart. I've stopped returning my mother's and Gwen's phone calls. I'm floating on the dance floor, not at work. My savings are nose-diving into the danger zone.

When I broach our class schedule for the following month, Jack tells me, with suspicious breeziness, to do whatever I want. Before I have a chance to sign him up, he shows me an article describing how medication affects the way you hear music. Based on a minor study, he's now convinced that the sacculus, a structure in the inner ear that responds to decibels and maintains balance, is dulled by antidepressants. Surprise, surprise! His brain's greatest pleasure is lying around feeling depressed, not moving his feet in time to the beating of his heart.

"Don't you think the study was probably done on monkeys whose idea of great dancing is playing tin cymbals and jumping up and down while scratching?" I protest.

"You can't ignore empirical evidence," he says.

I drag him out to a practice party, the post–junior high school torture session designed to remind grown-ups that they're still only wallflowers moving through the world. He trudges across the floor with his hands in his pockets, looking down at his feet. He stops in front of a woman sitting in one of the metal folding chairs against the wall. *No, not her!* I telegraph to him. I watch, helpless, as the woman shakes her head and turns away. I want to go up to her and hit her for doing this to his confidence. But why did he ask someone to dance who has such long, beautiful black hair? She looks as though she's been doing triple inside turns since she learned to walk. This isn't supposed to happen at dance school, although here, as in life, compassion and classlessness are a myth. This is classic Jack. Low self-esteem and a monstrous ego in one wrinkled-shirt package.

He sits down again on the sidelines. I lose both my concentration and the beat. The guy I'm dancing with shakes my arm like it's a piece of wet laundry. I break away and walk off the dance floor, something you're never, ever supposed to do: Never abandon your dance partner, even if the music stands are sliding off the deck. Some night when this stranger is the only man in the room and I'm the only woman and he looks right through me and chooses the water cooler instead, I may regret this. He immediately asks another woman to dance. She jumps up eagerly. Right away, they seem to be having a much better time than he did with me, and I'm jealous.

A merengue comes on. This is supposed to be the simplest dance on earth. I ask Jack to dance. We seesaw our way into the corner where there are no mirrors and slowly wind down, a dying battery toy. He stops abruptly, then bends me back over his arm in a hard dip and keeps me there until the blood rushes to my head and starts pounding in time with the music.

"I can't do this," he says. He's staring into my bulging eyes. For a minute I think he's going to drop me. I brace against the pain of a three-foot fall. His face is serious, gorged with blood. The two of us could service the whole Red Cross. He leans down and kisses me, then jerks me upright and spins me away, looking astonished at his own instinctive reenactment of some long-ago Fred Astaire/Ginger Rogers routine. He whirls me back into his chest, looking more confident, suddenly Mr. Ballroom. About-facing crisply, he walks away. Even his shirt looks less wrinkled.

"Why haven't you danced this way before?" I call after him.

He doesn't answer. Just shrugs and keeps walking. My suave mambo guy.

I plunge into the world of unlimiteds, finding a whirlwind comfort in this candy store for grown-ups. I charge a block of fifteen private classes with Carlos, busting the limit on my credit card. I do this deliberately, knowing I have to use the privates up in a certain time period, like when you take steaks out of the freezer. I have this idea that I'm going to quit my job and just dance. I think of Ballet Michael and the yearning, soaring grand jeté feeling I've been searching for ever since. Maybe this is it. I imagine announcing my career decision to my father.

One night at the studio, I call my mother from the studio's one pay phone. It's like calling from a college dorm. Behind me, there's a line of students itching to get back to class. A turned-out foot taps, impatient quarters click against the bannister, throats clear with raspy deliberation.

"Hi, Mom," I say. "I can't talk long." I hunch over the phone, the recipe one part shame, two parts regression. I should have called from home this morning. I'm pretty sure I hear glasses clinking in the background. Maybe Gwen's over and they're polishing off the one-bottle wine cellar. I don't want to know.

"I'm at dance school. How are you?"

"Fine, perfectly fine," says my mother. My finger is plugged in my ear against the rhumba music that's wailing a couple of yards away. A woman leaves the phone line in disgust, but her stomping turns to animated dancing as soon as she reenters the classroom. "I'm going to get cut off," I yell, as though my mother's in Havana. "I'll call you soon." I'd wanted to ask her if I could borrow money, but couldn't bring myself to. (Dance Druggie. Homeless Hoofer. Mambo Bum.)

I apply for a new credit card and get it in three days. (Your father never charged, your father had no debt.) I buy two new pairs of dance shoes.

Pair #1: Black, T-strap, soft leather with a heartbreaking squashed heel, the kind of shoes a Broadway dancer would wear.

Pair #2: Pinkish nude satin with two-and-a-half-inch spike heels and a rhinestone design on the cross strap (admittedly age/ability inappropriate, I can tell by the look on the salesgirl's face). A pair of sheer black stockings with a design of tiny rhinestones on the ankles to match the shoes.

Standing in front of the long mirror in my bedroom, I practice my turns. The rhinestones hardly show over the tops of the shoes, but I know they're there, glinting devilishly. My father's dead and all I want is to be a great dancer: early in the morning before coffee or sex, late into the night on champagne and no sleep. I want to turn so fast, I'm a blur. I want to dance beautifully with every man in the world. They say you can die in the throes of sex. What about dancing?

Jack calls and tells me, "I'll come back if we can stick to the fox-trot. Or waltz. I was programmed to do those dances back in sixth grade. I can't do anything that requires hips."

"I'm sorry, but I need hips right now," I say.

nine

The dance studio bustles like a rush-hour train station. Today's cast of characters: Zorro, six foot two, with a couple dancing the tango tattooed on the back of his neck. He stares up at some religious point above my head while we dance, his eyes wide and earnest, black as patent leather. His step is so wide and loping, his legs so long, I've invented a little hop to keep up with him. This hop is the first in my developing lexicon of personal style, so important in dancing. So far, mine is on the sparse side, a brand-new wardrobe with spaces between the hangers.

Geisha Girl's hair covers one eye. She's dressed in diver's black with frog buttons slanting across her chest. She keeps time with a little tick of her tongue against the roof of her mouth. You can hear it over the music as she passes each man. She won't lose the beat just because she's losing her partner, won't raise her eyes or crack her caked white face in a smile.

Shuffle Bum practically stands still when he dances, not bothering to move his feet except for the occasional lackluster stumble that gets the two of us around eventually, a little shy of the beat. Next to his, my feet are large and frantic, big American cars vying for a lane. I want to report him, get him arrested for low-rent footwork. I deflate when I dance with him. He makes me remember how much I want time to stop, why I want to rush forward into the next dance, vaulting over the timid beginnings and the tragic endings, to stay in the middle where nothing else exists.

Velcro Sally never lets go, has to do the combination one more time or she won't get it, holds up the line, ruffled pink top riding up her ribs. The men eye their next position in the circle, dying to shake her loose.

To dance with Shortest Man I have to stoop. I become lost in the cave of our arms. His are thick and hairy, a meaty warren, patched with deodorant. This dance is low-ceilinged, oddly comforting. I dance with my knees bent, close to the ground, expecting not grace and air but a few solid moves, a short, filling meal of bread and cheese.

Spider, natural eyeliner, tight black jeans, long guitar-plucking fingernails on one hand. Every move is slide and parry, delicate as a web. He makes darting eye contact, sucks on menthol drops in time to the music.

No one's sure why she's here, but Cha-Cha Queen knows how to dance, fast or slow, with total disdain. The men can't wait to get to her, yet are afraid to arrive. Carlos tangles with her octopus arms as she unlearns the way she's learned and relearns his way. We all eye this premiere couple, the Ones Whose Hips Already Know.

Nasdaq arrives late, never apologetic, carrying his briefcase, with his suit jacket over his arm as though this is just another meeting. He rolls up his crisp pinstripe shirtsleeves twice, holds out his hands for me like claws on an instrument panel. Clomping in his shiny wing tips, his rhythm is buttoned down, boilerplate perfect. Narrow hips thrust at me like a small dog's.

I pray that class will end before Warlock comes around to me again in this mandatory game of musical partners. With his damp black T-shirt smelling of layer upon layer of old sweat, his fingernails digging into my palms. Even worse, the look of frantic, passionate focus in his eyes. How dare he try so hard. I imagine some young ballet dancer working at Capezio's staring down at his grizzled head and laughing as he bends to lace up his new dance shoes. It's my responsibility to make him feel graceful and accomplished. This is the definition of a good dancer, to become the selfless mirror for the other. But his eyes are so afraid as he counts out loud, staring at my breasts. When he tries leading me in Suzy Q's, the saucy step in which you're supposed to prance on tiptoe, leaning coquettishly forward and bracing against your partner's spread hands, his balance totters and he has to keep adjusting his feet. I feel like a wide-load prefab in need of special steering.

Fay wears a blond wig and has large yellowed teeth. A bright gash of red lipstick leaks into her mouth seams, her strappy silver-sprayed sandals shed paint across the floor. Carriage perfect, she throws back the stiff tresses of the wig flirtatiously, delicate calves bulge veins in support stockings. Her partners lean in attentively. I can tell that she feels beautiful. Dancing, after all, is like sex. It's all how you feel about yourself inside while you're doing it.

Hovering too close is the ghost of the aging ballet student who was in Madame's class when I was a teenager. With her wrinkled neck and bony blue hands, the hand-knit, hard-orange leg warmers and ballet sweater imported from England—she was everything I didn't want a ballet dancer to be. The woman stood in the corner, pressing the tops of her toes into the floor, again and again, as though she still wore toe shoes. She'd once danced onstage, I knew, had been a swan in the corps de ballet. The way she cast her eyes down, you could tell she still imagined herself there. No one wanted to stand next to her in line. Her brittle movements and failure to stay young might be catching.

As though to make up for my past cruelty, I always take Fay into my arms with courtly tenderness. At first I held my breath against her sweet, powdery smell. But now I breathe in as we dance, welcoming that smell, curving my arm happily around her dry, brittle weight. She beams up at me, head cocked, flirting with me out of faded, velvety eyes as though she sees the cruel young ballet dancer inside me and forgives her.

I know how much I know only when my feet are tired. I've cracked my dance shoes, joined the shoe leather hoofers, Cyd Charisse, James Brown. My father wore such sensible shoes, walked with a steady tread, watched where he stepped.

I'm a social worker in mambo class, pretending to find the best in people, overlooking the alcohol shadow on someone's breath, another's sifting dandruff. It's easy with The Kid. He has shoulders like sturdy planks beneath his shirt, and tight blue jeans, a cowboy. Gazing off into space, he dances with an out-of-body indifference as though his mother has sent him. I look forward to when he lands in front of me in the ever-moving circle, enjoy the way he trails one big warm hand around my midriff, ropes me in during turns, making my belly button twinge, transporting me back to ballet class with Michael.

One evening I go to class and there aren't enough men. "Would you mind being a man tonight?" Carlos asks, walking across the classroom to whisper his question. I suddenly find myself standing in the men's circle, facing the outer circle of women. As each one passes through my arms, I see in their eyes, in the way they move their arms, their hips, their necks, the way they flirt with me, a reflection of what I've felt on that side.

I try to make my hands lyrically supple. Providing the essential dancing hook of melded forefinger, middle and ring fingers around which a woman turns, I'm strangely confident. The mirror image of the woman's part comes to me intact and I don't falter. I'm a mambo savant.

"You're a great lead," Cha-Cha Queen whispers in my ear as we line up for the ladies' room during break. She squeezes my arm as though to feel my biceps and presses lightly against my side with her upper body. "Better than any man in the class. Except for Carlos," she adds. She brings her lips unnecessarily close to my ear.

"Thank you," I say, pleased. Spider and Shortest Man are watching us. A few men seem to admire the way I have so quickly picked up their part; others seem annoyed, as though there will be fewer women for them to seize upon, which is in some ways true. What do women want when they dance? To be held, yes. But what more? I think of my mother dancing in the laundry room in her apron, gazing up at her tall, invisible partner.

During break, I don't know whose side I'm on. Couples break apart and head for the water fountain, then reconfigure. I stand near Spider and he looks at me searchingly, as though he can learn something revelatory about women.

"Did I hurt you before?" he asks.

"When?" I ask, trying to remember his particular crime in the swirl of moving violations, the bumps and the crashes, elbow to tit, forearm to cranium.

"I don't know, I don't remember," he says. (The worst crime, to not remember.) "Didn't I smack you in the chest? I smacked some woman in the chest." He's staring at my breasts, as though he can read the answering bruises through my top.

"I was a man for the last few dances," I say. "I don't think it was me."

Carlos is watching us. He's talking to his circle of students, but he keeps looking over at me. I wonder what this means. When class resumes, he again pulls me out of the women's line into the center of the room. To demonstrate how men must not behave. He places one slim hand on my shoulder in the woman's position. With his other hand, he takes mine and plants it in the small of his own back. I like the way he's so casually possessive with my body, as though we've been dancing together for years. Then he takes my wrist and slides it around his own rib cage toward the front of his chest to show how easily a man can come too close to a woman's breasts, sometimes even touch one while dancing. Jumping at this imagined injury, he spins away from me, glaring. I step back. Suddenly we're doing a tango. The class laughs.

We separate. He reaches for my hand and we step back in toward each other. I bow and he curtsies low. The class laughs harder. Carlos smiles. I'm not sure why he enjoys this so much. Returning me to the women's line, he whips me around in a fast double turn. When I return to face him, I see a few fine beads of moisture from my nose on his red, beautifully knotted tie.

The next evening, Carlos asks me to dance the man's part again. Five minutes into class, Jack walks in. He sits on the bench at the side to change into his best-man's shoes. As he laces them up, he scans the lines of students, looking worried. As far as I know, he's never come to a class alone. I wonder if he'll give up and take his shoes off and leave if he doesn't spot me. "Jack," I say in a loud stage whisper over the music. He looks up and down the women's line. Then again, louder: "Jack!"

He brightens, and then his face falls into a puzzled look and he cocks his head, trying to figure this out. We haven't spoken in close to three weeks. I'm not home at night. I'm not returning his calls.

"Choose a partner," Carlos instructs, clapping his hands. Jack jumps up and is coming toward me when he sees Cha-Cha Queen plant herself in front of me and put her hand on my shoulder possessively. He does a deer-in-the-headlights freeze, then veers left and heads over to Fay. He takes her by the hand, giving me a hurt look over his shoulder, and escorts her to the opposite side of the circle. It's the man's job to rotate around the circle of women from partner to partner. Moving in the same constellation, Jack and I will never meet.

Plucking me from Cha-Cha's clutches, Carlos leads me into the center to demonstrate. He quickly reviews the combination we learned last night. I'm still the man. Through a complex merry-go-round of arms, I watch Jack's face. It looks frozen with worry, forehead wrinkled. I want to go to him, grab him away from Fay's old-lady grip, teach him what I know, give in to the fox-trot, be the girl again. With a little amused smile, Carlos returns me to Cha-Cha, who immediately puts her left hand on my shoulder and offers me her right one, with the long gold nails aiming for my palm. I shrug in Jack's direction, flashing him a half smile that he doesn't see, and take her in my arms. How easy it is to take women in my arms. Why was it that my father couldn't?

Once the music starts, I forget all about Jack. If drums are the heart, mine is fibrillating to distraction. But as soon as I land in front of Fay, and she beams me her big yellow smile, I suddenly remember him and sneak a quick look behind me. His shirt is stuck in a narrow line of sweat to the middle of his back. "Flop sweat," I can hear him say with relish tomorrow, leaning back in the client chair, his psychiatrist flipping his Birkenstock on one toe and nodding wisely as though he knows exactly what dancing terror is all about.

During the break I sidle up to Jack, who's standing in line at the drinking fountain. I feel like we're back in high school. I lean my face into his back, remembering for a second Gabriel's patchouli-scented collar. Jack smells of sweat and Tide. "Hi," I say.

"Well, if it isn't Signor Mambo," he says, not turning. He moves abruptly away from me and leans down to the fountain and gulps water with his mouth wide open for at least a minute straight. When it's my turn at the fountain, he takes this opportunity to walk away. Fay joins him in looking out the window and they stand there talking animatedly. He's waving his hands around as he talks, and once he gestures over in my direction, without actually looking at me. I'm pretty sure he's not telling her what a great dancer I am. He's probably talking about his meds and his unreliable sense of rhythm.

After the break, Carlos requests that the women step back and the men come to the center of the room and face the mirror. At least I've remembered to wear pants and shoes with low heels so I don't stand out too much. I push by the other men and position myself so that I'm standing next to Jack, figuring he might need me. He won't meet my eyes in the mirror. I remember our first class together, his impromptu gangster shuffle.

Carlos has the men review a tricky side step. Suddenly he stops dancing, walks to the tape player, and shuts off the music. He turns to face us. I can feel everyone steeling for a group lecture. He passes right by me and stops in front of Jack. "You're not dancing on the two," Carlos says in a surprisingly mild tone, referring to the correct beat of the music on which to start dancing mambo. He studies him for a minute. He reaches for my hand and joins it with Jack's, and holds them together, as though he's a priest, marrying us. "Demonstrate to my friend how to dance on the two," he says to me.

I want to say no. I want to tell him Jack is all wrong for this. I want to tell him that I can't change dancing genders so quickly. I want to tell him that my father has died. But I have learned my lesson well from Madame. When it comes to dance, you only say yes.

Jack and I bounce up and down in place, marking time, trying to synchronize our starting beat. We step out together and our two right knees collide. A wave of laughter from men and women, both. Carlos hides his mouth behind his hand.

We stop, drop hands, and Jack bends and rubs his kneecap. Still below waist level, he hisses, "Has mourning turned you into a man?"

"I'm a better man than you are," I hiss back.

At this point Carlos intervenes. Making Jack take him in his arms, he begins to push him around, counting in a slow, exaggerated kindergarten teacher's voice. "You . . . shouldn't . . . be . . . in . . . this . . . class . . . if . . . you . . . can't . . . count," he intones.

Jack's face is sheepish and sullen, a little red around the ears. Behind his glasses, his brown eyes are burning. He has his stampeding bull look. He could go off and write a blistering opening paragraph right now, but he can't figure out how to coordinate his brain and his feet. For a minute I feel guilty that I've involved him in this.

"Count it out loud with me," says Carlos. "The whole class." Suddenly we're all chanting primary numbers and moving in unison, without partners, one of the narcotic, childhood aspects of dance class.

When it's time for the last dance, Carlos doesn't have us switch partners. He sometimes does this to simulate a real-life situation in which we are made to cast our lot with one partner, and enjoy or endure that person for an entire dance. Cha-Cha Queen grabs me. She seems to have adopted me as her favorite male dance partner. The song goes on and on. Her silky blouse wrinkles under my hand. I'm staring into her eyes not so much because I desire her, but because this is what this music makes you do.

At some point in the middle of the song, we're perfectly in synch. I'm moving her turning arm in a sexy tick-tock, ready to spin her out, when Jack careens into us like a moving van changing lanes.

"What the fuck!" says Cha-Cha, jumping back, her eyes all big and incensed. She runs her tongue over her front teeth repeatedly, managing to avoid her dark red lipstick, as though she's literally lapping up the situation. She keeps rolling her eyes and making tsk-ing noises, looking around like she's waiting for the mambo police to come along and arrest Jack.

I'm irritated, but still not convinced that this junior-high-school, frog-down-the-shirt ploy of his was intentional. The art of staying in a small, proscribed area when you dance is only learned through practice and intention. I imagine Jack focusing on his feet and making these big farmhand, out-in-the-wheat-field moves until he blundered right into us. His radar is undeniably connected to me. I can't blame the guy.

He's standing there looking clumsy and out of place, as though he's waiting to fill out an accident report. Cheerful Fay has stopped patting him on the shoulder and is now smoothing her skirt and looking around for a new partner.

Completely ignoring our traffic accident, Carlos is packing up his tapes with his back turned, ready for class to end as soon as the song is over. I have this petulant urge to go over and tug on his balloon sleeve, make him get involved. This somehow seems his fault, the result of his Machiavellian doings earlier on. I sometimes forget how bored dance teachers must get, how insignificant these dance-floor dramas become to them. It's obvious that Carlos doesn't give a shit. I realize that I'm more in love with Carlos and Cha-Cha Queen and mambo right now than I am with Jack. No matter that this has more to do with mourning and dancing than love or sex. On one side my mother is clapping, on the other my father is checking his watch and turning away. Unlike the rest of my life, dancing feels intense and real, accompanied by horns and bongos and heavy breathing, so I don't care.

"I'm staying for the practice party," I tell Jack.

A derisive look twists his face. "Basement rec room, low lights, necking?" He shoves his hands in his pockets and studies me. "Sounds great."

"No necking," I say.

"I miss you," says Jack.

"I'm trying not to miss anyone right now," I say, and turn away.

He leaves, and I go upstairs. For a while I'm lonely, a wallflower, thinking of limbo, not the dancing kind, and ashes. But then someone comes over and asks me to dance. I wonder what my mother said when the man in the photograph asked her to dance. "Yes, thank you," I say, sounding more English than I mean to. And I dance and dance until midnight and the lights go up and the school closes and the balls of my feet are so sore I can hardly walk.

On the way to the subway I'm walking through a maze of subway tunnels covered in tile like one big, echoey bathroom. Having not yet had my fill for the day, I'm still listening to salsa music, the headphones tipped back on my head. I pause in front of a subterranean drugstore window that holds a lunatic display of plastic and glass, glittering under fancy spotlights. My feet are still moving. A true mambo nerd, I still have on my dance shoes.

I sense someone behind me, watching. Whirling around, I'm facing a female security guard in her blue uniform. Her lipstick is the thick, granular red of cold tomato juice. Her feet are doing a little dance. Without thinking, I step up to her and hold out my arms. I reach down to my Walkman and press the speaker button. We stand this way for a minute, and then we start to dance.

This time, she's the guy. She has a loping, easy step. We hear the music emanating from my waist in distant, tinny miniature. She smells of a spicy man's cologne with a feminine base, saucy and edible. Up close her shirt is like a piece of sky. I worry that someone will come along and she'll lose her job. I wonder if she's crazy..

We stop right in front of the window with the cheap perfume and the Pepto-Bismol. We're both breathing hard. She kisses the air in my direction and walks away backward. I think of my mother and how she can't say no. I think of my father and how he couldn't say yes. I wonder if there's something in between that actually works.

ten

"Girl, Carlos is running late," the receptionist greets me, each fingernail a sunset.

The front desk is so high up, I feel like a kid back at the principal's office. It's filled with statuettes grouped on each end, black plastic and fake gold won at dance competitions in U.S. backwater towns (e.g., the Ohio Star Ball), as if to say: Sign up for a year of unlimited classes, and you, too, can win one of these!

I get my slip and head toward the classroom, automatically walking ducklike, the smell and soft sheen of the wooden studio floors returning me immediately to old ballet habits. I love the sound of a "private"—secretive, sexy, body parts whispering in a closed room. Some of the studios are as big as two-car garages, others aren't much more than cubbyholes lined up along the hall like cells in a brothel. The traffic is constant, the music loud and conflicting, the rooms so confined that at the end of the day they're a stew of sweat, breath, perfume, aftershave, damp feet and crotch.

Sometimes if you're in one of the bigger rooms, there are other people dancing with you. It isn't really private at all, it's all about making money, and nothing to do with art. Sometimes teachers even mix up the dances and take turns with the music. Suddenly there you are trying to hear the Latin beat, and listening to swing music. You just have to keep it going in your head (quick, quick, slow, 5, 6, 7, 8). They tell you that learning to dance is all about counting anyway.

Ten minutes late, Carlos sweeps into the practice room on a rush of aftershave. Although I normally don't like aftershave, his is overpowering in a way that makes me feel sexy and helpless. During the lesson, little puffs of his scent keep emanating from inside his ballooning pirate/poet shirt, first from the direction of an armpit, then from a deeper region, his midriff or his back. My mother always wanted my father to wear aftershave, and she used to buy it for him on Christmas and birthdays, but he never opened the bottles, and finally she just stopped.

Carlos keeps talking about "the man" and "the woman."

"The man needs to feel where the woman is at all times," he says. I like how elemental this sounds, Adam and Eve doing mambo in the Garden. He's carrying a cardboard case under his arm that looks old enough to have once held 45s. He places the case on the bench next to the tape deck and opens it and starts rummaging around inside, picking up one tape and reading the case sideways, then discarding it with a clatter and picking up another, as if they're battered old friends. "Today we're gonna review turns," he says, rubbing his hands together, acting all enthusiastic but looking bored, not quite seeing me. This is how they learn to do this, I think. Act all there on the outside, and intimate, but inside one big yawn. I want to be able to change that. I think about Jack's obsessional interest in his own depression. Probably if he grew up dancing from the time he could walk, he'd be as blasé as Carlos is.

"First of all, the hands," he says. "Think of pizzas. Our hands together should be like pizza dough." He comes toward me, closing his eyes briefly. I can see the lizardy movement of his eyeballs under his lids. He places his palm flat against mine, as though we're kids measuring fingers. We're standing about a foot apart. I'm tempted to slide my hand up and down his just slightly to warm mine, to create friction before we dance, but this would give him the wrong idea, that I want more from him than simply to learn how to dance. Really, this isn't true, although it might become true the more we do this.

I keep glancing sidelong up at the clock and then back at him, worried that he will notice and think I'm bored, or want the lesson to end. I want it never to end. It's not that I'm in love with Carlos. I can see that if he were ever in my bed I'd find him too thin. He looks as though he'd wear tiny black satin bikinis and have a single line of hair running down from his belly button. I would feel like a dough girl under him, large and soft and pale. Hands could be like pizza dough, but not your whole body. I want him to keep dancing with me, even when the hour is over and I've stopped paying him. Even if he wanted to, the school wouldn't allow him to. I want to be a good enough dancer for him to break the rules.

"I'm not sure I understand," I say. "About the pizza dough."

"Okay," says Carlos. "This is the story." He grabs my right hand and raises it high in the air. I feel as though I'm John Travolta in his white three-piece suit about to do that move from *Saturday Night Fever.* But the music is all wrong. While Carlos has been clattering around with his tapes, some other teacher has come along with his Viennese Waltz student and popped a tape in, and they're circling grandly around us, their heads poking forward like fancy geese. The heartbeat gone in an airy rush of strings. Jack would love this. My mother would love this. They should dance together. I can see her version of the royal wave as she waltzes by.

Carlos and I look up at our hands hanging together above our heads, fingers clasped and playing like we're about to get married. I try to keep my hands soft but not mushy, pliant but not too tender. I lodge a ball of pizza dough in my mind, and all my senses sit in it. Carlos is moving his hand around mine, grabbing my fingers, letting them go, then moving the flat of his hand around onto the flat of my hand. It seems very Italian, very Japanese, definitely not Latin. Then he takes his two fingers and forms them into a hook, and hooks my two fingers with his, and then I just grab hold, like a big baby capturing a twisting mobile. We both laugh and I flush from bottom to top.

Still holding our hands high, he does a smooth left turn. "He goes," he says. Then he guides me under his arm in a right turn. "She goes." When I'm facing him again, he does another turn, small and perfect. "He goes," he says. "Get it? He goes, she goes, he goes. That's the deal." Then he takes my right hand and places it on his waist and starts spinning and spinning, like a kid let out of school, so hard that my hand skates around his middle, bumping over his belt and his taut waistline. Every time my hand touches his hipbone, it rides up slightly. I have the urge to grab hold of his belt buckle and yank him to a stop, facing me. He isn't even breathing hard. I can't believe that anyone can move this fast and gracefully. Will I ever arrive here? The closest I've come to this is doing turns in ballet. But they were so stiff, one foot at the knee, spotting like a puppet. What comes closer, maybe, is sex, the moment when the breath rises and falls, rises and falls, your head is filled with sound and you no longer care that someone might hear.

I can barely manage a double turn, and here Carlos is doing four, six, ten at a time. I feel privileged to have a hand resting on this leashed tornado.

He goes. Will she ever go?

We're finished. It's the mourning that happens after taking the last sip from a glass of perfect wine. The longing to have just one more dance fills the room; the air grows pink with it. Carlos's back is turned away from me and he's reshuffling his tapes, returning them to their cases. I walk up behind him and just stand there. I want him to turn around and hold out his arms to me and glide me back to the center of the room and start dancing again, just once more, just because he wants to. I remember when I used to stand behind the chair where my father sat reading the paper, my eyes trained on the back of his head. I'd read about ESP and I wanted him to sense my thoughts. Behind the wide armchair, my feet did an intricate barre combination while I tried not to move my upper body at all so he wouldn't detect what I was doing. *Daddy, read my mind,* I'd be thinking as loud and hard as I could.

Once my father drove away from a gas station, leaving me standing there at the pumps. I'd been in the bathroom around the corner, and when I came out he'd already started the car. He'd forgotten me. I ran after him as fast as I could, then stood in the middle of the road, watching the silhouette of his head as the car chugged away. How could he not feel how hard my eyes burned? But he didn't turn around. A few minutes later, the car appeared again on the horizon. He did a U-turn and stopped at the side of the road next to me. I didn't say anything because it seemed like just another thing that was too late to repair.

Carlos puts his hand in his pants pocket and whistles and jingles some change. "Later," he says, and walks out.

Ten minutes after air-kissing him good-bye on both cheeks, a mandatory dance-school affectation, I run into Carlos sitting in the subway drinking beer out of a brown paper bag. It's like spotting your therapist on the street and realizing that he's actually a drug dealer. His elbows are propped on his knees. He's clearly tired, his salesman's smile swallowed. He looks up, sees me, and waves with the hand that isn't holding the beer. I blush and dip my head. It seems rude not to sit in the empty seat next to him. He's my teacher, not my father. It's a little tight, and instantly I feel the heat of his leg. I try to pull away, even though we've just been dancing and he's been holding me in his arms and I've felt the protuberances of his backbone under his black silk shirt, and my breast has brushed his arm at least three times while he told me how to hold my right arm in a T-square like the crank of an old-fashioned coffee grinder. He's still wearing his thin-soled black dancing shoes without socks. He leans back on the subway seat and sticks his legs, crossed at the ankle, straight in front of him, balancing the bottoms of his feet on the subway pole. He's short enough to do that. He's actually just the right size to be my dance partner.

I know it's too much to expect that Carlos will sit here with me and postmortem my technique. Shrinks can barely bring themselves to think about you after hours, although sometimes they tease you with this, as though they really are your loving, unconditional parent. For just a second one afternoon, you're there in their thoughts, and then, ha-ha, you're gone. Carlos is off-duty. He's heading home. Maybe he feels like he's dug ditches all day. The poetry of my basic step and the feel of my heart against his are the last things on his mind. He's thinking about paying his utility bill, or his girlfriend's *arroz con gandules.* He probably brushes twenty women's breasts just the way he's done mine today. He's probably bored with breasts by now. I'm sure you could rouse him from a deep sleep and instruct, "Cross body lead" or "Inside double turn," and he would take a woman in his arms and do the steps perfectly without ever waking up.

Would he think I was a good dancer if we slept together?

"Are you married?" he asks. "Do you have kids?"

Why is it that men always ask questions like this before they know you?

"No," I say, "but I'd like to." As though he's offered to father them. "Do you?"

"Yeah, two." He takes a long swig of beer.

Often I imagine what it would feel like to hold a child to my breast. Once while visiting a friend, I stood by her new baby's crib as she fussed, hungry, and wanted to bring her to my own breast, lift my sweater and pull it out, thrust it, empty and unenticing, just to see what it felt like to nurse, the existential tug. That tiny mouth, the feeling of tenderness. A dry run.

Every year that I don't have a baby, I add five dollars to the bottles of wine I buy. By the time it's really too late, I'll be sipping Haut Medoc every night in the bath, not giving a shit. Thea and I have this conversation a lot. She's decided to have a baby on her own but has yet to pick out the right man from her lineup of sitar players. I think she has some vision of herself continuing her catering business without skipping a beat, dropping the kid between buttering the phyllo and zesting the lemons. I've told her I'll be happy to baby-sit for her, as long as she lets me torch the crème brûlée once in a while. I tell her that sometimes I think my mother wants me to have a baby simply to carry on her dancing genes.

Carlos rises to get off the subway. Bending, he halfheartedly makes a kiss-kiss motion on either side of my face. Without planning to, I grab his hand, then immediately drop it.

"Do you have time next week?" I call this after him as he leaves, his bag slung over his shoulder, beer pumping at his side, as he steps out of my life and into his neighborhood forever. This is what it feels like when your dance teacher leaves.

He gestures with his spread thumb and pinkie to his ear to call him. I vow then and there that I will practice my turn patterns at home. I don't need Jack. I don't need anyone. I'll use a broom.

For a moment when we were turning, I'd felt an eerie, soaring joy, and realized I was starving.

I gather my courage and call Carlos, asking for a "home private." It's going to cost seventy dollars plus transportation, ten dollars more than at the studio. Although I know that he takes the subway, his travel plans seem too sensitive to discuss.

I take a shower and dab on a new perfume. I bought it because the shape of the bottle reminded me of a dancer leaning back in a swirl of hair and skirts. The scent is dark and oddly wet. I scrub most of it off with a washcloth, in a panic to achieve the right balance of casual, smell-good spontaneity and professionalism. I rub body lotion into my arms and hands and then wipe it off. Soft but not greasy. I go through a flurry of outfits. The long skirt will wrap around my own legs and his, ensnaring us both during double turns. The short skirt and stockings make me feel too perky, a flight attendant inside my own home. I settle on loose pants and a long shirt, a little too much like a midterm maternity outfit, but in the end the doorbell rings and saves me from my next skewed judgment.

He's standing outside my door, on time, his box of tapes tucked under his arm, looking over his shoulder as though he thinks someone is going to mug him. I immediately fixate on the pin attached to the lapel of his jacket, a one-inch silver brooch of two dancers in a serious dip, the pin not quite manly enough in my estimation, but clearly some kind of badge of ballroom prowess. I remember my father's favorite tie clip with the arching silver fish with the hook caught in its mouth.

Dancing is supposed to give you freedom, but so far it's only made me tremble on the edge of my worst frailties. I impulsively went shopping last night and padded my Latin music collection, the way you might buy five new lipsticks before a first date. I can't even confess to myself that I've changed the sheets for this occasion. The last thing I want (not an unconscious wish, I'll stake my life on it) is to go to bed with Carlos. It's a precaution bound in superstition, like preparing yourself for an unforeseen car accident by putting on clean underwear. Why, there might be a dance accident, right here, this evening, in my living room. He could trip over my cat, Herbert, and break his ankle. I wouldn't want Carlos sinking back on my pillows, waiting for an ambulance, noticing the *TV Guide* under the top sheet, the nervous pinwheel of cat hair right by the pillow.

I predict that Jack will call in the middle of my lesson and I'll sound guilty, as though I'm in bed with another man. So I unplug the phone. I don't want Carlos's attention wandering from what I'm paying for. Three crisp twenties and a ten, and an extra five for travel, already sit in an envelope by the door. At first I'd written his name in a foreign, flourishy script, then simply *C,* wasting two bond envelopes, and finally opting for blank.

Will he expect a tip?

My father's ashes are sitting in their Tupperware container inside the plastic bag on top of my bookcase. Herbert is crouching next to it, a perfect sphinx, lazily turning his head once in a while to lick the still-tasty plastic. I keep looking up, expecting to see the container teetering on the ledge.

The first thing Carlos and I do is roll back the living-room rug. There's a mouse stuck to the underside, flattened into a form so dry, translucent, and weirdly misshapen, it looks like an organic potato chip with the skin still on. The mouse could almost have been part of the rug's design, one of the paisley shapes in the low-level Oriental. But the tail places it smack in the animal kingdom.

I almost let loose with one of those mouse screams women are allowed to make, the kind accompanied by full-body chills and an instinctive leap up onto a high surface.

Carlos's resort to Spanish seems ominous.

"A mouse!" I say, at least leaving out the organic potato chip observation. He looks at me strangely, as though I've offered it to him to eat. The rush of shame I feel is sudden and complete. Once again I'm overheated, even before we've started to dance. He'll make assumptions about my cleanliness, have doubts about holding my hands, scrutinize the bathroom with suspicion, be unforgiving about a stray, perfectly sweet pubic hair.

Uncertain what to do, I just stand there. I'm furious at Herbert. How dare he not have devoured this particular mouse carcass while it was alive? I glare up at him where he sits, blinking impassively down at us, one paw draped over the bookshelf. Herbert hates salsa music.

"Let's get started," I say. It's disorienting to dance with a strange man in my own living room, small and high-ceilinged and windowless. I've always joked about this room—the upended shoe box, the prison cell. I painted it as soon as I heard that my father was going to die, shedding my standard Linen White idea of myself and venturing into Vibrant Red. The room seems to throb now, a bead of blood along a pale vein, the heart of the house. This is the room where Jack and I slow-danced on our first real date. That was the night I learned that not only does he have no rhythm, but he also can't count his way out of a paper bag. I would find out later about his hips. He was happiest dancing in complete darkness, not because it was so romantic, but because my modest strip of track lighting gave him a migraine. It was only when we started to kiss that it all turned around.

Is it my imagination, or does Carlos hold me closer here in my home than at the dance studio? Even above the music, you can almost hear our mingled breathing. It's the good acoustics of the room, which he admired as we were sampling my CDs.

"He goes, she goes . . ." I'm chanting inside my head. He turns, then I turn. We're halfway through a complicated turn pattern when he steers me under his arm so that we're back to back. Still holding our hands in the air, he looks down at me from over his shoulder like a posing bullfighter. We freeze this way, the music careening on. I want him to kiss me. I keep breathing in and out through my nose, trying to keep the count going in my head, feeling dizzy and sensual. I remember Michael kissing me down in the laundry room, the way our hearts raced so fast from the exertion of him lifting me above his head, me attempting to hold a graceful pose, that we had to pause in the middle just to breathe.

"Make your arms softer," Carlos says. "You're fighting me."

I envision the bone marrow in my arms, then command it to melt. I wait for him to explain what we're doing, but we simply stand there looking into each other's eyes. Mesmerized, I stare back up at him. Does this mean anything? What if the neighbors can see in? I want them to. I think of my mother, knowing that she would understand. Why couldn't my father have given her this?

"Excuse me," I say. Extricating one hand from the jungle gym of arms, I reach behind me toward the stereo, arching, forcing Carlos to support my back, and turn the volume way up. I want to disappear into sound. Once we're back in position again, our feet begin the basic step automatically. I'm pleased to see that I'm this advanced already—my feet with a mind of their own. Even though Carlos is so skinny, my forearm feels fragilely beautiful and feverish pressed against his. The sleeves of my shirt fall back almost to my armpits. I let them stay that way, draped and extravagant.

Herbert is now sitting calmly at our feet, watching us. His stillness makes our fantastic whirling seem foolish. I'm afraid that we're going to knock into things in the narrow channel of my living room, but we don't. The furniture seems to have shrunk. Carlos holds me steadily, somehow returning me to a place directly in front of his chest each time as though invisible wires connect us. His black satin shirt is partway open to show a smooth chest, with no hair.

I meet Herbert's eyes over Carlos's shoulder, lose the beat, then find it again. Why do I have to have such a judgmental cat? Twice during the lesson I excuse myself and go to the bathroom, flush the toilet as background noise, pat cold water on my cheeks, reapply lipstick, and stare at myself, wondering if I'm the kind of woman Carlos finds sexy. More important, does he like the way I dance?

After the lesson is over, I offer him a beer, remembering the brown paper bag in the subway, his grainy, off-duty breath. I've bought a selection for him to choose from. We bend and peer together into my fridge, our faces close. I can feel the moisture jump off him, have the urge to turn and lick his cheek as though we've just made love. Hesitating slightly, he chooses a can of

Budweiser. I stare at his thin brown hand hovering inside my fridge. I notice he isn't wearing a wedding band.

Holding the unopened beer down by his side, he shoves the envelope in his pocket without looking at it, and is out the door within three minutes. I want to yell after him playfully, "How did I do?" I wish I spoke Spanish. I'll learn to cook *pernil* so that he will come over on Sundays. We'll have children who will also dance. But he bounds down the front steps, supporting the tape case against his middle, a kid eager to be let out of school.

I go back inside and walk around my apartment, looking at familiar objects, not seeing them. Somehow I thought he'd stay longer. Scooping Herbert up, I bury my face in his neck and dance with him for a while with no music on.

Any dance is always the beginning and the end of something, always at the same time, and yet it's the middle that you live for.

eleven

On my way to the grocery store, I pass the homeless man who always leans against a high wrought-iron fence in front of a nearby church. He's wearing my skirt. My whole body tingles when I see it. The skirt was a gift from my mother. I wore it enough times to wear out guilt, enough times for it to absorb my scent, enough for a tracking dog. The man is pulling at the waistband. I'd put the skirt out in the street, along with some sweaters and old socks.

The minute I see the skirt, I veer over toward him, then veer away again. What will I say, after all? His fingernails are dirty and elegant and long on one hand, as though he used to play classical guitar. I imagine dainty forms of cress growing from beneath them. Underneath the skirt he's wearing turquoise nylon leg warmers with a white racing stripe up the sides, the bottoms unzipped and flapping as though he's just won a 5K race.

He's dancing mambo right there on the sidewalk. How strange to see my skirt come to life this way. I stand there, respecting his invisible circle of movement, and watch him dance. The music is coming from the open door of a nearby car. A neighborhood guy is lying half underneath it on a flat wooden dolly, doing repairs. The homeless man pumps his elbows and does a smooth turn, lifting the skirt to give his knees room, twitching the hem flirtatiously. He sings, his head wagging, eyes closed. Then he looks right at me. He shuffles over to me, dancing as he walks. I don't move. He holds out his hand, the palm dry and cracked, a big dirty desert of a hand. I feel stiff and self-righteous. I think of Carlos and the way it felt to be turned and turned. I think of my father, who never danced.

He takes my hand and I let him pull me in. Even before I'm near him, I'm holding my breath, the thing you automatically do when you pass by a homeless person. Experimentally, I breathe out and in again, thinking I might catch a comforting whiff from my skirt. He smells of smoke and layers of overcooked food.

He's actually a great dancer, loose and easy, moving with a strange authority. An unreal feeling steals over me, an out-of-body sensation. I feel weightless. I remember square-dancing with my mother at a county fair, my father and Gwen off looking at the bulls, how they glanced curiously at us over their shoulders, as though we were strangers.

The homeless guy is looking my body up and down, admiring me. He laughs some more, a cackling hyena call up to the sky. Our timing together is perfect. How can this be one of the best dances I've ever had?

Abruptly, he lets go of my hand and then walks away, muttering, picking at his beard.

The guy repairing the car turns his radio louder, as though this will entice us back together again. He's sitting on the floor on the passenger side now, the door wide open. He holds both hands out to me, palms up, as though asking me to join him in the front seat of the car. I shake my head and walk away quickly.

I remember the time my father came to see me in New York and a homeless man asked him for change and he stopped and dug into his pocket and brought out a dollar and gave it to the man without saying anything. "That was nice," I said to him, starting to slip my hand through his crooked elbow, but he pulled away, shifting his briefcase so that it hung between us as we walked. "Nice has nothing to do with it," he said. I wanted to ask him why. But I remembered how he never let us thank him for our weekly allowance. "You earn it for being part of this family," he said, marking off the amount on a little piece of paper and returning his wallet to his back pocket.

As if he knows I'm in trouble, Herbert is waiting for me by the front door. I scoop him up and squeeze him so tightly to my chest he meows in protest. Tucking him under my arm, I carry him into the bathroom and wash my hands with soap and hot water. I want to wash Herbert where I've touched his fur, but you can't take things out on a cat. Together we stand over my answering machine and listen.

"Alice, this is your mother. I want your father's ashes back. I want to scatter him properly. I can't feel any peace." I think of my mother and the ashes spilling onto the kitchen floor, wonder whether she finished cleaning the corner with her Dustbuster, a ridiculous purchase in my father's estimation. Now there he might be, the dust of him, sucked up and stored forever in her kitchen closet.

"Please call me," she says.

I erase the message, then go over to the bookcase, reach high and pull down the plastic bag and open the container. Plunging my hand into the ashes, I stay that way, perfectly still, imagining that my hand is a plaster cast drying in cool sand.

I'm sitting up in bed with a glass of wine, Herbert draped ecstatically along my legs. I start calling old boyfriends. Jack's been relegated to a special limbo reserved for distinguished hangers-on who won't stop cooking in the face of no appetite.

"It's so great to hear from you," says the one who resurfaces in my life every five years like a shipwreck. We chat, stirring up old ground cover. "Yup, you were definitely a babe back then," he says, and chuckles.

"And what does that make *you* now?" I ask.

"Middle-aged," he says. And chuckles some more.

Another, living, breathing, judging ex actually went ahead and had a kid without me. Since his divorce, father and son walk up my street on his "father mornings" three times a week. He still calls occasionally in the evening when the latest girlfriend is asleep. He seems to know when Jack isn't here and I'm eating cookies in bed and drinking red wine, covered in Herbert's hair. He likes to remind me that we could be sharing a kid right now. I hear his voice on my machine in the other room, talking in a kid-friendly singsong. No more sexy rumble. I no longer jump up and grab the phone, the way his voice used to make me do. According to Thea, I don't know how lucky I am. But I miss meat loaf and homework with the kid.

"Send me a picture," says the next old boyfriend.

"My father just died," I remind him. "I'm not looking so great."

"I'll airbrush you," he says. "I'm a photographer, remember?"

When I run out of same-decade boyfriends to call, I decide to fire up the time machine and find Ballet Michael. I call directory assistance and give them his old address. Obviously his mother still lives there. I finish my wine in a series of courage-inducing gulps, then pick up the phone and call. A woman with a tiny birdlike voice answers. I have trouble imagining this as the mother of Thigh Boy. I mumble and burble sweetly. I say something about ballet so she won't think I'm a stalker. Turns out he's living in San Diego and works at a bank. I wonder if he's secretly in love with a floater. His mother gives me his work number, which means he's probably married. I don't ask if he's still doing ballet. I don't ask if he turned out to be gay or has kids or is happy or miserable. I hang up and dial his work number, even though it's eleven o'clock on a Saturday night. Amazing how tone and timbre jump right out at you. I gush lightly into my sweatpants at the sound of his voice on the message, a reaction less sexual than sentimental. "Hi, Michael," I say, trying not to sound too breathy. "I don't know if you remember me, but I'm the one you used to lift across the room a long time ago, in ballet. I just wanted to say hi." I don't say, *I've always remembered the way you performed oral sex on me up in the air, it's never been quite as strangely wonderful since.* I continue, "Remember how Madame used to yell at us when we talked in class? Anyway, I hope you're having a good life. I work at a bank, too. Your mother told me. This is Alice, by the way." I put the phone down quickly, a bomb about to detonate, and sit there, my heart beating. I realize I forgot to leave a number or an address or anything. I don't call back.

I can hear Thea walking along the hall outside my bedroom, her dress-up high heels clicking, a man's low, murmuring voice, her throaty response. I can almost smell the champagne and aftershave and Thea's spicy perfume cocktail through the wall. When was the last time Jack and I went out on a real date? I lean out of bed and reach over to the wall, but stop myself from knocking in time. Even Thea's good-natured sense of inclusion won't stand for this kind of interruption. I'm remembering another time that Thea filled the hall this way.

I made Cornish hens the first and only time my father visited me in New York on a business trip. I ushered him here, into my bedroom, where he would be sleeping, as if he were a customer at a hotel.

"Here are some towels," I said, "I hope you'll be comfortable. Please feel free to take a bath." My father hated baths.

The minute he went into the bathroom with his shaving kit and closed the door, I remembered that my underpants were drying on the showerhead. Probably he thought two bath towels was excessive, not loving.

The hens were too big for my plates. I knew I shouldn't have added the pistachios and currants. I was dying for a glass of wine, but I poured water for both of us, and later brewed cups of decaf. After dinner he sat on the sofa, reading the newspaper. Under the reading lamp, his bald spot looked shiny and naked, his hands holding the pages, old and still. Wearing an apron, I was my mother, drying dishes. I was dying to go to him and casually stroke the top of his head, the way Gwen might have. Turning both faucets on full, I poured a half glass of red wine from a leftover bottle and swallowed it in two gulps. In the bathroom, I brushed my teeth, turning the faucets on full in there, too.

During the night I lay awake worrying about the city, about the traffic and the sirens, wanting to reach a long arm down to the street and shush a drunken couple laughing too loudly after leaving the corner bar. Did my father know about corner bars? I worried that Thea might start playing her finger cymbals, a soothing, tinkling sound I usually enjoyed. What would my father do if a woman wearing a beaded sky-blue bra and a sheer skirt draped high on one thigh were to steal into his room, move her belly in exotic tremors at the end of the bed, and lure him in with seductive, circling wrists and offer him baklava?

At midnight I woke, needing to go to the bathroom. Inching off the sunken sofa bed, I scraped my leg. As I tiptoed toward the bathroom, I saw my father standing in the front hall wearing only his pajama bottoms. They were drooped low and slightly twisted. His feet looked long and pale on the dark wood floor. He was holding the metal peephole on the door aside with one finger and looking out. I stood there, not breathing. He was concentrating so hard he didn't hear me.

I backed away and returned to bed. Lying down again, I closed my eyes, trying to focus my hearing, muting every other sound. I could hear the murmur of voices now. There was Thea's voice, and a man's, too, coming from the hall, and low laughter. I strained to hear. Perhaps he'd woken and thought there was an intruder? Ignoring my bladder, I pretended to be asleep. I wanted him to come to the doorway of the living room and check on me, to stand there and watch me sleeping. This night was surely the only chance for this vigilance to occur.

He didn't. I heard the toilet flush. Not wanting him to know I was awake, too, I found an empty pasta sauce jar in the drainer and peed in it, then poured my urine slowly down the side of the sink so it wouldn't make any noise.

The next morning I watched my father buttering a square of toast and sipping coffee. He'd shaved and his cheeks were smooth and damp looking. He looked handsome, Italian, almost. The expensive preserves I'd bought sat there, unopened.

"How did you sleep, Daddy?" I asked.

"I slept well," he said. Talking about sleep is always shorthand for something else. I waited for him to mention Thea. I wanted to know if she'd been wearing her belly-dancing outfit under her coat and whether she'd stood out there and kissed the man. I wanted to know if he found her sexy. I wanted to know if he thought I was beautiful. I wanted him to ask me if I'd slept well. I wanted him to reminisce about our fishing trip years ago.

I helped my father get a taxi. I stepped off the curb, too far into the street, throwing my arm up high near my ear. "Taxi!" I yelled, thrilled when one veered over immediately. He let me open the door and I stooped to kiss him good-bye on the cheek and he turned his head at the same time and our mouths brushed by mistake. His lips felt dry and smooth. I tasted shaving cream. I blushed. He was looking at the cabdriver, giving the address of the bank. He glanced up at me once, and I closed the door. As the cab pulled away, he waved a stiff salute with his big white fisherman's hand.

The morning after my home private with Carlos, I drag myself out of bed to buy cat food, and end up sitting at a coffee shop. I'm gulping a latte as though it's the first and last drug, thinking about Gwen and my mother and how long it's been since we've spoken, when a man and his kid sit down near my table.

"Why do you think watermelon is the color it is?" the man asks the kid. "Is it red or is it pink?" He holds out a tub of pale grainy chunks to the small boy, stabs a piece with a plastic fork, and presses it against the kid's lips. The kid stares out the window at a group of boys straddling bikes further down the sidewalk. Still not looking at his father, he mumbles something unintelligible. The father keeps looking over at me.

Over the years I came to expect double takes from men. Something that life handed me, and then I grew greedy, waiting for the yes-no-yes, the certainty that I was a fleeting moment of pleasure in someone else's eyes. A sad need, a gift from a father who seemed not to look, whose take was through a camera or binoculars or not at all. Gwen was different. Walking next to her down the street, I noticed that she looked straight ahead, never bothering to collect glances. Double take, single take, an incidental issue.

I usually try to avoid weekend afternoons when couples radiating the tension of lost financial and intellectual opportunities congregate on street corners with strollers parked in a spoke shape and chat, keeping one eye on their children, who dart around in expensive oversized hand-knit sweaters. I'm jealous of the sweaters. My only power is to not smile at their children.

"I might want to have kids someday," Jack often says. I just nod, figuring that someday has already come and is on its way out of the station. Borrow a kid for the day, is Thea's advice. "You'll be thrilled to give it back when the day's over." (She always calls kids "its"). I've discovered that sharing your friends' children is impossible, and no longer try. "You're so lucky to have all that time alone," mothers tell me.

"It's not wed, it's red," the man is saying, shaking the fork in front of his son's face to regain his attention. "What letter does red begin with? Don't you think it's more pink than red, Jason?" The boy turns back and stares at the watermelon with a blank expression and doesn't open his mouth. "That's because it's a seasonal fruit," the man continues. "Do you know what that means?" Again he glances in my direction and smiles. "Name a season, Jason. What season are we in now? What season is November?" The man's hand waivers and almost misses his son's mouth as he looks at me again with a deliberately bemused shrug.

When I get up, my chair crashes to the floor. The man and his son look up at me with identical expressions, surprised and faintly resentful.

"Why don't you buy him a banana?" I say as I walk by.

twelve

My mother makes good on her answering machine threat, and formally phones in the recall order. She's decided that having her husband exist as three separate portions of ash in three separate states was the wrong way to deal with his death. Her bread-baking instincts have her wanting to bring the cupfuls of him together like so much flour, salt, and baking soda. I don't know why she didn't keep him all to herself in the first place, sift him, then bake him into a big loaf of bread, adorning it with the mysterious hieroglyphics she likes to carve on her loaves as though they're artifacts from Easter Island. It's another version of the story about the woman who kills her husband with a leg of lamb, then cooks it and feeds the evidence to the detectives.

My father's ashes probably mean more to me than they should. Some people wouldn't think so, judging by the plastic container inside a plastic bag I've kept him in all these weeks. Gwen tells me she immediately transferred her ashes into a heavy gilt bottle with a wide mouth and a stopper that once contained perfume.

"It's like I'm keeping him sitting around in a suitcase," I say. "The way I can never unpack after a trip." I tell her I'm worried that I might have blocked the transition of some part of his soul to God knows where.

"Do you think Daddy has a soul?" Gwen's voice is cool, almost amused. I imagine her staring off into space, the phone tipped slightly away from her ear to avoid pressing her hair flat. This is what happens to the favorite daughter. She steps out of the warm center of affection and pretends that she was never there.

I want to tell Gwen about Herbert's latest habit of licking the plastic bag that contains our father. Gwen hates cats, and so did he.

"Actually, he'd probably prefer a Tupperware to my urn," she continues. "He'd think your choice was more modest and practical, enough for him. You know how he liked to think that not too much was enough. He'd think my bottle looks too Catholic, incensey. But that's what happens when someone's gone. It's not up to them anymore, is it?" She sighs impatiently. In the background, her assistant's voice rises over the airplane whine of a hair dryer shifting to high. "As far as his soul is concerned, I have no clue."

"I know it sounds far-fetched, but don't you seriously believe he went somewhere when he died? You could feel it, a kind of rush in the room," I say.

"Actually, no," says Gwen. Her voice has become stiff, wary.

"What does Gabriel think?" I ask. "About the soul." I ask this casually, wanting to catch her off guard. I want to ask her if they've talked about this, maybe in bed, staring up at the ceiling after sex.

"I have no idea. We've never talked about things like that. I think he deals with the physical death, and the soul part is up to someone else."

"Well, I think that people like Daddy have to pay in some way," I say.

"Pay?" It sounds as though she's brought the phone close to her ear again and is pressing it hard against her head, not caring about her hair anymore. "For what?"

"For being selfish. Don't you think?" My insistence grates, even on me.

"No."

"Well, I do."

"So, where is he, then?"

"I think he probably ended up in some ballroom dance studio," I say. "Doing the cha-cha." I laugh. "It's a stage of hell. The devil is a dance instructor."

Gwen cuts me off, telling me that a client's just arrived. But then she adds, "Well, that's Mom's idea of heaven. Maybe they'll meet up one day."

I'm standing in my underwear listening to salsa, staring blankly into my closet. I'm having a clothes crisis. What to wear to go dancing, followed by a festive scattering in a small New England town? Is there a crossover getup for this? Each time I throw another dark skirt or dress on the bed, I do a few turns, singing in my fake Spanish.

The minute I hear salsa, even when I'm alone, I feel hopeful: warm air, clinking glasses, fried food, loose hips, a roaring car, café con leche, the kaboom of a heartbeat—life's possibilities.

The only way you could tell that my father even heard music was by watching the tiny muscle jump at the base of his jawline, right where the hardest chewing happens. Usually it caught him unawares, a few unexpected bars that slipped through after the news when he hadn't managed to turn the radio off in time. Gwen and I would both look up, watching for the same sign on exactly the same beat. If my mother turned the radio volume up when a waltz came on, he would do everything short of plugging his ears to avoid listening, clear his throat with loud extended harruumphing, the way a kid makes noise to distract himself from the sound of thunder.

Sometimes I feel completely at one with salsa, the clave, the conga, the timbales, the trumpets, the other dancers. Other times I feel shut out from the music, and the hiccupping, keening lyrics, my passion gone dull and dry as an old dance slipper. But it's the only music that lets me forget.

As a last resort, I reach deep into my closet and grab a short dress, pull on a jacket over it, the sheer black stockings with the rhinestones on the ankle, my dancing shoes. I stand in front of my bureau and stare down into the dusting powder. Talc to talc. Picking up the puff, I pull the neckline away from my breasts, swipe under both arms, of course streak the dress. I replace the lid carelessly and start sneezing.

Today Carlos has promised to teach me some new turn patterns. I'm still more comfortable dancing in my head than in my body, an action/repression ratio I'm working on. When I first started lessons with him, I'd write notes about what I'd learned afterward: *Always turn square to face the man. Your hands belong to him. Always move away after turns. Give him room. Keep your elbows close to your body to avoid accidents. Lean the weight of your back into the man's hand. When he pulls your arm, your body should go with it. Don't hold back. Try to smile and look welcoming. All beats aren't equal. Try thinking: I want to dance.*

Carlos saw me writing in my notebook one day after class and looked over my shoulder. I couldn't hide the page quickly enough.

"Throw that shit out," he said. "The only homework I want you doing is dancing until you drop dead."

Dance till you drop dead! I wrote later, at home.

I walk into the dance studio carrying my father's ashes under my arm. They started inside my backpack, but the container has the shape of a small melon and rests uncomfortably against the small of my back. Today's plan is to take as many classes as I can, including a double with Carlos. My goal is to store up the rhythm, the way you might beef up your blood before an operation. I'm scared to leave this world of unlimiteds and privates, but you can't send your father's ashes through the mail.

I'm nervous about entering that house again, into my mother's kitchen, into the range of my sister's hungry scissors, into my father's study, scene of my first dancing crimes. Whether it's exactly the same or transformed into some unrecognizable, pink-walled dance studio by my mother won't matter. He'll still be there, the guardian of all movement. The instant I walk into the house, I may forget how to dance.

For the first time, Carlos is waiting for me in the classroom. I say hi and walk over to the corner and casually put the plastic bag on the chair near the stereo. He closes the door, transferring the DO NOT DISTURB sign from inside to outside. He's wearing black flared pants and a black vest with a satin back and a little buckle, and a tight white T-shirt underneath. His muscles are compact and sleek, no visible body fat. He has a faint childhood-age scar running around his right biceps like one of Thea's bangles.

I step into his arms and we start to move before the music has even settled into its beat. His breath smells of milky coffee the way my father's used to in the morning. My arms are liquid tension, my feet have their own wisdom.

Today's dancing is a ride on the best horse on the carousel. Not one of the stationary ones, or the ones that go only halfway up. This is the one that lives right on the edge of the platform with the black mane and the neck at the funny angle in the middle of a wild toss, the one with the bared teeth and pink cement gums that rides to the top of the pole, so high it shows the grease in the joints if you're standing underneath and pretending not to look, so high it's going to topple over into the sky. The No Horse, Gwen and I used to call him because we weren't allowed to ride him.

Carlos and I are whirling in heaven. I want us to be on the boardwalk at Coney Island, have some huckster stroll by with an old-fashioned camera and a cloth hood to capture the moment.

You see, Daddy? I think. This is what you missed.

Carlos cocks his head in my direction as though I've mumbled out loud.

Dancing and crying don't mix. Your sinuses get stuffed up and you can't hear the music anymore. This affects your equilibrium and basically your rhythm is shot.

I can't use my hands to wipe anything away, so I just let everything run. I try to keep my face turned away, but Carlos must feel the change in my body temperature, that instant crying sweat that breaks out in strange places—your upper lip, behind your knees, between your shoulder blades, right where his hand is.

"You could be a beautiful dancer." Carlos's lips are right next to my ear. "If only you'd stop thinking. Dancing isn't a thinking thing. Can you stop thinking for a minute?" He pulls back suddenly and looks right at me, sternly. "Why are you crying? You shouldn't be crying. You're dancing." We're marking time now, not really doing anything.

"I'm sorry."

"This is what my daughter does to me, but I have a diaper on my shoulder."

I wipe my eyes and nose with the back of my hand, then on the back of my skirt. I stand there with my hands down at my sides, feeling like a five-year-old.

"When she cries in the middle of the night," he continues, "my wife hands her to me and tells me to dance with her so she'll fall asleep." He feigns launching a bundle to his shoulder and briskly patting a bottom with a one/two beat. "There's only one song for her and I play it over and over. Nothing slow or like a lullaby. No, baby, she likes to mambo. She likes those spins and dips, down to the floor."

"Actually, I was feeling happy to be dancing with you," I say. "I don't know why I'm crying."

He doesn't seem to hear me. "One day I pick her up and dance to this one old tune, and that was it, and now it's the only thing that will stop her crying."

I want to ask him if his wife dances.

"If I stop before the end of the song, she wakes up and I have to start all over again."

"So you never stop."

"You got it. You want me to play my daughter's song for you? It's in my box of tapes." He walks away. Even though his back is turned, I nod. He deliberately takes a long time, letting me blow my nose.

"This is Marianella's song," he says as we start to dance again. "But don't fall asleep on me."

I just graze his shoulder with my head, and we both laugh.

Before we part, I show him the picture of my mother dancing with the strange man. I've been carrying it around in my wallet. "Can you tell me what dance they're doing?" I ask.

Carlos takes it over to the window and holds it up to the light.

"That shit's old," he says. I look over his shoulder at the cracks and seams visible in the afternoon sun. Showing through the sepia figures is my mother's up-and-down script on the back: *My Wedding Day.*

"Yeah, way before I was born," I say, blushing. I've always wondered if Carlos knows my age. I wonder how much this matters with dancing, although of course it shouldn't matter at all. "That's my mother," I say. "She used to be a great dancer. Actually, she still is."

"I don't know. Fox-trot? Waltz, maybe? Definitely not mambo, definitely not West Coast Swing." He laughs, handing the picture back to me. "They look pretty good together."

"Thanks." I have no idea why I'm thanking him. "It's my mother's first dance as a married woman." Carlos is looking at me, interested, but drifting away. I'm about to lose him. "But that's not my father."

"It's a big world out there when you're dancing," he says. For a minute I think he wants to say something more, but then he shrugs and sweeps out the door, banging it behind him.

thirteen

I've taken four classes, one after another. The tinny music and fluorescent lights have spun me into their own Milky Way. I'm a man, then a woman, then a man. Between dances I keep going out to call Gwen and tell her that I'll catch the next train, and then I don't. Instead, I walk the twenty-two blocks to Jack's apartment and stand there in the front hall, not ringing, staring at his name on the buzzer. He comes in while I'm doing this, bulging plastic grocery bags twisted around both wrists.

"Hi," he says. I love him in situations like this. For all his nervous tics, he can be as implacable as Herbert.

"Hi," I say, feeling suddenly shy. I rest my backpack on my dancing shoes. My father's on my feet, I think. I remember how I always wanted to be able to stand on his feet and have him dance around the room with me, the way I'd seen a little neighbor girl do with her father.

"Did you come for supper?" he asks. Now he's not looking at me, all busy with extricating himself from the bags.

"What are you making?" He looks tired to me, and rumpled. And handsome.

He peers inside the bags, opening one, then

another. "I thought I'd make a marinara sauce, and I bought some pancetta and basil and a bottle of red wine. And some tiramisu for dessert."

"You're such a narcissist," I say.

Jack smiles, then looks sad. He's always said that the word *narcissism* sounded like a rich, silly dessert, a hybrid of tiramisu and sherry trifle.

"Yeah, a narcissist with a sweet tooth," he says.

"Is someone coming for dinner?" I ask.

"I don't know, maybe you are." He pauses, not even long enough for me to blink. "If not, I guess I'll be having leftovers. I finished my piece today, and I'm sick of takeout."

I don't actually say that I'm staying for dinner, just open the door for him with my set of keys, hold it so he can squeeze by, and once we get upstairs and into the kitchen, I automatically start helping him put the food away. Even though I'm happy to be here, I keep thinking about dancing and Carlos and what's going on without me.

"I've missed your herbs," Jack says. "I bought a couple of plants, but look." He gestures toward two small pots on the windowsill containing a few spiky dried twigs.

"It's hard indoors, even if you have light," I say, going over to examine them. "You don't have light." I rub the twigs between my fingers and they proceed to crumble into the pot. How long ago had he bought these? I'd lost track. I smell my fingertips. "Thyme?"

"Actually, it's Greek oregano. I was getting fancy."

"Let's take a bath," I say impulsively, and immediately wish I hadn't. Jack is the only man I know who will sit in a bath as long as I can, who will keep adding hot water and sinking down lower and keep the conversation going until full prune state occurs. We've had some of our best and longest talks in the tub, and this is why I suddenly realize it's a bad idea. I don't want to talk.

But he's already in the bathroom, turning on both taps as hard as they'll go (the city equivalent of a crackling birch log fire). "Maestro?" he says, gesturing at his shelves. I always like to add a swampy mixture of anything and everything to baths—oil (bath, olive, canola, corn, whatever's available except walnut, which is too expensive), kosher salt, Ivory dish liquid, old gift-pack Chanel, vanilla, cinnamon sticks, cardamom pods, twists of fresh lemon zest.

"How about plain water?" I say. Jack looks crestfallen, as though I've told him I'd like porridge for dinner and no sex afterward. "Well, maybe some basil," I amend. I pull off a few leaves, brushing away the sandy dirt still clinging to them, and grab the extra-virgin olive oil.

Even after a few weeks it feels awkward to undress in front of Jack. I wrap a towel around myself and shimmy out of my clothes from underneath as though I'm at a public swimming pool. Jack, too, turns away from me, undresses quickly and slides in. His tub is long and low and squared off, more like a coffin than my traditional cattle-feeding trough with sloped ends. We always use our respective tubs as a convenient point of impasse when we argue about whose apartment we'd move into if we decided to live together.

Instead of joining him, cross-legged, with my back to the taps the way I usually do, I sit modestly on the side of the tub with only my feet and legs in the water, my towel still on. We don't say anything. After a while he picks up my foot and opens the olive oil, which looks extra grassy against the white tub, and pours a wasteful quarter cup all over my foot. Some of it pools between my toes and drips down into the water. He catches most of it with his hand and begins briskly rubbing it in, the way he would prep a pork roast. Basil leaves are nudging around his penis and pubic hair like boats looking for the right slip. I pluck out a leaf and tuck it behind his ear. He rubs my foot until it feels slick and greasy, and then bends to examine it closely.

"Your feet are a mess," he says. He's right. Since I've been dancing so much, they've taken on the battered buniony look of a working ballerina or a veteran waitress. I've always wondered why feet must become hideous in the cause of beautiful movement.

"A dancer's day isn't done until her feet are bleeding," I say.

Jack makes a scornful snorting sound and drops my foot in the water, picks up the other one. He finishes this one up quickly, as though the project has tired him out. Usually by this time in a long bath, we'd be doing some kind of watery sex dance; that or dripping our way into the bedroom and either making love or falling asleep, still damp that way. A new formality has set in. Having suggested the bath, I find I'm not eager to get wet above the knees, remembering the way my hair looks after such baths, oily and dotted with odd detritus. Jack doesn't protest, simply heaves up and out and dries himself quickly and leaves the bathroom. By the time I make my way back into the kitchen, he's dressed and chopping garlic.

"Why don't you put on some salsa music," Jack suggests. This startles me, as though he's suggested I invite my lover in for a quick snack and a drink.

"I didn't know you had any salsa music," I say.

"Ah, what you don't know about me," he says.

A modest stack of salsa CDs is piled neatly separate from his others. I get the distinct impression that he's unwrapped them but not yet opened a one. I make a selection and turn the volume up.

While Jack cooks, I dance around a little in the living room. I'm absorbed in practicing some shines, when suddenly I look up to see that he's standing in the doorway holding a wooden spoon.

I stop, self-conscious. "Did you want me to taste the sauce?" I ask.

"No, I'm just watching you. Is that okay?"

"Of course," I say. I continue, feeling awkward.

"What the hell is that?" he says, pointing at my feet with the spoon.

"It's a step called Millie Donay. It's a shine, one of the steps you do when you're dancing alone, not touching your partner."

"Who's Millie Donay?" he asks. "Sounds like an Irish fishmonger's wife."

"I have no idea," I answer stiffly. "Shines all have interesting names, I'm sure with some historical context." I sound like a social studies teacher. I go to the stereo and turn the music way down. "You know what, I should go."

I move around, getting my things together. I'm waiting for him to come and stop me. I repeat some of the same motions more than once, opening and closing the zipper of my backpack a few times. Jack stays in the doorway, once in a while sucking on the end of the wooden spoon as though there's still sauce there.

"You'll get a splinter in your lip," I say. I'm furious at him for not begging me to stay and eat. A mere hour from now we could be full and cozy, lying in his bed and drifting off to sleep. *Is this some kind of strategy?* I want to scream at him, but I restrain myself. Really, I do want to go out dancing.

"Take care, sweetheart," he says as I kiss his cheek so fast and far away, it's hardly a butterfly kiss. I hate it when he tries to sound like a Raymond Chandler character.

"Bye," I mutter. "I'll call you." Suddenly I'm out in the hall and the door's closed and the garlicky smell of the tomato sauce rushes at me and I realize I could faint with hunger. But the last thing I'm going to do is knock on the door again. As I walk down the stairs and back into the night, I hear some jazz tootling safely behind me.

fourteen

I've been back at the studio for an hour or so when I decide to tag along with a bunch of students who are going to a club. At the door I entrust my father to the coat-check girl. She has a pierced tongue and is chewing multiple pieces of bubble gum.

The second I enter, I spot Carlos. He's changed into a cream suit with a black shirt and a black tie, a gangster outfit except for the ballroom dancer's pin, which shines from across the room like a sheriff's star. He's standing at the bar stirring a drink, hair slicked back, tight as a baby seal's. He's with a beautiful woman who looks as though she might have bad skin if the lights were up. Hair almost to her waist, a big dark curtain of it. I know what a great dancer could do with that hair. She swings it back, all of a piece, and smiles up at him with her too-white teeth. Carlos leans down and whispers something to her. Already, before making even a baby step onto the dance floor, before eating so much as a mini–egg roll from the free buffet, I feel like a failure. This has to be his dance partner. I know by the way he touches her, the way he's touched me so recently, just a glance here or there, waist, shoulder, not completely sexual, not completely fatherly, just familiar.

Once they start dancing, it doesn't take long for everyone to clear the floor. I move closer, too, into the crush of perfume and human smells. I hardly even recognize what they're doing, except for the occasional turn or movement of her feet, here and gone again in a fantastic blur. She isn't wearing student shoes. Hers are purely professional, heels like knives (the ones I've kept at home until I deserve them). Her slender arm, pale as skim milk, slithers up past her ear and on into the air, a move that somehow brings him in closer to her. Her long red nails point up at the ceiling. If I did that, I'd look like I was directing traffic.

It's impossible to count the number of times she turns. She turns and turns without beginning or end, her hair its own weather pattern. She goes and goes. His movements around her are almost in her, liquid and insinuating, a snake charmer's. Obviously they're ignoring all those silly spotting rules he's explained to me, Adam's apple rules, don't-touch-the-breast rules. His hands know exactly where to return on her body, beautiful homing pigeon hands. They're looking straight at each other, smiling as though they have a private joke. I could cut in on her. I could cut in on him.

Everyone claps and whistles and finally moves back onto the dance floor. Other people don't seem to mind not being that good. This is what happens after too many generations of not dancing. It all coils and burns inside and turns into something poisonous, jealous, the heart and soul of yearning.

I order a gin and tonic. I'm standing right where Carlos and the woman were standing, waiting for them to come back. I'm amazed when they do. As though dancers have no sense of direction. Carlos doesn't see me, or if he does, he's ignoring me. I stand there, taking lots of busy sips from my drink. Everything feels safer with the straw in my mouth. They're both panting lightly, foreheads glazed. The band starts up another song. I'm worried that they're going to move back onto the dance floor, so I press up against Carlos, as though someone is pushing against me from behind. This chain reaction is not my fault. I remember pressing this way into Gabriel as he looked down at my father.

Carlos turns around with an annoyed look. Something resigned and masklike comes over his face. I recognize this wary, closed look as one I've sent out to men for most of my life.

"Hi, Carlos," I say.

"Alice," he says. A big, flat statement with a lot of meaning behind it.

"How are you? It's been so long." I hadn't meant to sound so sarcastic. His partner looks down the bar, and then out at the dance floor, completely ignoring me, as though this stalker interaction happens to them all the time.

"Why aren't you dancing?" Carlos asks. This question clearly isn't an invitation. He takes a long gulp of his drink, and his Adam's apple moves like a perfect stone up and down his neck. I want to reach out and stroke it, stop it in its path. He drains his glass and places it purposefully on the bar, takes the woman by the arm. "Catch you later, Alice," he says. He nods at me as though they're stepping out of an elevator and I'm some neighbor he's glad to be getting away from.

"Carlos," I call after his retreating back. He's the last train pulling out of the station. "Carlos!" I call out again over the band and the bar noise. *What about this afternoon?* I want to yell after him. He must have heard me yell his name, because he turns around and disengages himself from the woman for a moment and appears to start back toward me, and then changes his mind and turns back to her and just waves at me. I can just barely hear him say, "Have a good time."

A man takes my arm and pulls me onto the dance floor. I follow him because I don't know what else to do. Dancer's training tells you, Always say yes. When he turns to face me, I see that he's probably in his early seventies, my father's age if he'd lived another five minutes. He's wearing a suit with military-style epaulets on the shoulders that give him a boxy *Music Man* look.

"Can you dance on the two?" he shouts.

"And how are you?" I hear him say. I keep saying, "Fine, I'm fine," and search the room. Where did Carlos go?

"No, the two!" he screams at me. "I like to dance on the two."

"Fine," I say, completely hating him, his suit, his damp hands, his eager acolyte's question. People who really know how to dance don't ask what beat you start on. They just do what the music tells them to do.

A lifetime's disappointment enters me. This is just one dance, but it feels like the verdict. His steps are slow and shuffling, a hair off the beat. His yellow-gray hair is waxy and strong-smelling. He holds me too close and I pull away from him with my whole back.

"You can't dance when you're tense," the old man shouts over the music. He moves his tufted eyebrows up and down as if to emphasize his displeasure, keeps looking over his shoulder, as though scouting a new partner. I hate that he isn't Carlos, whose touch and smell I would be drinking in, my eyes secretly closed, our ears almost touching, like delicate pieces of instrumentation sensing the other. I could right now be having the best moment of my life, instead of the worst. Strange what proximity the two have, the impossible and the inevitable. I suddenly miss Jack, wish he were here to put his arms around me, yank me around in goofy imitation of the other dancers.

A blink, a trick of light—I happen to look up just as Carlos and his partner open the door to leave the club. My partner has stopped dancing before the music ends and is walking away from me, breaking our contract, for which I'm grateful. I can't tell whether this is in response to my indifference or to my dancing. I fight my way through the dancers, all the deadness of this one dance leaving me in a rush of flight adrenaline. At the coat check I drum my hands impatiently on the edge of the counter. The young woman with the pierced tongue plops my bag in front of me, and I take off at a run.

They're already halfway down the block, walking slowly, arms around each other's waists. I walk quickly, halving the distance, then slow down to match their pace. I study them from the back. Their intertwining could be that of friends or lovers or dance partners.

They stop by the subway entrance and I stay across the street, protected by the edge of a building. They're talking and laughing under a streetlight. She puts one hand on the pole and leans sideways, stretching her arm out like a kid's, her hair nearly touching the street. Carlos bends down as though maybe he's trying to kiss her, but instead he gathers and holds her hair so that it doesn't touch the sidewalk. I wonder if he's ever danced with her to Marianella's song.

As though by prearranged signal, she pulls herself upright, turns and walks quickly away. He bolts down the subway stairs. I'm near enough to the entrance on my side of the street to hear the train coming. I only have time to make it through the turnstile and dive into the next car before the doors close and the train pulls out. I am not myself. I'm a runaway.

Once again resting my backpack on my feet, I stand there like a teenager riding the cars, watching him through the dirty square of window at the other end of the next car. I feel like my father must have felt looking through the peephole in my apartment. Carlos is slumped low on the seat, both hands pulling down his jacket pockets, staring at the floor. I imagine sitting next to him, my head on his shoulder, our hands together in his pocket. I stare at his face, trying to make my gaze burn. I wonder if he's thinking about the woman he was with. I know I'm not there, even as a flash card in his thoughts. If Gwen were here, she'd march right into the car and sit down next to him.

I plan to get out at the very next stop, and then I don't. A local now, the train trundles out of the tunnel into dark, mysterious night somewhere else. I haven't traveled this far in the wrong direction for a long time. I'm still standing, peering into the next car. Sitting near me is a man who studies me as though he isn't sure he wants to be so close. After a while he gets up and moves to the other end. As long as I can still see Carlos, I feel safe. We're in a musical. Right now I could slide open the heavy subway door and careen through his car in a lightning trail of turns and there he'd be, leaping up to join me. There'd be no ashes in my bag or muggers in the street. I should have worn my rhinestone shoes.

After a good dozen stops, he finally gets up, straightening his jacket, and stands at the door, smoothing his hair back with one hand, looking at himself in the window. I have no idea what his secrets are. If I don't act now, I know I'll keep sitting in the train from one end of the city to the other, in an endless loop until morning, never able to make the decision to get off. I hadn't planned to follow him so far. He gets out, and at the very last second I bolt out as well, waving at a man and a woman in matching black raincoats who turn their heads to stare after me.

At the end of the platform, Carlos stops and bends into his cupped hands to light a cigarette with a movement tenderly familiar. He pulls the collar of his jacket up past his ears and hitches his bag up high on his shoulder. Even from this far away, I can hear his tapes and CDs clattering.

He finally notices me at the cuchifritos place a couple of blocks from the subway. He's sitting at the counter bent over a mound of greasy fried things, drinking a beer under the bright operating-room lights. I stand out in the street for a few contemplative minutes, staring at him through the window, past all the jewel-like mounds of fried food heating inside the golden incubators.

The counter guy beckons me to come inside, so I do. I slide onto a stool, two away from Carlos, and order *café con leche* in the smallest, airiest, least Anglo voice I can summon, but still he recognizes it. The shocked look on his face as he turns sharply, the way he swallows several times, and puts down his fork with a clatter, all this pleases me.

"Alice. What the fuck are you doing here?"

"I used to date someone who lives in the Bronx," I say. "On Jerome Avenue." And shrug. It seems important to use names, places, dates, like a police report.

He wipes his mouth with his napkin several times, takes a sip of beer, picks up his fork again. The guy who's beckoned me to come in is leaning on the counter watching us.

Carlos pushes his plate away and pulls out a wad of bills held together with a gold money clip in the shape of a cross. He waves at my cup as if to say he'll pay. "No charge," says the guy behind the counter. He looks amused. I feel special and set adrift.

When we're outside, Carlos turns and just looks at me. He lights another cigarette and keeps it in his mouth, inhaling and exhaling from his nose without removing it. I watch this trick, mesmerized by his nostrils. As much as I'm not thinking anything, I know his mind is busy. He can't very well stick me back on the subway alone at past midnight, and there are no taxis around. He can't take me home. (Would he like to? I imagine leaning over Marianella's crib.) He looks the street up and down for an answer. I wait, expectantly, all future plans suspended.

"You're crazy, you know that?" he says. Then, "So come on."

This club is a hole in the wall with an unmarked door. A guy in a black silk shirt frisks me carelessly up the insides of my legs, then waves me through. The place is packed and hot, the music loud. Carlos is moving forward, not looking back or worrying about me. Focused on the hem of his jacket, I push through the crowd, squeezing by men's shiny shirts and women's soft breasts. I'm not even worried about this being a firetrap. I want to stay here forever.

Without taking off his leather jacket, Carlos pulls me onto the dance floor. It's so crowded I don't see how anyone can dance. Every move is just smaller and tighter and faster. His concentration looks angry. He doesn't look blank the way he does in class. He starts turning me faster than I know how to turn. Our arms weave magnificent patterns. My eyes stay right on his. I don't want to tell myself that he's enjoying dancing with me because then I'd stumble and lose the beat. I'll see the end of joy in his blink, in his turning away. The music stops and I wait for him to walk away from me, but the band starts another number and he doesn't leave.

An old guy is playing a set of bongos braced between his knees, hardly looking at the dancers. He's wearing one of those English tweed caps pulled low over his face, just like my father used to wear. Their profiles are the same, and the way he slaps and pats at the drums is just the way my father would have if he'd played.

I'm waiting for Carlos to come back and dance with me, but he's talking to a man and a woman sitting at the bar, leaning toward them, holding the straw in his glass aside with two fingers so he can gulp his drink straight. Two songs begin and end. My feet try to move, but my brain is telling them, No. Finally a man asks me to dance. I glance over at Carlos, but he's still deep in conversation. The man looks in his direction, too, and then back at me, and makes a hooting sound. He starts to walk away from me onto the dance floor, but then he stops and starts moving side to side. He's holding his hand out behind him, arm down, wrist against his ass, palm up. I know what this means. He's wearing a bright orange shirt. There are fine lines of sweat in his big palm. I take his hand.

Other men ask me to dance. Then a woman whose perfume smells of some over-ripe fruit. I take this younger, juicier Sister-of-Fay in my arms and lead her onto the dance floor the way I have learned. Each time I turn her, her smile is larger and more glistening. Her eyes stay on mine.

Carlos sits at the bar and drinks beers and shots of rum, studying the bottom of his glass. When I take a break, he buys me a rum and Coke. I take one sip, then another, then leave my drink at the bar. My mouth is filled with cool, confident spit. I've never danced this much. I know the secret my mother wanted to teach my father.

At three, Carlos's eyes are heavy-lidded and bloodshot. His breath is smoky. He already smells of old drinks.

"You should go home," he says. "Can you get home?" I nod and return to the dance floor.

At four, I reassure Carlos that I'm on my way.

"You have to take a cab," he says. "I'll call you a car." He lifts one hand and waves, as though something will happen.

"Thanks, but I'll be okay," I say. I don't want to tell him that I'm not going home. The second longest day of my life is about to begin. "I'm fine with the subway."

"You have to."

"All right," I say.

"Promise?"

"Promise," I lie. "Are you okay?"

"Sure," he says. He puts his head down on his hands, which are folded next to his drink, and seems to fall instantly asleep. I stroke the back of his jacket a few times, up and down over the leather, then around in circles, feeling the unreachable warmth of his body inside. I consider kissing his neck.

The band is packing up, the fluorescent lights are on, and the bartender is swabbing down the bar. The place feels like the end of the world. Something slow and jazzy is playing on the jukebox, an unexpected relief after hours of galloping drums and squalling horns. I remember that I forgot to call Gwen one final time to tell her that I wouldn't be taking the train last night, wouldn't arrive until this morning. I think of calling her now from the phone at the back of the bar. With the harsh sound right by her ear, she'd jerk awake from her dream of bad haircuts, then be captivated by the hypnotic swirl of sax on my end. She'd get over being angry. She'd want to be here with me. We'd pick out songs to play.

Leaving my knapsack and jacket on the bar stool next to Carlos, I wander over to the jukebox and lean on it, enjoying its warmth. It's the old-fashioned kind, with red song titles in rows of boxes. After a few minutes the old drummer in the cap comes and stands next to me. He runs one long finger up and down the glass, and stops. His fingernails look mottled and strong, like tortoiseshell. He punches several keys and then keeps standing there. He's tall, a little bent over, as though a lifetime of leaning over his drums has permanently curved him. His selection begins in a gush of strings, and a throbbing, sentimental man's voice instantly swells my nose and eyes, then the music settles into a soft thud of drums. He turns away, satisfied.

I sway in front of the jukebox. Next thing, he's come up behind me and is pulling me by the hand and we're slow-dancing in the middle of the empty, fluorescent-lit dance floor. He enfolds me, resting his chin on the top of my head. He's tall enough to do this comfortably. The front of his vest smells like old cigars, pungent and rich as smoked sausage. His glasses poke out of his breast pocket. We swoon together, knees buckling, as though we've known each other forever and are close to sleep. I imagine him napping after lunch this afternoon, sitting up in a chair, his grandchildren tickling his ears.

When the song is over, we move apart, the cooling down a solid block of space between us. I blink, newly woken. He squeezes my hand and walks back over to his drums, already loaded into a battered case. Whistling, he puts on a jacket, waves at me, talks to the bartender for a few minutes, takes some money, and then leaves. We haven't spoken a word.

At the bar, Carlos is awake, his head in his hands. "Fuck," he keeps saying. "Fuck." He's pulling at the dancers' pin on his shirt. I push his hands away and undo it, close the clasp and put it in the breast pocket of his leather jacket, zip it closed.

"Will you remember where this is?" I ask, and he nods.

I wait for him outside. It's near dawn, but the bird wings of the music are still flying in my chest. The air is cool and perfect. A lone car drives by, its muffler crying.

We go to the same cuchifritos place to get coffee. The frying smell is even denser than before. It doesn't seem to make Carlos sick. It makes me feel like I've never left home, in that good way that grease can make you feel. We order café con leche and ham and eggs. I eat two pieces of his white toast with margarine and grape jelly, lifting the soggy points above my mouth and chasing them playfully. We speak in breakfast-time "ums" and grunts. I'm glad I didn't leave lipstick on his neck for his wife to find. I have that released, empty feeling, as though I'm embarking on a trip around the world with nothing but a thermos and a map.

I offer to walk him home, but it's obvious that Carlos doesn't want me to know where he lives. He walks me to the subway, twice dodging behind me so that he's walking near the edge of the sidewalk. Hands deep in his pockets, he pulls them out to light one cigarette with another. He stands at the bottom of the stairs, watching until I enter the shabby wooden entrance at the top. In a travesty of a third-grade school morning, I turn and wave good-bye. Without taking his hands out of his pockets, he waves back, flapping his elbow. Then he turns and heads back the way we've come.

Along with the first city workers, I wait for the train at the end of the platform, hugging my knapsack. High on the elevated outdoor platform, balanced on splintery stilts, I watch the city spread out before me, unrecognizable this far uptown, so elegant and pink, majestic with pollution.

ashes

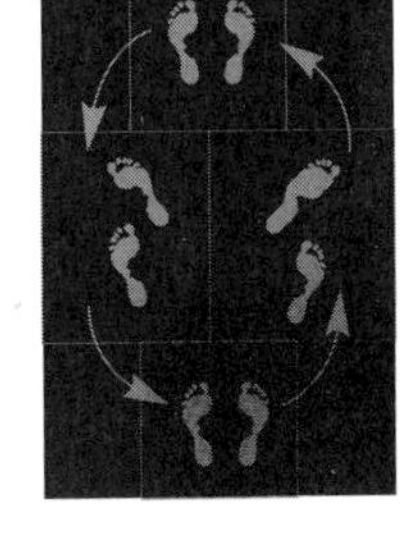

part three

fifteen

At six A.M., Penn Station is already moving. In my short skirt and my dancing shoes, I look like one of the river girls coming off duty. Being out and about so early reminds me of when Gwen and I would get up at dawn with my father to go fishing, a feeling of butterflies and thrilling, sleep-deprived doom in our stomachs.

I drink two cups of coffee and read the paper, then finally call Gwen to tell her what time my train will arrive. I'm still lingering in my post-dancing high, a shred of twirl and damp and buzz.

I can tell right away that Gwen hasn't had caffeine. "I thought you were coming yesterday," she says.

I tell her I changed my mind. When I ask her if she'll still pick me up, she says, "You leave me no choice," as though I'm blackmailing her.

"We'll have fun," I say. "I'll buy you coffee and doughnuts. Or a glass of wine. As long as it's noon."

She doesn't laugh. She seems to have forgotten our ritual.

Sitting in the train, I tug at the hem of my dress, pull it down, a familiar action. I remember years ago sitting on a bar stool wearing this dress, and a stranger putting his hand right up the front where the fabric stretched between my knees, a look on his face both possessive and melting. "Is this all for me?" he said. My father always hated my short skirts, although he was never able to tell me so himself.

As the train rushes by a stand of trees, I hold my hands up in front of my face and let the patterns play across the backs. The ads on TV would call them age spots. The freckles appeared suddenly. All those pamphlets with pictures of melanomas. I bought a magnifying glass, telling the young guy at the store it was for fine print. They make me think of my mother's hands.

My life has hardly begun.

The train conductor takes my ticket, his gaze slipping from my face down the front of my body. I look back up at him, lingering on his creased, sunburned neck with the thrust of reddish hair. It's only habit to need him to want to fuck me.

A man sits down next to me on the train. I'm looking out the window, so I see only his reflection at first, an impression of a big shoulder, a gleaming, newly shaved cheekbone. His aftershave is the kind that smells like deodorant, but some essence of him comes through. I immediately think of fucking.

Half turning to the man, I imagine sitting on the toilet and looking up at him as he shaves. I remember when I used to sit and watch my father. Once he dabbed shaving cream on the end of my nose, a gesture so playful it now seems as though I made it up. When I asked him if I could lather my whole face and pretend that I was shaving, too, he became silent again, running his badger shaving brush under the hot faucet, his long fingers squeezing out the soap, as though he was embarrassed. When he visited me in New York, I realized I was waiting to watch him shave, wanted him to leave the door open and stand there in his undershirt the way he used to. Of course, he closed the door. I went up close and stuck my nose in the crack of the door and breathed in the familiar shaving-cream smell of a man in the morning, which always makes me sad.

This man has a goatee, silky and pointed. He's probably younger than I am, but I'm not yet ready to do the math. Without looking at me, he settles back into his seat, pulls his trousers up to let his knees bend comfortably. The material of his suit is expensive. He's vain, I can tell. He hasn't even turned to say hello. I pretend that I want only this, but really, I want more.

He opens a briefcase, revealing a tiny, expensive computer. "Excuse me," he says, leaning over me and holding out the cord and gesturing for me to take it and plug it into the wall outlet near my hand. "Do you mind?" Now he is appraising me. Hating myself, I drink it in.

Ever since my father died, I've wanted everything accelerated, have no patience anymore with slow, unfolding situations, things taking their correct course. I imagine his mouth pressing hard against mine and his tongue poking my lips open and running along my teeth, lightly shredding the inside of my upper lip with the pressure, a souvenir to play with when I'm with my sister and mother. I miss kissing Jack.

I wanted everything to matter less once my father died, but this hasn't happened. Now he's vanished, leaving me with my thoughts and my short skirts and my cat and my future and two-left-feet Jack and forty-odd lipsticks in my bathroom cupboard. Wanting to throw things away after he died, I'd taken the lipsticks out and wound them all the way up, some brand new and pointed, others worn down to the metal lips of the cases. I arranged them in a row so they looked like organ pipes. Then I swept them into an old shoe box. One day I'll melt them down and see what color all these years of my lips will turn into.

The man turns on the computer and begins punching keys. I like his hands. I remember the old drummer's hands last night, like warm bowls, enfolding mine.

I fumble at the outlet, unable to see below waist level in the subdued lighting of the train. Close to the floor, the engine hums inside my head and chest. I feel him watching me, impatient to get to his spreadsheets. *You'll die before you know it,* I want to hiss. All my warm, pink dancing feelings are sifting away along the train tracks. I want to take the ashes out of the plastic bag at my feet, open the container and stick his nose into the future.

The prongs of the plug don't go in at first, and I jam them at the outlet, like a baby with unformed motor skills. "Careful," the man warns, and puts an arm out to take over. His hand hovers, then lights on mine for a moment, warm, so warm. "Actually, I can manage a plug all on my own," I say. "I wasn't born yesterday." Then I flush, because what was supposed to sound amusing has come out sounding bitter, and because it is clear that I wasn't born yesterday.

I wonder if he is now appraising my face, the lines around my eyes, in the way men feel entitled to do, as though they are counting weeds in a garden. I want to put on my sunglasses, but don't want him thinking I'm vain, which of course I am, although probably no more than he. "You didn't answer my question," says the man. He's typing at the same time that he's talking, staring into the screen.

"Which question is that?" I wonder if subliminally he's thinking of using me for secretarial duties while on the train. Working as an office floater, I have a sixth sense about this kind of need.

"I just asked your name," he says.

"Don't you prefer your train encounters to be anonymous?" I am relieved to hear the lightness again in my own voice.

"In that case, don't tell me." He continues to type, smiling and shaking his head. I resume looking out the window, except that now I'm not seeing the trees with their baked-potato-brown leaves, but am mesmerized by a one-inch-square patch of skin near my eye, the oil and pores exaggerated by the angle of the sun and the tilt of the glass, the hairs of my eyebrows like separate crisp spider legs. Turning to face front again, I lean down to rummage for my compact, watching his hands out of the corner of my eye.

Abruptly I excuse myself and edge out, stumbling over his lap as he holds the computer up in the air as though it's a tray of cakes. Lack of sleep is catching up with me, making everything surreal. Bumping down the aisle, swaying as the train picks up speed and then slows, I avoid making eye contact with other passengers. At the same time I peer into each seat trying to memorize landmarks—a red shirt (Carlos!), a book, a curled sleeper. I have a fear of getting lost in trains.

When I reach the café car, I note that I've traveled four and a half car lengths, and that on my return, my seat will be on the left-hand side. I buy a cup of coffee and then on impulse buy one for Goatee, piling extra creamers and packets of sugar and stirrers into my cardboard carrier. I have this fleeting idea that we'll become friends, then lovers, then grow old together, a cheap fast-forward trick I often do with complete strangers. I resent the way I can suddenly feel such an enormous, deranged sense of comfort with an unknown man. When I was two years old, my mother tells me, I used to run up to men in truck stops and hug their legs.

On my way back, my hips hit the seats on either side of the swaying car. I'm halfway there when I regret my impulse. I wait until the train slows down near a station and then hurl one of the covered cups out a half-opened window. The wind snatches it from my hand and the coffee flies back up my arm, instantly infusing my sweater with a hot caramel smell.

I duck into the tiny, ammonia-steeped bathroom in the next car and grab a wad of paper towels and dry myself off and then stuff them gingerly into the hole in the sink counter, already congested with used ones. This is exactly the kind of place I always expect to find an abandoned baby, a small mouth pressed against a dry-cleaner bag.

When he sees me standing at his shoulder, Goatee moves his knees sideways, performing a dainty dance step on his toes, and I slip back in. The backs of my stockings brush his legs.

"Smells good," he says.

"Train coffee?" I say. I wonder if he smells my generous impulse on my sleeve.

"I think I'll get some, too. Can I trust you with my whole life here?"

"I'm sorry," I say. "I could have saved you the trouble." He takes off his suit jacket and folds it the way men are taught to do, inside out and in quarters, like a satin pillow. His starched shirt rises up from his waistband, a jagged, blue-white iceberg.

"Of course you can trust me. Aren't we practically best friends?" He smiles down at me.

As soon as he leaves, I lean over onto his side, pretending that I'm looking at the train literature in the seat pocket. I stick my hand down into his open briefcase. On rare occasions my father allowed us to explore his briefcase, a boxy salesman's model, the kind that always made me sad. The structure seemed too large for the rattling collection of objects inside; it reminded me of playing office when I was small, with a row of pens and pencils, a single pad of paper, a plastic telephone, no one on the other end.

My father should have been a real fisherman, going off to work in waders with suspenders and a blue wool cap pulled low. Bringing home a mess of striped bass. My mother was not a woman to welcome that. She hated having chapped hands and was sensitive to bad smells. Once, my father brought home a fish and slapped it down on the bare counter in front of her and she screamed and hit his arm. His face pulled tight as though all the moisture had suddenly left. She pushed the fish into the sink with the point of the knife she was using to slice apples. "Disgusting," she said.

He looked so clumsy standing there, as though he'd never been indoors in his life. He took the fish by the tail with his bare hand and walked out the back door, the fish slapping at his leg, the screen door banging. He came back within the hour and we all sat down to spaghetti. Even though I knew the fish was dead, and the ocean was too far away, I still hoped he'd thrown it back into the water.

All through dinner he chopped up his spaghetti with his fork, instead of twirling it on a soup spoon the way our mother was trying to train us all to do. After every twirl, Gwen and I would cut a mouthful of spaghetti, glancing at our mother, then our father, until finally we were only cutting, not twirling properly. We kept looking at him, waiting for a smile, or a wink, but he cut and ate, cut and ate, until it was all gone, then pushed his plate away. He wiped his mouth hard with his napkin, looked at my mother, and left the table.

The scarf balled up inside this soft leather briefcase feels like cashmere and I bury my hand in it. A cell phone rings, vibrating next to my hand. On the third ring, I pick it up, flip it open, and bring it to my ear. "Hello," I say. There's a woman on the other end, probably his wife. "He's not here right now," I say in my best office voice. "He's stepped away."

"Wait a minute." The woman's voice is cold and liquid, like a martini. I snap the phone closed, then open it again. A gay guy I once met at a party called me a home wrecker. The tone of voice he'd used had been a perfect balance of sarcasm and pity, and I'd laughed along with everyone else, until I got home and thought about it.

I have the urge to call Jack. He'll be sitting at his computer, or interviewing on the phone, his hands stuck in the pockets of his bathrobe. He has no idea that after I left him, I stayed up all night, dancing in the Bronx. He has no idea I'm on a mission now to deliver my father's ashes. I close the phone again and slide it back into the briefcase. If I were there right now, we'd be eating yesterday's cold leftover pasta together.

Goatee comes back with a cup of coffee and a small bottle of Chardonnay, a bag of salted peanuts and a cinnamon Danish. I can tell that the Danish has been microwaved because the icing looks sandblasted onto the plastic. Automatically I look at my watch, the clear sign of a problem drinker who's stuck on allowable hours. Alleged experts say that people without a drinking problem will have no guilt about having a drink at eight in the morning. I've always found this logic to be faulty. It's ten minutes past eleven. I don't tell him that his wife called.

"Would you like a sip of wine?" he says. "I brought an extra glass."

"I thought you were working," I say.

"The two aren't mutually exclusive in my book," he says, and pours me an inch.

I take it politely and hold it to my chest and don't drink. It looks like a urine sample. Then I change my mind and just wet my lips with the wine, then take a little sip, the way you might do for Communion, not to actually taste the wine, but to have it turn into something else. It flowers in my chest. I can smell it on Goatee's breath, and it seems to join us in some way. I feel our shoulders move slightly closer together in those fractional shifts that happen on trains or planes when comfort is finally achieved, the body loosens, the knee relaxing past the invisible middle. Maybe his wife disapproves of drinking during the day. Here I am, an instant vino buddy.

"Do you have kids?" he asks.

My heart always does this sinking back flip at that question, as though my body is eager to give a different answer. Why don't Gwen and I have kids?

"Why do you want to know?" I ask.

"That's not a normal question?"

"Am I supposed to whip out my wallet now?" I know I sound angry, and I wonder if this suave, handsome businessman with the shiny cheekbones with whom I am sharing wine is thinking I'm crazy and dangerous. I usually have a good nose for that, but a good nose can go at any time. "No, I don't," I say. "Have kids."

"We do," he says. The royal "we" right now annoys me. I want to tell him that I've already spoken to his wife and could have asked her myself. He resumes typing furiously. I lean over to see what he's writing, but can only make out the silvery swirl of the screen. Maybe he's writing, *I want to fuck you,* or *Go fuck yourself.* Probably he's typing a sales report. Since when have men added typing fast to their pissing contests?

"Where do you get off?" he asks.

"Are you dying to get rid of me?"

"Just the opposite," he says, turning to me and smiling again. "I'll hate to see you go." With his left hand he deliberately moves across the space and picks up my hand that's lying half under the opened tray. As though I'm expecting this, I've already turned my hand palm up so that he won't have time to study the back. He starts kneading one of my fingers the way a masseuse would, starting at the base and working his way up, cocking his head this way and that, coyly studying what he's doing. His hands are warm and dry.

I close my eyes, not caring that the woman across the aisle has glanced up from her book and is looking at us strangely, or that the conductor might come by and see what he's doing. There must be something wrong with me, that this will do. I wonder if my knuckles feel swollen to him. I wonder if I will ever again strip off my clothes and jump into bed with a man without worrying about how some piece of me looks. Jack claims to like all parts of my body, even at rest, under natural light, although I generally try to engineer a smoke-and-mirrors show.

When I feel Goatee's lips, I'm not even startled, just sink deeper back into the train seat and accept them. His mouth tastes foreign, a little sour on the edges of his tongue, as though he comes from a home that stocks things unrecognizable to me in the fridge and cupboards. I picture the bumps on a gherkin. This strangeness makes me open my eyes and pull my head away, back into the plush. I watch the trees flash by beyond his hairline. His face is much too close, staring at me, almost cross-eyed, and I gulp for air as though I've been swallowed by water. Instantly I think of Gwen. I see her sitting in her battered Volvo station wagon in the parking lot, rubbing her eyes, unconcerned about damaging delicate skin, sipping a cup of tea from her plastic to-go cup. This man's arrogance, his little pointed beard, would disgust her.

Goatee puts his hand on my knee and slides it up and down. Without thinking, I grab his hand with both of mine and start twisting back and forth—Indian wrist burn, we used to call it when we were kids. I have no idea why I do this, and immediately start stroking and patting his wrist and apologizing. He grabs his hand back and cradles it with the other as though it's filled with shrapnel.

"Crazy bitch!" He yanks the cord of his computer so that it jumps out of the wall and skitters across my lap, the plug hitting my hand. He hasn't saved his work.

"Wait," I keep saying over and over, "please, wait." He stands up and shoves his computer into his briefcase and shrugs on his suit jacket and grabs his raincoat from the overhead compartment. I'm surprised that he's not afraid to expose himself to me this way, his arms up, his pants right there, his fly.

Goatee walks away, trailing his iridescent raincoat behind him down the aisle. He looks back at me once with a red furious face.

Two stops later, I go looking for him. I take my backpack and the bag of ashes. He's sitting two cars past the café, eyes intent on his computer, working on what I assume to be his second miniature Chardonnay. His eyes travel slowly up my body, starting at my knees, until he's made it to my eyes. I stare into his furious blue ones. He exhales a rush of sweet, winey breath in my face. Is this how my father felt about my mother's drinking breath—repelled and pulled?

"I wanted to apologize," I say, already not liking him again. He doesn't remind me of my father, who seemed like only the shadow of a businessman.

Goatee is still on the aisle, the window seat empty, all his familiar things piled there, the cashmere scarf, the cell phone. He stands and, without discussing it, we walk to the end of the car, open the door, and stand out there on the metal platform, our legs spread for balance, like bareback riders.

"You're crazy," he says.

I'm getting off the train, and temporarily dying of loneliness, although I know by experience that this could last forever. He leans against the wall and I stand on tiptoe, kissing him, pressing against him hard until I feel his hipbones, his erection. A little shorter, a spicier smell, and he could be Jack. I don't care. I want skin and arms more than I want integrity or revenge. The ashes bang against our legs with the movement of the train in a one-two rhythm, first my knees, then his. The backpack keeps pulling me away from him, toward the emergency exit. "I'm sorry, I'm sorry," I keep crooning, my words keeping time, as though something real has happened between us. What is it about someone dying that makes you want everything to have meaning?

Had my father ever been this intimate with a stranger? My mother said he'd had only one girlfriend before her, a pretty, plainish woman, except for beautiful black hair so long she could sit on it when it was braided. Supposedly she was part Cherokee. My mother used to mention her sometimes in a funny voice, make a face and gesture with her hand as though she were yanking a curtain pull. I figured this reaction couldn't be anything to do with our father. It was strange to see her jealous this way. He wasn't a lady killer who had finally settled on our mother. I tried to imagine what it would be like if my father had married the other woman instead, and spent his life combing and rebraiding her hair before bed.

A woman sometimes comes to dance class with a thick gray-black braid that hangs straight down her back. She moves stiffly and majestically in an up-and-down posting motion, without engaging her hips, as though she's wandered in from country dancing. Her almost-black eyes fix above her partner's head. Sometimes I pretend that this is my father's long-lost first love, and that he sits in her faraway gaze as she dances. When I'm her partner I become courtly and shy. "Did you ever dance with my father?" I want to ask her. Perhaps, in the nature of the cruelest fairy tales, this woman had been his dancing love and he vowed never to dance again after she left him. This woman's braid follows her slowly after she turns, an afterthought.

"Thank you," I say to her after our few minutes are over and she moves on in the circle, and I bow just slightly.

Goatee helps me get off the train—"disembark," he calls it—suddenly formal, although my lipstick still stains the outer edges of his mouth like early-summer tomato sauce. He gets out first and helps me down the steep metal stairs, taking my backpack and the plastic bag of ashes from me first. He squeezes my hand and then jumps back on the train and stands there, both hands on the rails, leaning out boyishly, the way they always do in the movies, yearning after the one staying behind. I stand there and wave at him as the train pulls out, feeling swollen and sentimental, prickling with tears.

sixteen

As soon as I see Gwen standing at the end of the platform waiting for me, I want a glass of wine. Whenever we haven't seen each other for a while, this is what we do. Drive immediately to a bar to have lunch and order big goblets of red wine. We gulp the first glass in ten minutes or less, devouring bar nuts or corn chips, whatever there is, scattering debris around us like monkeys, forgetting about real food. No need to flirt with the bartender. Instantly we talk, deeply, about everything.

Gwen's black Lab, Sam, is right there in the parking lot, faking that he's happy to see me. He's the one positive result of Gwen's brief marriage that ended five years ago. The dog's frantic over-attention to her every move is the antithesis of her ex-husband's, who developed marital glaucoma soon after their wedding day.

Gwen's neck smells good. Even though she cuts hair professionally (maybe *because* she cuts hair professionally), at home she still uses some kind of cheap herbal shampoo from high-school days. The sheen of her hair dazzles me. Automatically, I put a hand up to my own, tuck a few strands behind my ears.

She smiles, then immediately frowns. "Have

you been drinking?" Without waiting for me to answer, she continues, "How the hell are you going to walk on the beach in that dress? And those heels?" I look down at my dancing shoes and the thin black stockings that show the veins at the top of my feet. I see Goatee's hand slithering up my leg.

"No one told me we were going to the beach." I imagine the ashes flying away in a salty mist, the impossibility of trying to gather them back. "But I'll manage. You know me, I can walk through anything in heels."

Gwen doesn't laugh. "A guy on the train forced me to have a sip of his wine," I continue, thinking this will intrigue her. She shrugs, stoops to pound Sam on his rib cage with hollow thumps. Gwen is wearing jeans and work boots, the laces doubled-knotted and caked with mud. She walks her dog every morning for two miles in the woods.

She loads my pack into the backseat. I hold on to the plastic bag containing the ashes and, when she doesn't say anything, place it carefully on the floor between my feet.

We drive for fifteen minutes in silence. She doesn't once mention lunch or a drink or stopping anywhere. For some reason I'm unwilling to bring this up, as though in this part of the world she's the hostess. I just keep staring out the window at the delicate bare trees and pale sky, waiting for her to say something.

Splayed on the car floor is a naked Barbie, probably belonging to her roommate's kid. The doll's bare arched feet turn directly inward as though she's been in a car accident. I pick her up, smoothing the wild blond hair, and with my fingertips bring her face close to mine and kiss the cool plastic lips. My mouth envelops her entire pointy face. I hope Gwen's caught this in her peripheral vision and will laugh, but she's looking straight ahead at the road. Perhaps all my humor is about to be revealed as immature and drinking-based, even when there's not a bottle of wine in sight.

Gwen pulls into the parking lot in front of the giant year-round Christmas store that's stuck in the middle of nowhere, the pride of this area. This is the last place we'd work before committing suicide, we've always joked, a kind of terminal stop on Santa's route for the emotionally downtrodden in need of Xmas angels.

She turns off the engine and we sit there listening to the silence settle. The way she's gripping the steering wheel with both hands and staring straight ahead reminds me of my mother, and how she used to sit out in the car. After she'd been grocery shopping, she often did this for a long time, staring at the back wall of the garage where the rakes were lined up, the claws turned outward, and the huge dusty wheelbarrow protruding like a man with a hunchback. We had already clambered out of the car and gone into the house. We would look back at the empty doorway and know that she was still out in the car. She wouldn't yell if we went out to check, but she also acted as though we weren't really there. She just sat, not taking her gloves off in winter, the windows closed even in summer, both hands on the steering wheel as though she was still driving. When we became frightened at her stillness and knocked on the window, she would say, "Just a minute more" or "I'll be right in," mouthed through the window, and then she would continue to sit, sliding her hands up and down the steering wheel, polishing it. Sometimes she would take out her lipstick and put it on. We always waited for the day that she would start up the car and simply drive away.

Gwen suddenly gets very busy rolling up the window and gathering her bag and restraining Sam. Now it's my turn to just sit there, still holding naked broken Barbie in my lap. "Things are this bad?" I ask. "You hate this place."

"I want to pick up some vanilla candles," she says, still not looking at me.

"Since when do you like flavored candles?"

"I use them for meditation," she says.

"Since when do you meditate?"

"Since I gave up drinking."

Her statement thuds in the car like a rock out of the sky. I don't know what to say, so I say, "Don't you think the vanilla ones smell too much like cookie dough?"

Gwen shrugs and ignores my attempt at humor. "I was bombed out of my mind the night Daddy died. I remember cutting Gabriel's hair and drinking wine and smoking Mom's cigarettes, and that's it. Even his dying is a blur."

Because every second of that evening is clear to me, I, of course, want to ask if she remembers whether or not she slept with Gabriel.

"I think I stopped because I figured that if I really cleared myself out, the whole deathbed scene would come back to me," she continues. "I still like to think it's stored somewhere in my mind, but with a shroud around it. Unfortunately, I think maybe it's just gone." She starts crying, sniffing and blinking hard as though she's still driving and is trying to see the road. "It seems like such a betrayal of Daddy, to not remember when he left the world." I lean over the gearshift and put my arm around her, pull her head down to my shoulder and stroke her hair over and over again with a firm downward movement, the way you're supposed to pet skittish, resistant animals. Neither of us says anything. The air around us feels delicate.

"Do you feel better?" I ask. "Since you stopped drinking? What does Mom think?"

"I haven't told her. Hey, she's just been invited to life's cocktail party." Her voice is bitter. "Why should I ruin her freedom?"

This sounds ominous, but I decide not to grill her. I feel shut out. The last thing I want to do is tell her how much I'd been looking forward to a long lunch together over red wine. It's as though she's just had surgery and anything I say right now is going to tug at the sutures.

We go directly to the German-theme coffee shop and settle in at a table. The whole place smells of scented candle wax, the 255 advertised scents, from Piña Colada to Newly Mown Grass, mixing into one big sensory headache. A waitress dressed in a dirndl that pushes her breasts up under her chin stands at our table. She hums along with the accordion music. I glance at Gwen, longing for her to humor me on this one. Again, she won't let me read her eyes. Not drinking seems to have swallowed her sense of humor whole.

I order a double espresso, Gwen asks for tea. The urgency with which Gwen orders her Earl Grey with milk and sugar is reassuring. She hasn't given up on all poisons.

The waitress brings our drinks in cardboard cups. Once again, hot beverages to cure all discomfort. We decide to walk around. I leave a two-dollar pity tip and Gwen rolls her eyes. With me trailing behind, she heads for the Nutcracker Room as though she knows exactly where she's going and why.

It's like walking into a fairy tale in your grown-up body with all its tired, dark feelings. I have the urge to sink to the floor and cry my eyes out, but Gwen is going from one frame to the next, her head cocked as though she's in a real art museum. A guard dressed up as a Santa's helper is standing in the corner watching us. I'm sure they're instructed to keep a sharp eye on all the frustrated Sugar Plum Fairies who want to leave their husbands and children and disappear into one of these inviting sets.

I join Gwen in front of a scene where hundreds of white branches rise sharply into darkness, their bases covered in soft folds of glittering fake snow. A dozen miniature ballet dancers skate on a mirror, their outfits tiny and accurate.

"That one looks like Michael." Gwen leans over the railing, her finger almost touching a little pink-skinned figure with pronounced bullet-shaped buttocks under a green tunic. The guard has moved in closer, his elf hat pushed way back as though any minute he might reach for a gun and a walkie-talkie.

"Michael who?"

"Michael who?" Her voice soars derisively, then nose-dives in the empty room. "Your great ballet love? How many Michaels have there been since?"

"A couple," I mutter. I move closer to look. Actually, he does remind me a little of Ballet Michael, only without the red hair.

Gwen is staring into the branches with eyes fixed wide open, gently pounding the railing with both open palms. "I wonder what secrets you've kept from me?" she says, almost to herself. "You know, part of being in AA is making amends to the people you've wronged." The very idea of Gwen and pro-active forgiveness makes me nervous. Will this involve parading out our every wrongheaded act together, and restitching them into wholer cloth? Wouldn't a nice cash settlement, or some free shampoo and hair conditioner samples from the salon, be easier?

"I don't know," I say. "I don't think I have any secrets." This, of course, isn't true, but it feels safer to say.

"Everyone has secrets," says Gwen, as usual hearing my thoughts. She walks away, hands behind her back in a scholarly pose. She stops to study each diorama, her head turning this way and that with irritable birdlike precision. The old feeling rises in me, thick and warm. She turns and stares straight at my hairline in that fixed, accusatory way she has when she thinks I need a haircut. In a slow voice, as though she's watching something unwind, she says, "Remember the Sunday you went to church and I stayed home? How we traded places?"

Gwen always liked church, the ritual and order of it. I used to make fun of her. She'd had a sore throat that day. She made tuna fish sandwiches with no mayonnaise for lunch. We were all angry at her for producing such a dry, flaky offering. Where was Alice's delicious curried tuna pie? my mother kept saying to Gwen. What did you do all morning?

Gwen turns around so quickly that I step back and almost lose my balance. "He came by to see you and you weren't there, and I was." She says this as though the very simplicity of her presentation, the Dick and Janeness of her delivery, will make it all right.

I go back to the miniature skating rink and stand in front of it, staring at little big-buttocked Michael, frozen forever with his leg in an arabesque, the runner on his black ice skate glued on at a suicidal tilt. "Just that once, or more than once?" My lips are tight and buzzing. She's come right up behind me. Strange how something so old, an admission dusted off after more than two decades, can return with summer thunderstorm violence.

The guard turns away and in that moment I reach over the railing, past the magic white forest that plucks at my sleeve, and into the diorama. I seize Michael with two fingers. He's glued on, but I feel him wobble, so I tug. He comes loose in my hand, leaving a small dark patch on the ice and a gap next to the smiling girl in the blue skirt. I pocket him and walk away with shoplifting cool, my body language whistling a light tune.

I'm sure Gwen hasn't seen what I've done, but she follows me anyway, as though she senses a shift in power. I'm squeezing Michael in my pocket so hard that the two ends of him, his pink head and his dull, misshapen ice skates, dig into my hand. With my forefinger I search out and stroke his round plastic butt.

Safely in the deserted Alpine Room, I pull the figure out of my pocket and thrust him in Gwen's face. "You fucked him?" I yell, knowing that I'm risking the guard running in and making his first official arrest.

"Calm down. That was such ancient history. I can't believe it still matters to you."

I remember her sitting next to Gabriel and looking up at me and talking about our married man with the same expression on her face, perfectly controlled, majestically condescending. I take Michael by his poor paralyzed legs and hurl him up toward the electric train that chugs endlessly around the perimeter of the Alpine Room near the ceiling. By some miracle, he lands headfirst in a conveniently open coal car, his arabesque leg sticking out. The train continues on its way with a manic choo-chooing. "There goes your first amends," I say. "On the train to nowhere."

Gwen stands there, looking blank. I have this urge to run out to the car and get my father's ashes. The whole place is filled with so much fake snow, it would be perfect. His body stuck forever in a purgatory of scented candles and everyday, ordinary need.

As we walk across the parking lot, the dog is pawing at the windows of the car, silently barking. "I thought it might be comforting to have Sammy along," Gwen says. She looks worried. "I shouldn't have brought him." I think of Herbert, the careless piles of dried food I've left for him, the dripping tap and open toilet for emergency hydration, the primary signals of abandonment. Thea offered to check on him every morning, and I agreed, but I worry about her ability to focus that early, except on a cup of coffee and a cooking list. Or she'll decide to indulge Herbert with leftover salmon *en croûte* and crème brûlée from one of her jobs and I'll have a monster on my hands when I return. I'll call Jack and have him go over and administer some tough-love, dry kitty food, even though he's allergic to cats. (Why do we even get along?) Surprisingly, Thea likes Jack. "He worries about what's for dinner," she says. "And wants to do something about it. That's good in a man, and rare. Keep him." She doesn't consider it a problem that Jack has two left feet. "As long as the two left feet don't jump into bed with you, who cares? It's better to dance with strangers anyway." I'm sure my mother would agree.

Sam has ferreted the Tupperware container out of the plastic bag, but his attempts to open it have only resulted in a little slobber. At last Gwen and I laugh. We lean back on either side of the hood of her car, the doors wide open next to us in crazy welcome. My back feels the faraway heat of the engine. We're facing up to the sky and the sun's intimate warmth, as though it will give us another chance, but only this once.

seventeen

Gwen and I hear the music from all the way down the driveway, Herb Alpert and his Tijuana Brass, our mother's scratchy old record from when we were kids. Instantly I see the palm trees, the raised trumpet, the white dress on a woman with large breasts and laughing red mouth on the record sleeve from so long ago, marimbas and hope. We would stare at it as we listened, wanting to blend into the cover. When he put the record away, my father would slip it into the sleeve without looking, and place it at the back of the shelf, shoving it harder, we knew, than a record should be shoved.

Before Gwen and I open the front door, I try to envision what dance our mother will be doing. Rhumba, I decide, or cha-cha. I love the movement of rhumba, the slight downhill tilt in the hip. I've recently read that Marilyn Monroe wore one high heel shorter than the other to make her hips sway when she walked.

My mother is lying on the couch with the next-door neighbor, Mr. Clayton, the guy she was planning to call if she had problems with the pipes. No nakedness, no expanse of flesh to telegraph the message. It's a few seconds before Gwen and I realize that they're making love.

She's lying stretched out, her legs barely spread. My first unbidden thought: This is the same position in which I come most easily.

My mother's scuffs are sticking up in the air, half off her feet, making them look twice their length. She's wearing her green velour bathrobe, the collar turned up to her ears, giving her the regal look of an off-duty queen. She's gazing over his shoulder with her eyes wide open so that when we open the door she's already staring in our direction, as though she's expecting us. It wouldn't surprise me if she put a finger to her lips, telling us to be quiet. Let him finish what he's doing. She blinks and then taps the neighbor on the shoulder.

The minute Mr. Clayton stops his elegant thrusting, it's as though she wakes from a trance. She pushes him away with a familiar clumsiness, sits up and fiddles with the neck of her robe, pressing the collar up against her neck. He looks back at us over his shoulder, apologetic but unhorrified, a look that is oddly comforting in its calmness. This is a different house now, the look says. He zips his fly and threads his belt methodically through the loops of his khaki pants. After tightening the belt, he pushes the tails of his shirt down into his waistband. I remember my father doing this in the same illogical order.

The neighbor stands over six feet tall. The first thing I imagine is my mother dancing with him. I know that he's been widowed for a good ten years, and occasionally dates women who wear cardigans buttoned all the way up the front and leave in small station wagons late in the afternoon. He's good at getting these women to help him with yard work, the way his wife used to, raking and stuffing leaves into plastic bags. "His gardening harem," my mother always says contemptuously, flicking the living-room curtain open, and then closed, then open again.

I stare at the sofa, which seems to still bear the imprint of their bodies. This is the same sofa where I made love with Michael all those years ago. Probably Gwen did, too, and is having the same thought. It's been reupholstered once since then. Right before my father died, when no one else was in the living room, I turned the sofa cushion upside down and unzipped the new cover and peeked inside to check if there was a stain after all these years. I was sure I saw a faint spot, dull as an old coin.

"Hi, girls," says the neighbor, smoothing back his hair in a curiously youthful gesture. They're both standing now, close together. "Hi, Mr. Clayton," we chorus. This is the way Gwen and I used to greet him when he stopped to wipe the mower blades and his forehead, looking over to where we pranced half naked through the sprinkler.

"I expected you yesterday," my mother says, her voice rising. "I wasn't sure when on earth you were planning to arrive." She's standing there with her robe half open. After her first instinctive clutching of the collar to her chest, she has let it go. She doesn't rush to retie it, or bring the collar up around her neck, and I can see the inside slope of her breasts. There is something languorous and decided, almost defiant, about the way she stands there in her own home in front of her daughters. The flush in the center of her chest is sweet rather than scary. Who knows how you're going to feel when you walk in on your seventy-year-old mother making love with the neighbor? This is it.

"He came over to help me with the fireplace," she says, waving vaguely behind her shoulder. "There was something stuck in the flue, and I couldn't tell if it was open or shut. You know how I always have trouble with that. I thought there was something up there, maybe a squirrel." Her voice is bright and interested.

She eyes my dress and my dancing shoes. Especially my shoes.

We all stand there without saying anything. I think Gwen and I are still mentally somewhere back in the doorway, digesting the hard evidence of our mother fucking. The thought of our parents and their separate beds and temperatures is almost impossible to reconcile with the reality of her lying casually beneath a man's half-clothed body, a man other than our father. That, in its own way, might have been even stranger. As though she senses my need for reassurance, my mother walks over and gives me a long hug and a kiss on the mouth. I've always wanted to belong to a family that cried and yelled and kissed on the mouth. Her familiar powdery smell envelops me. I breathe in deeply, wanting life to slow down.

Herb Alpert has stopped playing, leaving total quiet except for the familiar sound of a needle clicking at the center of a scratched album in the next room. I'm oddly relieved that my mother has not yet replaced the ancient stereo.

"Well," says my mother, "shall we three girls have a glass of wine?" As though by prearranged signal, she nods at the neighbor. He turns and, with a wave, walks out of the house. Through the window we watch him cross the street toward his house, his hands in his pockets. When he turns sideways to look down the street, his mouth is pursed as though he's whistling. In his front yard, he crouches and studies the grass.

I glance at my watch but catch myself, worried about looking too eager for a glass of wine in front of Gwen. Never before have I thought of her as a cop. Not saying anything, she walks over to the sink, turns on the tap and runs the water for a long time, and then fills a water glass to the very brim so that some spills as she walks back to the table. My mother is busy pouring three glasses of red wine, bending down to eye level with the table. Gwen and I keep staring at her mussed hair and exposed cleavage.

We stand around, sipping, my mother and me drinking wine, my sister, water. After a while, with her nose inside her glass, my mother says to Gwen, "Why aren't you drinking your wine?" She says this in exactly the same teacherly tone she used to talk about us eating green beans.

"I didn't actually say I wanted wine," Gwen says. She's holding her water glass against her chest, right under her chin, her knuckles poking out white.

"But darling, we're all here together again. Wine is so festive."

I'm waiting to hear how Gwen is going to explain her desertion from my mother's late-life watering hole.

"Not every occasion demands wine," says Gwen, sounding like she's reading from an abstention manual. "Someone has to drive us to the beach. Haven't you ever heard of the designated driver?"

"Oh, we won't be going today," says my mother. "Stan and I are going out dancing later. I have to get dressed and do my hair and makeup. I don't think Daddy would really mind, do you?"

Gwen and I exchange glances. When did the neighbor become Stan?

"Daddy's not here, Mom," says Gwen. "Alice and I came here because you asked us to bring Daddy's ashes back. I think maybe *we* mind."

"Do you, darling?" She wheels toward me. I shrug, not wanting to get involved. "Let's ask Daddy if he minds," she says, turning back and forth to take both of us in at once.

"How do you plan to do that?" Gwen's voice is tight. She gulps her glass of water to the bottom, goes over to the sink, runs the water, testing with her forefinger, and fills her glass again. She turns around to face us. "A Ouija board? A psychic?"

My mother takes a long gulp and then walks over and flings her arms around me, pressing her head against my chest. Her breath is hot and damp through my clothes. "I can't seem to miss your father," she says, her voice muffled. I pat her on the head, then on the shoulder, smoothing the back of her robe.

"He wasn't an easy man when he was here, why should he be easy to miss?" I say. Gwen is staring over my shoulder and out the window into the garden, her face unreadable. I gesture at her to come closer, to join me in comforting our mother, but she just looks away. I wonder if she's remembering that she also left this job to me when our father died. She keeps taking sips of water, as though she can drink herself out of this kitchen and to the other side of the world.

Just after dark the neighbor returns, wearing a bow tie dangling around his neck. His black patent-leather shoes have faint cracks across the arches as though they've endured years of spins on half-toe. We're all still sitting there. My mother jumps up from the table and hands him her glass of wine. He takes a couple of long, slurpy sips and hands it back. Obviously they've shared a glass before. "I told the girls we're going out dancing later," she says, turning and backing up against him. "I don't think they believed me."

He looks embarrassed, but steadies her around the waist and takes the glass again and brings it up in front of her shoulder, takes a sip. She turns around and fusses at his neck, starts tying his bow tie, then yanks it undone and starts again, as though we're not there. How does our mother know how to tie a bow tie?

She looks over her shoulder and smiles at us, a girlish grin that cuts into the seams of her face. "We're practicing for a dance contest to win a ballroom-dancing cruise. Would you two like to come?"

What had I expected? Maybe an evening of looking at old photograph albums or home movies. Or just sitting together and not talking much, but with my father's elusive spirit, his disapproving not-thereness in the room with us. Now it seems as though he's going to have to sit up all night in the kitchen, waiting for his wife and daughters to tire and come home.

I look down at my shoes. Here my mother is, inviting me to go out dancing. The unheard of, the longed for. For the first time, I know exactly what my father felt, and I'm filled with a weird elation. I feel left out and strict, knowing and unknowing, filled with stopped-up desires and crusty, packed-down fury. I feel like the kid who doesn't go to the party and wants only to ruin it for everyone else.

When neither of us answers, my mother shrugs and heads for the stairs, holding the edges of her robe to her chest as though now, finally, she needs protection from us. Her wineglass sails along ahead of her. She's humming something Cole Porterish.

"Your mother's a beautiful dancer," says the neighbor. I remember Carlos's breath when he said this in my ear. I wonder if my mother thinks too much when she dances.

Without another word, Mr. Clayton wanders away. From where we're standing, we can see that he's settled in our father's armchair, the corner of his angular knee sticking out, inches of thin dress sock showing and his patent-leather shoe gleaming in the lamplight, jigging and jerking occasionally to some silent music.

"Do you want to go?" I ask Gwen.

"Watch our mother drink and act like she's twenty years old? No. Why, do you?"

Hesitantly, I say, "Maybe it would be fun. How much do you think Daddy would mind? Hey, I have an idea. We could invite Gabriel as our date." At his name, Gwen's face undergoes a series of softening/hardening changes. I continue, "But probably he can't dance. Well, maybe he only dances with Death. Do you think Death dances Latin?"

Staring down at the floor, Gwen continues as though she hasn't heard me. "Do you remember the night of the father-daughter dance?" She's referring to that milestone of sixth grade in which little girls on the brink are requested to rope their sheepish, luggy fathers into bringing them, in thrall to their cuteness, to the auditorium, and spirit them around the dance floor.

I remember Gwen's dress as though it had been mine. Black velvet with short sleeves and tiny pearl buttons shaped like daisies with ebony centers that sparkled. It fell straight from her armpits down to her knees with perfect pubescent elegance. My father wore his good dark suit. They drove away, both of them looking straight ahead and Gwen not waving at me, my father's face dark under his hat. The next day she refused to say anything about it.

The next year, when I was in the sixth grade, I was too afraid to ask him if he'd go with me. Several times I sat on the stairs around the corner from his armchair, my heart thudding, practicing what to say. Instead I came down with a flu so profoundly miserable, complete with high fever and shots of penicillin by a visiting doctor, that I fooled everyone, including myself.

"He never danced with me," Gwen is saying, hypnotized. "We sat on these metal chairs against the wall, and he folded his arms and watched everyone dance. He didn't talk to one other father. The only thing he did was drink the punch. He kept getting up and walking over to the table and ladling out punch, and walking back slowly carrying two pleated paper cups and handing one to me as though that made up for not dancing.

"I think my teacher saw what was happening and must have asked one of the other fathers to ask me. Because this strange man came over and bowed in front of us and said, I'll never forget it, 'Sir, would you do me the honor of allowing your beautiful daughter to trip the light fantastic with me?'

"I didn't know what he was talking about, or what to do. Daddy looked at the guy and then at me and just shrugged."

To my knowledge, Gwen has danced only twice since then, both times with me. Once was in high school, up in our bedroom. We said we'd take turns being the boy, but I had a knack for leading, so it was always me. I remember the waxy, scalp smell of her hair, and how I wondered, looking down at her part, how a boy would feel doing this. The second time was on her wedding day.

The night before her marriage, Gwen and I slept side by side in our old matching twin beds. I waited for her to suggest that we kneel and say our dumb childhood prayer (*Now I lay me down to sleep . . .*). I'd never understood the pretend-virgin ritual that forbade you to spend the night with the guy who was about to become your husband.

"Wait until you get married," she said. "Then you'll understand."

Somewhere in the middle of the night I heard a rustling noise from her bed. At first I thought she was masturbating. When I realized she was crying, I automatically got up, pulled back the sheet, and climbed in next to her. We used to do this a lot, lie side by side, our hands outside the covers, weaving stories. Now we hardly fit. The bed no longer had any spring or buoyancy. Our hips dipped toward each other. I strained to stay on my side, but felt the heat of her body anyway. We turned so that we were facing, and looked at each other straight in the eye, our hands in prayer shapes under our chins. She leaned over and kissed me, a dry, soft kiss, a cross between a kid's kiss and a woman's, filled with anxious spit and worn-off perfume.

"Do you think I'm making a mistake?" She moved even closer, not quite pressing her body against mine. Her toes curled against the tops of my feet like small frozen shrimp. "I used to dream about Daddy kissing me good-bye on my wedding day," she said. "In the dream we actually kissed, not father-daughter, but a real kiss. I wanted him to rent a tux and wear a carnation and drink champagne."

I put my arms around her and cradled her head. Her hair was tangled and smelled dirty. I thought of the way we used to dress up in long, tattered sequined dresses and marry each other in the basement playroom.

After the ceremony, Gwen cornered me at the drinks table, where there was no champagne. She picked up the hem of her long white dress and hooked it over her arm. She took my arm by the inside of the elbow and we walked slowly toward the dance floor. I felt gentlemanly and protective, nodding slightly at friends and relatives, as though I were her new husband. He stood across the yard in a circle of friends, not looking in our direction. I think he hated me. A woman reached out to touch my sister's dress. We were within brushing distance of our mother who was dancing with Mr. Clayton.

The band broke into "Bewitched, Bothered and Bewildered." I turned toward Gwen and held out my arms. I wasn't sure what I was doing, but dancing the man's part is only hard if you can't count. I pulled her in close to my chest and started steering her around the floor in looping circles. I didn't pretend I was just any man. I pretended I was my father. He was sitting by himself across the lawn drinking a cup of coffee, looking up into the trees.

My sister's long dress got caught between my legs. I twirled her one last time and deposited her in a chair next to him. She was crying a little, and laughing. I bowed and kissed her hand. My father didn't say anything. Instead he leaned over and carefully, as though he were saving a cobweb, unfurled the bottom of Gwen's dress from around the leg of the chair and arranged it at her feet.

Gwen and I are both tilting our heads up toward the ceiling, listening to our mother bustling around upstairs in her bedroom, humming. I'm remembering the dead, hopeless silence that used to fill the house when she would disappear for the afternoon with one of her migraines. How evening would fall and there would be no supper smell, no downstairs lights.

It's my theory that she stopped blushing because it was something my father liked. Instead she got migraines, headaches of monstrous, biblical proportions complete with a stunning visual show. When she got a migraine while we were in the car, she would grip the wheel, focusing intently just beyond the windshield. I think this must have been why he never liked her to drive. Each time we made it safely through a traffic light, Gwen and I would exchange a scared, relieved look.

At home I automatically went straight to the bathroom and filled the metal salad bowl with cool water and carried this, along with the bottle of Alka-Seltzer, into the already-darkened bedroom. She would be lying flat on the bed, one wrist on her head, the lines on her forehead curved into furrowed S's of pain. Removing this hand and placing it down at her side, I'd wring out the washcloth, aware of the deafening plink each drop of water made into the bowl. Then I'd smooth the cloth along the length of her forehead and press it there as though she were a child.

Tipping two Alka-Seltzers out of the long bottle, I dropped each one into a glass of lukewarm water and waited until they had barely stopped fizzing, the way she'd trained me. I propped her head in the crook of my arm and helped her drink to the bottom of the glass.

"Remember, don't tell your father," she whispered.

Throughout the afternoon, I'd crack open the bedroom door and slip inside and stand there watching her, motionless under the bedspread. She would have thrown off my washcloth, and her wrist would be back, pressed against her forehead, the S-furrows deeper than ever. Sometimes she would murmur, making sounds but no words. I tried to match images to the sounds, knowing that she was caught in a swirling nightmare of shooting stars gone mad, bolts of lightning turning on her for the kill.

Once she spent the afternoon sleeping with her blanket thrown off and her wide, gathered Guatemalan skirt twisted up near her waist so that her high white panties shone in the dark bedroom like a phosphorescent paper-doll cutout. I blushed at the sight, but made no move to cover her, worried that she would wake up and catch me. Her migraine and my blush seemed to fill the room, sucking out all available oxygen, creating a kind of internal combustion all its own.

Now the whole house is humming, bright with lights. On her way upstairs, my mother has clicked on every lamp, as though following around the ghost of my father, who had extinguished each one along the same path.

Gwen and I look at each other. "I guess I'll go up," I say. My voice sounds apologetic. I'm admitting to wanting to join the teenager upstairs. "I'll try to figure out what she wants."

"She's all yours," says Gwen. As I move toward the stairs, she adds, "You'll want this." She's holding out my half-full glass of wine.

eighteen

"I never knew you could bring this many dresses home, and try them on and then return them," says my mother. I'm sitting propped on her bed with all her pillows behind me, my wineglass tilted against my inner thigh, watching her zip up her third evening gown. This one is ivory satin, a dead ringer for a wedding dress. She hasn't drawn the curtains, and already the dusk outside cocoons the house. She doesn't seem at all worried that the neighbors can see in. "I've even heard of people who will wear a dress out for one special evening and then return it. Isn't that awful?" Her eyes gleam.

This new life suits my mother. Nice fabrics, collarbones showing, tinkling ice, meatballs in chafing dishes, glasses chilling, just for her. I can see her on board a cruise ship, strolling the deck with Mr. Clayton, tossing her newly streaked gray hair back in the breeze to cool off her neck, damp with the rigors of mambo. She looks off at the horizon, aware of the picture she makes this late in life, turning to pose against the railing, a lady beyond her prime, just come into her own. The Merry Widow at Sea. Too bad the neighbor isn't rich.

I want to feed her a man story of my own. I

consider telling her about Jack, or Carlos, but can already see her blank, puzzled look. *But what kind of a relationship is that, darling?* I settle on Goatee.

"I met a guy on the train," I say, pulling a pillow tight against my chest.

"Oh?" Her sly, knowing look would be grotesque if there wasn't something so newborn about it.

"A businessman. We talked for a while, and had a glass of wine together."

"Should you have been drinking with a strange man on a train? Do you think he might be a prospect?"

"A prospect? Like mining for uranium?"

"Darling." My mother turns toward me, half in, half out of one of the borrowed dresses. She moves over to the bed and sits on the edge, lets the dress go completely so that the bodice falls down into her lap. She's wearing a black orthopedic-looking bra, the color and the shape somehow at cross-purposes. I pretend she's back in her bathrobe and try not to look below her neck. Her cleavage is the fine line of an arrow, pointing down.

"I just want you to be happy," she says.

Does she even notice I'm changing the subject? "Hey, how come I've never worn an evening gown in my life, and here's my mother modeling a whole line?" I pick up the dress and patch it back onto my mother's frame, as though I'm dressing a doll. I want her to get the hint, but she pulls it back down, happy as a kid to be almost naked, her freckled hand stroking the swooping satin collar on the inside, then the outside. I join her, placing my hand next to hers. I want to see all that together, our two hands, her freckles, my freckles, her age spots, my pre–age spots, her knuckles, my knuckles, our two lives.

"What size are you now?" My mother jumps up, looking me up and down. I don't want her scrutinizing my body, this woman who has just had afternoon sex.

"I never go by size."

"One of these dresses should fit you. We'll each wear one." She looks so proud, how can I tell her that the thought of putting on one of my mother's cast-off evening gowns makes me feel as though my life is over?

I want to sleep. I want to get drunk. I want to fuck. I want to dance. I want to bring back the bird wings in my chest. But my mother is tugging me to sit up, gently slapping my cheek, forbidding this luxurious catatonia in her bustling, newly eroticized boudoir.

"This one would be perfect on you." She's standing over me holding a lacy beige dress with a piece of material standing stiffly up around the neck, the collar a little Catholic, a little medical.

"I don't think it's my color. It would wash me out."

"Or this one!" She's almost running across the room, holding her half-zipped dress up against her stomach with her forearm. "This one" is black, on the plain side, a cross between a choir robe and a hair-cutting smock. I hold it against me without sitting up, barely lifting my head to appraise it, a laid-out corpse. I have this terrible feeling I'm going to put on this dress and end up at the Ramada Inn, drinking a whiskey sour, a wallflower to my mother's belle.

"Your father never wanted to go out. Don't be like your father."

Before I know it, I'm standing in the dress and my mother is kneeling at my feet with pins in her mouth.

"You shouldn't be filling it with holes," I say. "Don't forget, you haven't bought this." My voice is sharp.

"Stand still." She gives me a swat on the bottom. "Oh, they won't care. You and Gwen aren't the only ones with credit cards, you know." These oblongs of plastic were just another tool of the devil to my father, the glittering gold logos in the corners, like something out of Perdition or Las Vegas. Never a man for wads of cash, he used plain green checks, made out in black ink. Small amounts, neat zeroes, always filling in the memo, never a zany purchase. Now here's my mother with credit-card fever, firmly pinning an expensive dress that she doesn't even own far above her daughter's knees. At least she knows it needs to be short.

I want Gwen to barge in and point and hoot, break me out of this trance, save me from a suburban dancing fool's fate. But all is quiet down below. I imagine the neighbor dozing in my father's napping chair. His head won't be falling sideways, the way my father's used to. More likely, he'll be sitting there, waiting, his foot bopping to silent music, filled with as much manic elder-energy as my mother.

"He was married," I say. "The guy on the train." My mother pauses mid-pleat. I look down at the full set of pins sticking out of her mouth.

"It would be one thing if you were in love. But how well can you know someone from one train ride?" she says.

"Didn't you go out with a married guy once? Wasn't Rafe, the ballroom dancer, married?"

"I've told you, things were different during the war." I sense her mood plummet so fast, it's as though her body temperature has dropped. She turns to stare at her bed.

"I don't mean that as a criticism," I say. I want to grab her back. I've come to rely on this new hot shade of my mother.

"How well do you know Mr. Clayton?" I ask, trying to distract her.

One by one she removes the pins from her mouth and sticks them into the bracelet cushion on her wrist. She stands in front of me and starts playing with the collar of my dress, tweaking it this way and that. Her mouth falls open into a soft, sad pout that turns her face slack. In a panic, I squeeze her tightly to my chest, push my nose into the hollow of her neck. Her back arches. I realize how easily I could hurt her. I used to dream this when I was a kid, pretend that someone had pushed her, or hit her, and that I pulled her to safety. Then we would sit for hours at the kitchen table and we would drink tea. Every few minutes she'd reach over and touch my cheek and thank me over and over.

"I'm so fond of Stan. But he's just there," my mother says,

pulling away. She's stroking my hair and making little tsk-ing sounds with her tongue. I can feel the hot, optimistic sap rising up to fill her body again. "Do you understand?" She presses my cheeks with both hands until the skin inside my mouth squeezes painfully against my teeth. "I've decided that it's all right to dance a little before I die." With each word she nods my head up and down.

My tears come instantly.

"Remember how I used to tell you what my mother always said?" she asks.

Dutifully I recite: "That life is a dance, and if you don't let someone fill your dance card, you'll end up a dried flower."

"A wallflower," my mother corrects me, smiling.

"I always liked dried flower better," I say. "Like a milkweed pod." We stand that way for a minute, looking into each other's eyes, something we hardly ever do. I need a Kleenex. Then I blurt out, "You weren't a wallflower at your wedding."

My mother doesn't say anything for a minute, but lets her hands drop from my cheeks. I go over to her bedside table, take a tissue, and blow my nose loudly.

"What do you mean, darling?" she asks, suddenly sounding very British. I can't tell if she's really puzzled, or just stalling.

"I found a picture down in the basement. In Daddy's tackle box. It was buried under a lot of flies and stuff. Inside a little envelope. Here," I say. I've been carrying it around in my pocket, waiting for the right moment to pull it out. Somehow I hadn't envisioned it taking place quite this way, both of us upstairs in borrowed dresses, me in tears.

My mother pulls the photograph slowly out of the envelope and stares down at it for a long time. She starts blushing, the prickly, interminable kind that I know all too well, the body invaded by a heat monster that lets go only when it's good and ready. With the strange involuntary connection that blushers seem to possess, I start blushing, too.

"Who is he?" I ask.

"Your father's brother," she says. "Your uncle Daniel. Actually, he died the day this picture was taken."

"You're kidding," I say. I'd known about my father's brother, of course, killed suddenly in a car accident, but had never known the exact details. The basic facts, we'd always just known, the way a family story becomes locked inside amber, intact and unchanging.

My mother and I move together and sit down on the bed, each of us holding a corner of the tiny square as though we're afraid that we'll drop it. I've scrunched the glassine envelope into a sharp ball in my other hand. We both lean over and gaze closely at the picture. I glance sideways at my mother, studying close-up the wrinkles on her cheek.

"He was handsome, don't you think?" my mother says. Her voice is strangely prim. "He was hard to resist if he decided to turn his charm on you. Unlike your father, he was a real flirt. He loved women. He and your father were so close. Your father looked up to him." I take the photograph from her and carry it over to her bedside lamp and tilt it under the light. I can just make out the bright buttons, the military cut of a uniform, now smudged. He isn't wearing a hat.

She's continuing, "He missed the church ceremony, and arrived right as the best man was giving the toast. I'd never seen your father smile quite that way before. Daniel didn't ask me or your father's permission, he just came up and took me in his arms and twirled me onto the dance floor in my white dress. He was the first man I danced with as a married woman. He was the most wonderful dancer I've ever been with."

I interrupt, "I thought you always said you asked Uncle Edward to dance with you? Didn't Daddy leave, and you asked Uncle Edward because you thought it was bad luck not to dance at your own wedding?"

My mother shrugs, and then laughs, looking sad. "It was easier on your father for me to tell the story that way, and then it seemed to become the truth. I did dance with my brother Edward, and he did ruin my shoes, but that was later. First I danced with your father's brother. I was having such a good time, it was the first time that day I felt like a real bride. I think your father knew that, because as soon as we started to dance, he turned and walked out." Suddenly, she says, the man she'd just married seemed to be someone else, and she wasn't quite sure what she'd done. Uncertain in a different way than she'd been just moments before. How could he go off and leave his bride to be with his brother? "I wanted to stop dancing and go after him, but Daniel wouldn't let me. He held me tight and kept turning me, and I remember he whispered in my ear, 'I wish you all the luck in the world, beauty.' Your father could never have said something like that to me."

She found her new husband out in the garden, smoking a cigarette. He didn't smoke, had always been passionately against smoking, and it shocked her to see him standing behind a tree that way, inhaling clumsily, furtively knocking the ash off by tapping along its length with his whole finger, as though he were a child with a stick. She grabbed the cigarette from him, burning her fingers. "I wanted the dance not to matter, for him to laugh it off and be glad I'd done it. But that wasn't your father. I don't think he was used to being mad at his brother, and that upset him the most.

"Later that night came the phone call saying there'd been an accident. Of course, I've always felt guilty for that one dance," my mother says.

We walk downstairs, my mother and I, arm in arm. My mother's decided to wear the almost-wedding dress. A transparent panel in the ivory satin gives her cleavage a gauzy mystery. I'm wearing the black dress, adding at her insistence a pair of earrings and a hankie tucked up my sleeve. Something old, something borrowed. (The new is not only the dress, but my mother; the blue is my mood.)

Faces turn up as we walk down the stairs. There's the neighbor in the armchair over by Daddy's radio, and Gwen, with Sammy's muzzle covering her foot.

And Gabriel, standing across the room, his elbow propped against the fireplace.

We stop at the same time, on the same step, as though it's been choreographed. I have an overwhelming sense of toppling, of inevitability, of local headlines. I could fall right now, take her with me. And then I steady both of us.

I have a sudden sharp memory of Gwen on her way downstairs for the prom. Although we'd practiced slow dancing together for hours upstairs, this lone school dance, Gwen's, was the only one that either of us would ever attend after grade school. She wore a drapey lavender dress that didn't suit her at all. My mother had tried to dissuade her, but she'd picked it out herself.

The word *luminous* came to me much later, a kind of inward shining as though a candle was burning inside her skull. Gwen looked straight down at our father as she walked, floating, almost, as though she were coming downstairs for her wedding. By mid-stair, I'd stopped watching her and was watching him watch her. His newspaper half-lowered, one side bent in as though he were trying to mark his place with the corner of the page, he looked wondering and disapproving at the same time, in the same proportion, a look that created war on his face. Had he ever looked at me this way? Something free and young was fighting with the old stopped thing inside him. Had he ever just once been able to say, "And where are you going, young lady, with those shiny lips?" or "How beautiful you look," life for all of us would have changed into that other thing.

That night Gwen came home at four in the morning. Ours

was not a house where the doors would be locked in protest, lights extinguished in disapproval. The door was open, the hall light giving off its reassuring eight-inch golden glow on the hall mail table. In another family, the father would have still been up, smoking a cigarette, sipping a drink, pacing, ready to curse, then to embrace, the beloved errant daughter. Instead, he had gone to bed, leaving his leather slippers sitting there in front of his chair.

This was the night Gwen gave Eddie a blow job on the banks of the reservoir, the lavender skirt showing the next day the slipping, scrabbling stains of someone trying desperately to stay abreast of a situation, and wearing the wrong dress. Our father said nothing to Gwen that night, or the next morning, or the next night. She was on her own in a perilous new world of grass stains and semen and impossible requests. She stuffed the dress in the back of the closet. Secretly I pulled it out the next day and tried it on, sniffing the material, trying to imagine the pleasure (years later, the pain) trapped inside the cloth.

"How nice to see you, Gabriel," says my mother. "What a perfect surprise. Where did you come from?" She stops on the stairs, pressing my arm. I feel like her lady in waiting. She nudges my side and we continue down.

"I invited him," says Gwen. Her voice is flat, a far lower register than normal. Gabriel's hair is longer, but I'm not sure by how much. Gwen can tell almost to the hour just how long it's been since someone's hair has been cut. I wonder if he's been visiting Gwen regularly at the salon. Maybe they make love after she's done a single process and he's helped someone to the other side.

"Why don't we have a glass of champagne?" says my mother. The way she says this, it's not a question. Gwen and Gabriel exchange glances. I catch this and mentally deflect it, turn it around and throw it back into space.

"Mother, where are the ashes?" Gwen's arms are crossed over

her chest, her voice stern. My mother's trying to have a party, and Gwen is turning out the lights, dumping out the drinks.

"Why do I have to tell you that, darling? Isn't that my secret? He was my husband, after all." My mother is talking to Gwen, but her tone is directed toward Mr. Clayton, flirtatious and filled with extra meanings. I want to grab Gabriel by the hand and have the two of us run out of the house and into his truck, careen off down the road somewhere. But already he's pushed off the mantelpiece, is moving closer to Gwen and sitting down next to her on the sofa. He doesn't pick up her hand and hold it, the way he did the night my father died. But it's as though a private shadow of him is doing it anyway, even as his real hand is sitting there on the leg of his jeans, not moving.

I politely escort my mother over to her chair and settle her into it. We've done this dance before, all of us, the do-si-do, the four corners, the change your partners. She adjusts the bosom of her dress and then the skirt, as though she's lived all these past years in satin, and understands its moods. I hadn't noticed when she was pinning up the dress, but she's wearing nail polish again.

"You want ashes, I want champagne," my mother sings. "You say tomato, I say tomaaahhto . . ." She rolls forward, laughing. "He's still in the linen cupboard," she says. She's sulky now, the party not going well, no drinks clinking, one of her daughters still in pants and boots, a smelly dog in the room, nothing quite pretty enough. Where was the music? "I thought he'd stay dry and warm in there. You know how he hated damp. Remember how he always talked so much about dry rot? Doesn't that come from damp . . . sweetheart?" She looks over at the neighbor, who shrugs.

I'm waiting for her to offer drinks again, to start on the ritual of polishing glasses, opening and pouring wine. Gwen is bound to be thinking the same thing. But when I turn to exchange a look with her, she and Gabriel are whispering together, and laughing. I turn away, anger fizzing through my body. Since the beginning, my sister has found a way to dive into the heart of every situation with the insistent radar of a bat.

My mother rises gracefully and swishes over to the farthest window, and starts pulling the drapes as though she is taking it upon herself to close this scene of a play. She looks regal, beautiful. I'm shocked to realize that I feel jealous of her, her nervy confidence, her floaty energy. We watch her silently. Taking each curtain by the edge, she draws one, then another, steadily across, shaking the heavy material until each panel is smooth down to the hem. Closed, they give the room the cloistered symmetry of a church.

Turning to her audience so fast that her dress swirls around her legs, my mother is suddenly an army general. "Gwen, go change your clothes. You can't go out dancing looking like that. Stan, how many cars shall we take? Gabriel, are you coming with us? Good. Ride with us, or do you have to drive that truck in case of an emergency? I think it would be fun to all go in one car. We can coochee up."

I haven't heard this since we were kids, when we'd kick off our shoes and climb into her bed with all our clothes on and snuggle under the covers. "Coochee up closer," she'd say, dragging both of us into her sides and pulling the covers to our chins. And she'd press each of our bare feet with one of her stockinged ones, pressing down hard as though this was the only way to keep us and the bed from flying up and out of the room the way people and beds did in magic books. She never invited our father to coochee up. When he passed by and stopped in the doorway to watch us, a stillness would fall over the bed. I would have trouble breathing for a minute, and then my mother's feet would press down on ours again, and with loud laughs, we would reenter the game. And he would move on.

Gwen stares at the floor, not moving. Gabriel is standing now, rubbing his hands nervously up and down his jeans as though he's preparing to rope a steer. Mr. Clayton looks expectant, swiping the tip of his patent-leather shoe over and over again with a neatly folded handkerchief.

We wait and wait, as though what we decide in this moment will determine the rest of our lives. Finally Gwen says, "Okay, but I won't wear a dress," and this somehow seems to break the spell. We all stand up and mill around the living room, then the kitchen, waiting for Gwen, who comes down after about ten minutes wearing black slacks and a turtleneck and a pair of my mother's silver earrings. We continue milling around, in coats now, bumping into one another. It's patently clear that no one knows how on earth to go out dancing.

nineteen

We take two cars and a truck, getaway vehicles—not "coocheeing up"—on our minds. The Glory Inn is a second-cousin-once-removed to a Ramada Inn, with the same lonely smell and squishy, bad-dream carpeting. We march along behind my mother and Mr. Clayton through connecting low-ceilinged corridors toward the Grand Ballroom. The hall floors and the walls, halfway up, are covered in teddy-bear brown shag. Our footsteps are completely muffled, as though we're private dicks in search of tacky infidelities. Hunched into my collar, I feel trapped and skeletal in the unfamiliar black dress. I'm trying hard not to sweat. I have the feeling this is the dress my mother plans to return to the store after its big night out. I have no wish for her to be sniffing the armpits and discovering signs of my dread or insurrection.

At the reception table, we cluster behind her skirts like six-year-olds. My mother and Mr. Clayton are already signed up. Gwen and Gabriel and I are added to the list of "Guests of Dancers." She pays for all of us by credit card. Despite our second-class status, the woman at the desk assures us that we are perfectly free to dance during breaks. She's close to my mother's age. Underneath the table her feet in white ankle socks and cross-strapped white dancing shoes keep time to the music.

My mother writes our names on paper tags, which she insists we stick on our chests. When I surreptitiously slip mine into the side pocket of the dress, she digs her hand in and yanks it out and slaps it across my left breast as though she's plastering up a sign on a billboard.

Our table is right next to the dance floor. As dancers careen by I can practically feel the breeze up my loaner dress.

"Let's order some champagne," says my mother.

"Can you do that here?" I ask. It looks more like a Kool-Aid and coffee-with-creamer-in-cardboard-cups kind of place.

"Of course," she says. "Look." In the corner there's a long cafeteria table covered in a white paper cloth set up as though for a wedding toast, with dozens and dozens of plastic champagne glasses. A little old man in a neat suit with a yellow tie is carefully unsnarling the wire around a bottle of cheap champagne, as though he's defusing a bomb. I suddenly miss my Father of the Bride.

He was Thea's doing. He was wide through the chest, wearing a light gray suit that exactly matched his hair. I stood behind the drinks table at the back of the banquet hall, serving at his daughter's wedding. Everyone started clapping and a few people were crying as he moved her slowly around the dance floor. There seemed to be no Mother of the Bride. The bride was the same height as her father, and she stared into his eyes as they danced. He bunched the back of her dress until the hem came off the floor. This was the only way you could tell he was nervous. They danced simple steps, the same pattern over and over again: slide, together, slide. Neither of them smiled.

As the dance floor grew crowded, I waited on the sidelines to serve cake. As usual, I was ready with a sharp knife and a bowl of hot water to dip the way Thea had instructed me, to "always shield the bride from the lifelong memory of crumbling, unattractive slices." The father of the bride moved to stand beside me, hands clasped together in front. He looked sideways at me and smiled. "Would you like to dance?" he asked. I gestured down at my uniform, my black skirt with the tiny, near-invisible crust from prior parties, and my white blouse, unbleached and unloved; my black shoes with the rubber soles and old food in the treads. He shrugged. "Everyone should dance at a wedding," he said.

While we were dancing, I kept pulling my hand away and wiping at my nose, then giving my hand back to him a little damp. Dancing always makes my nose run, a genetic inheritance of the repressed. I kept sniffing. I thought he would pull a handkerchief out of his pants pocket, but he didn't. That was my father. This father let me manage on my own. Slide, together, slide.

He brought me back to the table, returning me to exactly the same position in front of the cake and the knife. He gave a small, courtly bow. He went to kiss my hand, and I pulled it away. "Don't," I said, "it smells." He asked for my phone number.

We went out to dinner twice and he kissed me in the front seat of his car. I told him I wasn't much older than his daughter. He told me I reminded him of his wife, not his daughter. I told him he didn't remind me of my father. He took me ballroom dancing at Roseland. He wore the same suit he wore to his daughter's wedding. I lied and told him I was between boyfriends, and maybe he lied and told me he'd never dated anyone but his wife. Why me? I wanted to know. Because of the way you cried at my daughter's wedding when we danced, he told me. What did that mean? I wanted to know. It means that you have a soft place in your heart, he said. I have lots of soft places in my heart, I said, that's my problem. Don't ever say that, he said. What did your wife look like, I asked him, do I really remind you of her, or is it just my soft heart? She had dark hair like yours, before she went gray. And the same eyes. My father refuses to dance, I said. He wouldn't even dance at his own wedding. My mother would have been happier with you as a husband. And you, what about you? he asked. Me? You mean a husband? I don't know. Maybe he'll have to dance. Is that crazy?

Not to me, he said.

Gwen and I are sitting directly across from each other at big patio tables. She's jiggling her foot nervously up in the air from a cross-legged position. We look like a pair of ghouls, me in my oversize black crepey dress with the flapping sleeves and the hem that my mother hastily tacked up somewhere above my knees, Gwen in her jewel-thief attire. We've both paid enough attention to the task ahead to wear leather-soled shoes. Gabriel, on the other hand, has tractor-tire tread on his feet. What will I do if he asks her to dance before me, and I'm left sitting here alone? Lit by a big dirty-looking chandelier, the room has the grandeur of a retired airplane hangar. Couples dressed in formal clothes are sitting around the dance floor next to couples in fancy gym clothes. The median age is sixty-nine-point-five. I try to imagine Carlos here, and fail. The piped-in music is a lifetime away from the dense smoky drumbeat of a few nights ago.

Gwen and Gabriel and I start playing Name That Dance Step, matching the barely recognizable music to the barely recognizable steps. "This is the warm-up phase," interrupts my mother knowledgeably. When they play a few bars of each kind of music and couples have to shift to the next dance without missing a beat.

"So let's see what you can do," says Gwen. She's just incorrectly identified a rhumba and my mother has slapped her on top of the head with her rolled-up program and told her to take some dance lessons or she'll end up just like her father. Gwen's tone is sadder than it is belligerent. My mother only looks pleased. She toys with the stem of her plastic champagne glass, taking a few sips, looking over at Mr. Clayton.

"Will you please ask her to dance," Gwen and I say in exactly the same intense way, at exactly the same moment. We all laugh. Suddenly my mother starts crying. It's the first time I've seen her cry since before my father died, when he was sick in bed and she dropped a pan full of newly baked bread on her foot.

Mr. Clayton jumps up and lunges down to hug my mother, his wide brow furrowed, a warm, anguished look in his eyes. For the first time I feel a surge of tenderness toward him.

"What's wrong, Ma?" says Gwen impatiently. I have the feeling she knows exactly what our mother is going to say.

"I'm so sad that I've missed out on this my whole life and now I'm old and how many more years will I be able to dance?" She ends on a wailing note, discreetly muffled by the front of the neighbor's jacket.

He takes her by the wrists and pulls her to her feet. "Wait, wait, wait," my mother keeps saying, reaching back to the table to grab a napkin and dab at the mascara stains under her eyes, and blow her nose with a honk, and fluff the skirt of her dress with her free hand. Then they're heading out to the dance floor, Mr. Clayton weaving her expertly through the other couples until they reach the center of the ballroom. There he turns to her, already dancing, his hands held out, one at her waist, one hovering above her shoulder, guiding her. How much better for her, I think.

The three of us have been sitting here watching our mother dance forever. I reach across the table for her champagne glass and drain it, adding my lipstick print next to hers. As I'm pulling my hand back, it takes a detour and of its own volition reaches for Gabriel's hand, grabs it and squeezes so hard he can't possibly let go. "Let's dance," I say, and drag him up out of his chair. I don't look at Gwen, but out of the corner of my eye I see her face fall, then stiffen that way, sad and jealous. A lifetime tally reveals itself, like falling dominoes.

Clomping in his truck-tire boots onto the dance floor, Gabriel follows me reluctantly as I weave us through whirling couples. Bending our heads against the tornado of flailing arms, we make our way onto the floor until we're right in the middle, next to my mother and Mr. Clayton. I turn to Gabriel with my arms open and waiting, remembering not to assume the man's position this time, but the woman's waiting one, and the next thing I know, the Archangel and I are doing the mambo.

*By the middle of the second number, we're slow-*dancing, even though the music continues to jump and fizz around us. Gabriel is graceful, his side-to-side movement so minor, it's barely discernable. I can feel how strong he is under his shirt, the kind of thin-strong that's coiled and waiting to lift dead bodies if called upon. I think of Carlos's bony, elegant frame, Jack's lurching cuddliness.

Next to us, my mother's dress floats, a soft, elegant meringue. I notice her looking over at us critically. We're not keeping proper time. We're not doing the right dances. We're draped on each other like high-school sophomores without chaperones. She and the neighbor are dancing in classic position, heads high, backs beautifully erect. They execute spins and dips, a shared horizon in their gazes. I'm seeing the neighbor in one of those powder-blue tuxes. If I ever get married, Mr. Clayton will be the Father of the Bride, and he'll be dancing with me. I pull Gabriel closer. Each time we turn, I notice Gwen sitting at the table, her chin on her hands, watching us, her expression a blur. The next time we turn, she's gone.

I grab Gabriel's hand and pull him across the dance floor, and we cut out into the shag-lined corridor. I want to find Gwen. The hall is deserted. We lean against the wall. We start kissing. From inside the ballroom comes the muffled sound of the music and the circus-bark of the MC. Not saying a word, we kiss for a long time, a long tonguey one that doesn't require air. His lips feel thicker than they look. This is definitely not the kiss of an angel. I forget all about Gwen.

Finally we break apart. Again, I drag him by the hand, in the direction of a brown sign with an arrow and yellow lettering that says THIS WAY TO ROOMS. Dodging a cart piled with ice buckets and more fake champagne glasses, I start testing doors in another corridor, this one carpeted bright blue. Finally one gives and I push it open and pull Gabriel in after me. We're in a small linen closet stocked floor to ceiling with towels and sheets. The smell is antiseptic and a little greasy.

"Wait right here," I say. Darting back out of the laundry room, I grab a DO NOT DISTURB sign from one of the guest rooms, hang it on our door, and dart back in. Gabriel is leaning against the wall of towels, his hands in his pockets, eyes closed. His hair is ruffled, his mouth faintly stained with lipstick.

I start unbuttoning his denim shirt. I hitch up my mother's black, for-hire dress and pull down my underpants until they're looping off one ankle. I scout either side of the tiny room for hand-holds. Making love standing up always looks so easy in the movies. As though he's about to hoist a beam, Gabriel automatically moves to support me with both hands. I remember those hands on my father's dying body.

I'm still working on unbuttoning Gabriel's jeans, when suddenly he pulls away. He's holding on to the back of his hair with one hand and pulling at his scalp, as though searching for the ghost of his lost ponytail to rein himself in. He shakes his head. "I can't."

"Why not?" I ask. My heart is pounding. I have towel fibers on my tongue.

"I just can't."

I step away from him. My skirt is still bunched around my waist.

"Why the fuck not?"

He considers this, as though he's weighing life and death on either side of a butcher's scale.

"Let's just say I wouldn't be helping your family."

"You mean because of my father?" This last comes out as a shriek. My father is still controlling my sex life from beyond the grave.

"Actually, it has more to do with your sister."

"Gwen?" My throat is tight. "How mysterious."

"Not really. I just can't talk about it."

"Am I going to have to murder you both?"

Gabriel laughs. "It's not that horrible an offense. Trust me on this."

"Why should I trust you?" I grab at the front of his jeans and start wrestling with the buttons of his fly again. He puts both hands over mine. Their size and calm warmth enrage me even more. I push them away. "Alice, Alice," he says in his soft, there's-life-after-death voice.

"Don't fucking try to comfort me," I yell. I can't catch my breath. My face is tingling and my vision is going all the colors of a fresh bruise. Reaching as high as I can, I start toppling towels—bath towels, hand towels, washcloths—down from the shelves. I stop only when I can't reach any more. The towels form a snowy moat around our feet. A washcloth is hanging off Gabriel's shoulder. A bath mat covers his head in a cowl. Pushing these away, he grabs my arms and holds them down at my sides by my wrists, imprisoning me in a straitjacket shape. "Shh . . . shh . . ." he croons. He lets go of one of my hands long enough to firmly cup the back of my head and bring it in to his chest.

My breathing is still harsh but slowing to a shudder. I hold my breath, trying to rid myself of the pins and needles the way you'd cure hiccups.

"Sometimes I think he didn't really die," I say. "He breathed in, and that was the end," I say. "I'm still waiting for him to breathe out."

He lets go of me slowly, prepared to reimprison me. "When someone dies, it's actually kind of fifty-fifty," says Gabriel. He's back to his angel-caretaker voice, and I know I've completely lost the lover. He stoops and finds a bath sheet with one hand, then drapes it around my shoulders so that it's covering my breasts like a cape. I'm shivering now. He strokes my hair from my brow to the base of my neck, then scratches lightly behind my ear. Not very sexy. More like I'm the neighborhood cat come by for scraps. "It has to be one or the other," he continues gently, "and one doesn't mean more than the other."

Suddenly cold, I throw off the sheet, bend down, and shimmy my underpants back up. I'm embarrassed at how mottled my breasts look under the fluorescent lighting. I unbury the black dress, which is covered in towels, and pull it quickly over my head. Gabriel is buttoning his fly. We stare at each other in the blank white room.

"I've seen a lot of people die," he finally says. "It doesn't mean he wasn't able to let go and move on. You should stop worrying about that."

We move back in together, and I put my arms around his neck and we start shifting our hips side to side, back in high school again, fused together in a friendly way, dancing with our eyes closed in the towely silence. I kiss his neck, innocently, not lingering. My pins and needles disappear out the ends of my fingertips.

Finally I pull back. "We should go find Gwen."

Gabriel nods. Smoothing his unangelic hair back with both hands, he retucks his shirt into his jeans. And then we go off to do this, marching around all the shag corridors still holding hands.

At the front desk they tell us that Gwen checked into a room about an hour ago.

twenty

"What the fuck are you doing here?" I ask, so relieved I start to cry.

Gabriel and I had tried calling Gwen from the house phone in the lobby. I dialed her room and let it ring at least twenty times. I dialed the operator and asked if I could leave her a voice mail and she told me that the Glory Inn doesn't have voice mail. I kept seeing Gwen's face when she was sitting at the table, her head propped in her hand in a mockery of alert pleasure. The way she disappeared in the space of a spin. I saw her spread-eagled on her back across a king-sized bed covered in a fuzzy brown bedspread, having done something stupid.

Far away there's the distant ocean sound of applause. I wonder if my mother and Mr. Clayton are performing. Here my mother is, fulfilling her lifelong dream, and we aren't there to see it.

"I was taking a shower," she continues in a matter-of-fact voice, as though taking a room at the Glory Inn and jumping into the shower is the most logical thing for any wallflower to do.

Gabriel had followed me to the second floor and we stood in front of the door to Gwen's room. I was afraid to knock. I tried finding significance in the number 204. After a minute or two, he reached past my shoulder and gently rapped with one knuckle. I said, "Gwen, Gwen," in this voice that started out low. I was worried about waking the hotel guests, but then I stopped caring and started yelling.

There was no answer for a long time, and then finally we heard some sounds inside—water running, rustling, and then a dead bolt turning and a chain rattling. There was a tingly feeling in my cheeks. Gwen threw open the door with enough energy to suggest that she hadn't swallowed a bottle of sleeping pills.

One towel is wrapped around her waist, one around her chest, a third around her neck, and another wound turban-style around her head. She looks rosy-cheeked and innocent, a religious convert, a towel bride. My first thought is that she's probably already called downstairs for extra towels and a pot of tea. Gwen always likes a full-service establishment. She puts one arm around my waist, another around Gabriel's, and pulls us inside, shuts the door with her bare foot.

She goes to the oversize television, turns it on, and starts flipping channels with the mute on. She stops at a reddish grainy tangle of nude bodies, sits on the edge of the bed and watches interestedly, toweling her hair with the other hand. Gabriel looks embarrassed. He heads into the bathroom and closes the door, and once again I hear the sound of water running.

"Because I wanted a drink," she says.

"You should have said something," I say. "Isn't this a little drastic?"

"You didn't exactly look like you were in the mood to be interrupted, and besides, you were dancing with my sponsor."

"Sponsor?"

"The guy who I'm supposed to call when I feel like I'm going to drink. My crisis person. The one who's supposed to help me not slip."

Suddenly it's clear why the two of them seemed so interested in their seltzer this afternoon, passing the bottle back and forth as though it were a rare and valuable vintage while the rest of us were guzzling house wine. I rewind the tape of my encounters with Gabriel, and mentally smell his breath: sweet, untainted.

"I'm sorry. It's not really his fault," I say.

I sit next to her on the bed. On the screen a man with a chubby hairy belly is lying back on a striped bedspread with his eyes closed. Two women are kneeling on either side of him taking turns giving him a blow job. I take the remote from Gwen and adjust the color. I change their bodies from burnt orange to a normal flesh color to a pale sickly green. Is Gwen also remembering when we knelt this very same way over our married man so many years ago?

The word *menage* would have sounded to us back then like a good kind of cookie. That Sunday morning we sat around Gwen's kitchen table sharing doughnuts and tea in cardboard to-go cups. She'd carved each of the pink and chocolate and sprinkled things into dainty thirds as though it were a tea party. Alan Mason, whose wife was working, turned on the radio and took turns dancing with each of us, close and old-fashioned, the way our mother danced, until we fell in a heap on Gwen's bed. Alan kissed Gwen, then me, and then gently, almost absently, started pulling off our clothes. Gwen and I knelt on either side of the mattress, still giggling. But then we got serious, as though we suddenly remembered that sex was for grown-ups. I wanted to rewind time so that it wasn't happening, so that we were still grimacing our pink-icing teeth at each other over his shoulder as we danced, and hoisting up our sweatpants.

At the same time, I didn't want it to stop.

I avoided looking at Gwen's nipples, which thrust out more than they did when she took a bath, and were a different, darker color. Our hands suddenly met behind his back and we recoiled from each other. Guiltily, I reached around and stroked her shoulder, then her back, safe, familiar areas we both knew from giving back rubs while we watched TV. It was unclear who this was for. I felt both in it, with pins and needles in my cheeks, and detached, hovering somewhere over the bed.

I turned away as he touched her between the legs and she closed her eyes and tilted her head back and parted her lips and stuck the tip of her tongue out between them. She looked like our mother did when she was dancing. I knew that this would be a different face if she and Alan were alone together. Sex could be such a lie. I knew this already. It made me wonder when it ever wasn't.

Easier to focus on the man between us than on each other. We touched him as though he were a large melting snowman in the backyard that needed shoring up.

"Oh, there, right there," he said, and our glances flickered at each other and away. I knew we could have burst out laughing, but we didn't out of respect for his idea of us.

"Baby," Gwen murmured, and I tried to remember if I'd ever heard her say this before, and tried also to remember what I said in bed, and couldn't, although I knew it wasn't baby.

Afterward, with our heads on either side of him as he lay lightly snoring, we stared at each other across the low hedge of fur on his chest. We began to giggle as we used to when we were six and seven and would look over our father's head when he read to us, sharing the joke of him.

We shook the bed. We looked down at his penis, curled and exhausted-looking on his thigh. Our crushed young cleavages moved and shifted, hers deeper than mine, and browner. All our sex smells mingled together strangely, like perfumes that have fermented in different ways and don't quite blend. I thought this meant she and I could always be together, this perfect warmth, the men would come and go.

Our married man shifted and stirred, woke, looking as though he didn't remember who we were. Annoyed, he mumbled and turned away, burrowing deeper into sleep.

Gwen and I got up and put on sweatpants and T-shirts. We gulped down the rest of the doughnuts until we almost choked, as though the size of these doughy bites would be enough to sop up our sin.

As soon as I hear Gabriel opening the bathroom door, I switch channels. It's my turn to start flipping around. He sits down next to Gwen on the bed and puts his arm around her, then stretches his other arm to include me. Gwen gets up and moves to his other side so that he's sitting between us, his two arms spread over us.

On one of the channels there are couples dancing. I flip right by, then backtrack, trying to adjust the color back to normal. There's our mother in her floaty dress and Mr. Clayton with his perky bow tie and slicked-back hair. They're the only ones on the dance floor. They're both smiling.

"Closed-circuit TV," says Gabriel.

"Is this the contest, or do you think they've already won?" I ask.

"They don't look very nervous," says Gwen. "I think we missed it. Maybe they did win." She doesn't sound in the least bit guilty. I want to tell her that she always ruins everything.

"Are you staying here tonight?" I ask.

"I don't think so. The bed sucks."

"Expensive shower," I say. "How did you pay?"

"Credit card."

"Maybe they'll give you a refund. If we leave now."

"They gave me the special rate because Mom is a ballroom-dancing guest of the inn." She snorts.

We help her straighten out the bed. I hang the towels back in the bathroom in neat rows. They look unused, although they're all damp. For some reason it seems important to have the room look as though Gwen was never here.

Gabriel goes to turn in the key at the front desk while Gwen and I find our way back to the Grand Ballroom. We're in the middle of the brown bear-shag corridor when she takes my hand and we walk along, swinging them, the way we did when we were children.

The ballroom is half empty, people scattered at tables, sipping from the plastic champagne glasses. Our mother and Mr. Clayton are sitting at the table. She's kicked off her shoes and he's holding one of her stockinged feet, rubbing the ball with his big wrinkly hand. There's a shiny gold cup sitting in the middle of the table. I reach for it and heft it. It's light, with a hollow base.

"We saw you on closed-circuit TV," I say. "You looked great."

"We won second prize," says my mother, beaming. "In the mambo."

ashes and dancing

part four

twenty-one

Tonight the house is so quiet, without music, the spirit and the life have crept back into the walls. It's late, and again I can't sleep. It's like the night my father died, only longer, with bluer shadows.

I carry my container of ashes downstairs to the kitchen, tucking it under my arm, tight by my waist. My father's closer than he's ever been before. We start walking around. This feels pretty good. What would I be saying to him if we'd ever done this when he was alive? Walked around the house in the middle of the night in the dark, stopping to look out windows, stroking a wood surface here, touching a silvery mirror there, straightening a shadowy picture. Did he and my mother ever do anything like this? A survey of the property before bed, like going out to do a last check on the farm animals? Our trip to the beach tomorrow seems so far away; inevitable, yet certain never to arrive.

I wonder if my father even liked this house with all its pictures and lamps and mirrors and curtains. Was he at home here? Maybe the woman with the braid would have given him a simpler life, a home where he could bring a fish into the kitchen and slap it down on a wooden table and slice it down the middle with his knife, gut it right there in front of her while she stood pouring oil into a frying pan, looking pleased. Maybe my mother should have ended up with the guy who was light on his feet and could hum "Begin the Beguine" and drink Pimm's Cup.

I'm going to end up with someone with two left feet.

I tune in a classical station on my father's old radio. Mozart. I twirl on. The local college jazz station is playing a slow saxy ballad and I leave the dial here, continuing my tour, humming in a low moan the way you do when you can't sing. I stand still and sway a little, cradling the bowl against my stomach. I'm in this great, hopeful mood, and I don't know why. I feel like calling Jack, but he might be in the middle of a difficult sentence and take me down with him.

In the kitchen I sit at the kitchen table and place the container in front of me, centered on a place mat as though it's dinner. I feel like pouring myself a drink. There's a half-bottle of wine open in the fridge, and some brandy on the counter, but instead I get out a bowl and fill it with cereal. This bedtime tradition, started by my mother, was something my father never shared. He didn't say so, but I know he thought it was decadent, having cereal at night. When she had trouble sleeping during the war, my mother would go down to the mess kitchen and have a bowl. The milk calmed her down. She'd go back to bed and stick the second knuckle of the forefinger of her left hand into her ear (it fit perfectly) and she'd fall right to sleep. I wonder if my mother and Mr. Clayton indulge in this homey nightcap together.

I sprinkle a teaspoonful of my father's ashes over the cereal, then fill the bowl to the rim with two-percent milk. The ashes don't melt. They look like granules of sugar floating in the milk, gritty and separate. I add brown sugar, some raisins. After stirring and mashing the whole thing vigorously, I eat it right down. I'm of the school of thought that cereal is better before it's soggy. My father tastes so sweet.

Wandering around the dark house again, listening to some

blues dirge, I look out every window, waiting to feel sick. They say you're supposed to store people inside you, even when they're no longer there. Outside, the dark purplish houses and trees look like a stage set. A light goes on in Mr. Clayton's house and then off again, on again, off again as though he's sending my mother a signal from a lighthouse.

I carry the container back upstairs and stow it safely back on my bedside table, then go and stand over Gwen. She looks beautiful and calm and young. I tried to smother her once when I was thirteen. I could feel the individual feathers inside the pillow as I pressed it down on her face, the way the quills poked through, sticking my palms, as though there were chicken heads inside, trying to breathe.

I bend down and kiss her forehead. She stirs, sighing. I'm sure I hear her saying my name. I stay down there close, drinking in her innocent sleeping breath. Returning to my girlhood bed, I lie down and curl up on my side and stare into the dark. There's grit in my back teeth.

With my father's body inside me, why wouldn't I dream?

He's fishing at the edge of the ocean. I'm standing behind him watching, wanting to go up to him and hold his hand, but I'm scared he'll pull away. He doesn't like to be disturbed when he's fishing. I know this even in my sleep. I move closer, studying his hand, shoved half inside his jacket pocket. He keeps looking up at the tip of his fishing rod, and then out to sea.

Slowly, I raise my hand, the way you do when you want to kill a fly. Just as I'm hovering there, ready to slip my hand into his, he shoves his hand deeper into his pocket and pulls out a crumpled white handkerchief. Instead of a normal size, the handkerchief goes on and on, changing colors, flying out of his pocket. The wind whips it away and sends it coiling down the beach like a circus banner. I run after it.

When I come back, trailing it behind me as though it's a kite, he's pulled his hat low over his eyes. As soon as I hand him the handkerchief, it returns to normal size, becoming a dull white square again. I haven't done anything in particular. He returns it to his pocket, stuffing it down, still looking out at the water.

It's morning, and his ashes haven't killed me.

twenty-two

When we get up, there's no hot water. My mother says she can't scatter her husband's ashes with dirty hair. She puts one hand to her flattened curls and strokes them as though they're someone's pet. Her nails look like bright cranberries, leftovers from a party.

I tell her I'm going to keep the dress. "I'll wear it out dancing," I say, not wanting to tell her that it's wrinkled beyond repair, covered in white towel fuzz.

The three of us sit around the kitchen table, not sure what to do. Then my mother jumps up and starts bustling around the kitchen in a storm of activity. Out of the cupboards she pulls flour and oil and salt, a rolling pin. She gets down on her hands and knees, peers into a bottom cupboard, rummages around, and triumphantly holds up a heavy black skillet. Peering into it, she blows hard, dislodging a fine dust. "This is the pan your grandmother used to cook in," she says. "We'll fry bread, the way I used to when I was a girl."

"Mother," says Gwen, exasperated. "What does frying bread have to do with scattering Daddy's ashes?

"Nothing at all, darling," she says gaily.

"Why don't we go to the shop and I'll wash both of you," says Gwen. I like the way she says this, as though she's transformed a childhood game into something grown-up. Today she seems calm, removed.

Ignoring her, my mother hands me the pan, then clambers up off her knees. I go to help her—she's seventy, after all—but she's already upright, bustling around. "Your father never liked my Indian bread. He thought it was too greasy, bad for his stomach. That's why I never made it. Do you remember how we used to bake cakes together, Alice?"

Instantly, I'm back in the pantry with both doors closed, the swinging doors, one leading into the kitchen, the other into the dining room. I'm eleven. It's August and I'm wearing shorts. My mother is wearing a white slip, hurrying to finish so she can get dressed. She's having a ladies' tea. Both of us are sweating, drops beading on our foreheads and dripping into our eyes. My mother insists on keeping all doors and windows closed when she bakes. "Cakes will sink and dip in the middle with the slightest draft from the crack in a window," she says.

I'm sitting on the edge of the wooden counter, banging my heels against the drawers, hitting my heel bone every once in a while too hard, and stopping. My mother has just knocked the cake out of the pan and onto the tea towel, and is rolling it up with jam and chocolate-cream filling. I'm holding the bowl in my lap, gathering cream worms the length of my finger, and carefully transferring them whole onto my tongue.

Just as I'm wiping cream from my mouth with the back of my hand, my father pushes open the swinging door.

"We're baking," says my mother in a flat voice.

"I can see that," he says.

I hold out the bowl of cream. "Would you like some, Daddy?" I ask. He's eyeing the messy tracks in the bowl. I know for certain that he wants some, but I also know that he won't let himself. He stares at my mother's shoulder where the white strap of her slip crisscrosses the white strap of her bra. I know he wants to touch her skin there, even more than he wants a swipe of cream.

Abruptly he says, "Why don't you two get dressed?" and lets the door swing closed. It swings back and forth a few times, and my mother and I watch it. When it finally settles, she goes back to spreading the cakes, and I to making paths in the cream bowl, but something has happened. The giddiness is gone, and the cream tastes a little funny, the way milk does when it starts to turn sour.

Now she rolls up the sleeves of her bathrobe, measures flour and salt and oil into a mixing bowl, and plunges in her hands. Gwen and I stand and watch, mesmerized by their arthritic strength. She hasn't taken off her wedding ring. Did she put it in the pocket of her robe yesterday when she and Mr. Clayton were making love on the sofa? I didn't notice.

Finally she turns the mound out onto the table and starts kneading. As she works the dough, she's begins the story she's told so many times. How she cooked bread as a child in England with her Indian nursemaid, Tulsie. How she remembers standing in the kitchen in her underpants and watching her cook, her skin so brown against the white shirt with the white apron over it. My mother put her hand up to her face, so pale next to Tulsie's brown skin. They made paratha together. "I couldn't pronounce it. I called it parrot bread," my mother laughs. She cooked it in this same black frying pan. The fat would burst and spit and Tulsie would tell her to stand back. But she'd let her turn the bread. She lifted my mother, holding her around her waist like a sack of flour. Even though her hand was almost as small, she covered my mother's hand holding the spatula.

She would bring my mother a piece wrapped in a napkin when she had to take a nap. She sat on the edge of her bed and leaned down and kissed her and put the bread next to her pillow. My mother smelled it all through her nap.

"Sometimes when I'm just about to fall asleep, I still smell that bread. I open my eyes and I'm a child again, and I reach out to the table, but it's not there. Just a glass of water, and the alarm clock and maybe a book, and I feel so sad."

After the dough rises, my mother shows us how to roll it out into thin, layered triangles, which we fry on one side and then another until the surface is speckled and brown. The kitchen fills with a dense oily haze. The smoke alarm goes off and my mother laughs and climbs on a chair and pulls it off the wall, yanks out the battery. The pile of bread stays warm in the oven.

We sit around the kitchen table, each of us with one of my mother's good white linen wedding napkins folded at our place, a piece of bread tucked in the middle, seeping oil. We eat the bread slowly, tearing off pieces and wiping our fingers on the edge of our napkins.

"Isn't it delicious?" says our mother. "If only we had a glass of wine, but I guess it's too early."

Gwen and I both nod. We carefully don't look at each other.

Half an hour later, having unceremoniously rejoined her husband's ashes, my mother's shed her apron and is on her way out to Gwen's car holding the master container in front of her as though she's headed out for a potluck lunch. "We can't do the dishes with cold water, we might as well leave," she says over her shoulder. She sits in the front passenger seat, looking straight ahead, as though she's waiting to be taken to the zoo. We watch her from the kitchen window. Gwen rinses out our containers with cold water and Ivory soap, not wanting to leave them piled in the sink, soaking along with our oily bread plates.

Last night when we got home from the Glory Inn, we stood in a semicircle around the mantel for a while, admiring the gold cup she'd won. After Mr. Clayton had gone home, my mother, still wearing her dress, rolled up her sleeves, took out our three Tupperware containers, ready to put her husband back together again. We gathered around the kitchen table, discussing how we would scatter him.

"I want to walk along the beach and let him fall out of my pockets," my mother said.

"Do you remember that Guatemalan skirt you used to wear?" I asked. "Do you still have it? You need something like that, a big round skirt with deep pockets."

"I'm going to wade out as far as I can, at low tide, then release him into the ocean," said Gwen. "So he can swim with the fishes."

This is what I thought I'd wanted. To stand on shore, bring him behind my shoulder, cast him out into the crashing waves the way he used to cast out his line, not on the bay side, but on the stormy, wild coast side of the beach. Dare him to fly back in my face.

"I want to build a big driftwood fire," I said, "and let him go up in flames." I remember the smell of grilling fish.

"But he's already been cremated," said my mother. "I don't think you can burn someone twice."

I asked my mother if she would mind if we reunited the ashes in the morning. I didn't tell her that it felt too lonely, too final, to let my portion of him join the rest. I just told her I was tired.

"He never liked too much togetherness anyway," she said. And we all laughed.

I tell Gwen to go on out to the car and I'll join them in a minute. I have this urgent need to have the house to myself, to remember the way these rooms looked last night, blue and shadowy. In my father's study, I sit at his old desk and pick up the phone. As always, Jack answers on the first ring, barking his name.

"You don't have to bite my head off," I say.

"Alice," he says. He lets out a big breath and then repeats my name a few times, as though he's practicing a new language. "You're not picking up your messages."

"No."

"I've been worried about you."

"I'm safe in the bosom of my New England family."

"My point exactly. When are you coming home?"

I swivel back and forth in my father's chair the way I used to when I was a kid and he wasn't home, enjoying the give of my waist and hips, the silence.

"Home?"

"New York, your apartment, our dance classes, Herbert, me. By the way, Thea has a couple of big jobs coming up. She needs you desperately."

"*Our* dance classes?" I ask. I'm actually pleased that Thea has come to depend on me, but other things on his list interest me more.

"Actually, I had a private last night."

"A date or a class?"

"If you make fun of me, I won't show you what I learned. I signed up for tango. I know you think it's melodramatic, but I actually think it's the perfect dance for the depressive. That lugubrious music. The teacher thought I was quite good."

I try to imagine Jack sliding, with agile feet and noble head. Cool. I think about how he likes to sleep in an octopus weave, arms and legs tangled tightly enough to keep out the enemy. Maybe this is his dance and I don't even know it.

"I'll save a number for you," he says. "You do know that when you agree to dance with someone, they have power over you."

"Tonight," I say. "I can't wait."

I call my answering machine to pick up my messages. There are five from Jack, each one ending "I love you," intoned in a stern, embarrassed voice. I'd recently told him how my father had never said this to us. Obviously, Jack's trying hard to make up for lost time.

Thea's three messages become gradually more hysterical, the last one ending "Why the fuck aren't you back yet?"

Jack has called back immediately following our conversation to tell me he forgot to ask me to please bring over some rosemary from my window box when I get back tonight. He's making me a special dinner to celebrate my return, and rosemary is the one thing he forgot. I remember Thea's wedding bouquets and the bad-sex curse she'd lightheartedly wished on the poor couple and their guests. I decide that in combination with oil and garlic, rosemary is quite capable of rendering the exact opposite.

It seems like a dream. Leaning back in the chair again, I close my eyes and try to bring back my apartment. In my mind, I open the window and reach out with my scissors, dangerously, in the way I always do. Down below, taxis are gathered in a child's puzzle of color and noise. I drink this in. I cut the rosemary and pile it on the kitchen table. Herbert ambles over and sniffs at it, then leaps over the bag and onto the windowsill. He sticks his nose out, but just so far, his whiskers quivering. He likes a taste, but the world outside has never really tempted him all that much.

I open the freezer, and there it still is, next to the coffee, just where I left it, a Baggie holding a couple of tablespoons of white powder—like a minor cocaine deal. I plop it down next to the rosemary and let it sit in the sun to warm it up a little. Herbert continues to sit, a sphinx in the window, as I reach over his head and pinch by pinch sprinkle the contents of the Baggie around my herbs. Bonemeal, I know, is a primary ingredient in fine fertilizers. Some of the ashes land on the leaves, get caught in the branches of the rosemary, like snow on a fir tree. I gently shake most of the ashes off, then follow this with a good dousing of water. They fizzle for a moment, then seep into the ground, leaving a faint shadow in the soil.

Gwen moves around the salon, getting ready for us. She's put on a black smock that reminds me of my dress last night. Except that there are scissors sticking out of the pocket. My mother and I are sitting in chairs with big dryers attached, watching her.

My mother gets her hair washed first. She sits in one of the low, slope-backed chairs and Gwen helps her lean back, positioning her so that her neck fits right in the cutout of the shiny black sink.

As Gwen washes her hair, I watch my mother's hands in her lap. She's clutching her purse, a hankie twisted around two fingers. Gwen's hands make long soapy strokes on either side of my mother's head. My mother groans with pleasure.

Finally, Gwen squeezes the water from her hair, sits her up, one hand behind her head, the other placed on her middle, and wraps her head in a white towel, crisscrossing it snuggly on her forehead. I think of Gwen's swaddled head last night. She seems to have become more careful since she stopped drinking, the details taking exactly as long as they need to.

"Thank you, my darling," says my mother, patting her hand. "You're very good at that. I should come more often. I'll even tip you." She opens her bag.

Gwen rolls her eyes, goes to the front desk, and turns on the stereo. "You don't have to tip me. What kind of music do you want?"

"You think I'm too old?" she says. "Play anything. I would like a cup of tea, though."

It's embarrassing what the heart does when it hears certain bars of music. I've sometimes wondered whether my father ever had this pleasure: playing a song over and over and over again to hear one heart-stopping break that seems to contain the whole meaning of life and love and happiness in those few measures.

"You don't know what I had to take care of," says my mother. She sits up and straightens her smock. "What's wrong with asking for help?" This angry non sequitur seems a surprise, even to her.

"Didn't Daddy ever help you?" I ask.

"Of course he did," she says. She presses her temples.

"You have a hangover because you drink too much," says Gwen.

"And you don't have enough fun," my mother snaps.

Gwen looks surprised. "What's that?" she says.

Pushing her away, my mother continues. "Just because your father couldn't have fun doesn't mean you have to pay for the rest of your life." She pulls the towel out of Gwen's hand and slips it around her neck, holding the ends as though she's just finished ten rounds. "He just had something different."

"And what was that?" I ask.

"He just took life so hard." As an afterthought, "He loved you both, even if you didn't always know it."

That rare word *love* in our family invariably produces tears. For some reason, today no one's crying.

Gwen comes up close, tips the dryer back where I've been sitting, leans down and hugs me around the shoulders, sticking her face in my hair and breathing a big huff of air right on my part, the way you would on a baby's stomach. It reminds me of the night at the women's bar, except now her breath is sweet, with a faint morning tartness—safe.

"Your hair smells like the Glory Inn," she says. Then, "You're next," over her shoulder. And "By the way, Mom, Gabriel's my sponsor." The way she slips this in, I know she's been planning this casual delivery all morning.

"What does he sponsor?" asks my mother brightly.

"He sponsors Gwen—her not drinking, right?" I turn to Gwen and she's nodding at me as though this elementary explanation pleases her. "One day at a time," I say. "You've heard of that."

"It's how I've always lived," my mother says. Her voice is brisk. "Except that I do love to drink. Champagne. And wine. I even like Scotch sometimes." She pulls the dryer down over her head and signals Gwen to turn it on.

It's my turn. I move over to the washing chair, and Gwen stands over me, getting ready. She runs the water for a long time on her wrist, as though she's testing milk from a baby's bottle.

Finally she begins running it over my scalp. The temperature is so perfect, I hardly feel it. She digs in her fingertips. My arms resting on the chair break into goose bumps.

"Did Gabriel come in this week for a haircut?"

Gwen's fingers stop massaging for a split second and then continue automatically. I imagine the dirty suds sluicing down the drain.

"He's only come in once so far," she says. "A couple of weeks ago. I don't know how comfortable he is here. Too many women. Too much hair spray."

"I'm sorry," I say.

"For what?"

"Sometimes when you dance with somebody you feel closer than you really are, but it doesn't mean anything. And there's nothing else after that."

"That's not what I have with him. He helps me not drink, and that's it. He used to drink, too, you know."

"I can't imagine Gabriel drunk."

"The night Daddy died, Gabriel knew exactly what I was feeling. Being drunk at the wrong time, making a mistake like that, never being able to take it back."

"You cut off his ponytail."

"I know you thought I slept with him, but I didn't."

"It was the middle of the night."

"We talked for a long time while you were down in the basement, and then I asked if I could cut his hair."

She lets me sit up by myself and then stands in front of me and starts rubbing my head vigorously. From inside the safety of the towel I say, "What did you write on the window that night?" I stare down at her boots, waiting.

Again she pauses, then keeps rubbing. Her voice is light. "His name. I was wondering whether anyone had ever written his name anywhere."

I grab her around the waist and press my cheek against her

belt buckle. My brain tingles, reassembles. She strokes my hair for a second and then tips up my chin and pushes my bangs out of my eyes. "You need a cut," she says.

My mother comes out from under the dryer with her hair sticking up, giving her the startled, ageless look of a newborn bird. She's dancing around the salon to a throbbing country-Western ballad, still wearing her black smock and her white towel around her neck. She's stopping in front of every chair, using each one as a bulky, silent dance partner while she does some complicated footwork. Sam, who has been sleeping by the front door, jumps around her. She keeps pushing him away but doesn't seem to mind when he crowds back at her legs.

"I think I want to be auburn again," she says, stopping and touching her hair. "Stan and I want to try for the nationals."

Gwen and I both stare at her in the mirror. I suddenly feel so sad for both of my parents, the things they had to hide from each other.

"I used to have true auburn hair, before I got married," she continues. "Your father loved it. He said I had hair the color of a fox and eyes speckled like a trout's belly. He was good at nature compliments. It was just everything else." She sits down in one of the chairs and leans forward toward the table of supplies, her robe gaping. I remember the way she looked when Gwen and I walked in on her with Mr. Clayton, and wonder how soon it will happen again. Tonight?

She selects a can of mousse and squirts a big handful as though it's whipped cream.

"Let me do that." I scoop the mousse from her hand (I remember filling the jelly roll with whipped cream mixed with strawberry jam, our hands side by side, her big ones, my small ones, rolling, in summer, her sweat dropping down into the cream). I rub the mousse through her hair. By the time I'm finished, she looks like she belongs on the back of someone's motorcycle.

"Maybe I'll become a blonde," I say.

"Your father didn't know how to try new things," my mother says. "Before we got married, I thought I could change him. I thought I'd teach him how to dance, and he'd be happy. You always think that, and it's a mistake." She goes over to the sound system and pats the container of ashes that Gwen has placed in the space between it and a display of hair products. "If only he could have had a glass of wine once in a while."

She starts fiddling with the tuner. I can tell Gwen is about to say something about not needing a drink to be free, but she stops herself.

"But why couldn't you make each other happy?" I ask.

"I probably should have married Rafe," my mother says. "He was such a good dancer. But he didn't really love me enough. Sometimes two people just don't know how."

"Why don't you teach me how to waltz?" I say, changing the subject abruptly.

"No, why don't you teach me how to do what you do," my mother says. "I want to learn something modern. Isn't this what you like?" Wiggling her hips, snapping her fingers, humming, she turns to me. "Dance with your mother," she commands.

I hold out my arms, and with two graceful steps, as though she's about to enter her dance competition, she steps into them. Under my chin, her hair smells wet and loamy as newly turned ground. She used to be taller than me. I suddenly imagine dancing with her in strange places, a bar in Texas, a revolving lounge up in the sky. She places her left hand on my shoulder, the right one in my left palm. With two fingers, I curve around her dry, freckled hand. Gazing out over my shoulder, she lifts her chin. We cock our heads toward the music, listening for the starting count. I take a deep breath and let it out slowly, the way dancers are supposed to. Miraculously, my mother and I are ready at exactly the same moment.

acknowledgments

With heartfelt thanks to all the great and patient friends who read and commented and persevered with me through this project. With special thanks to Anne Hosansky, Robert Fagan, Carol Emshwiller, Anne Sandor, Lois Nachamie, Bonnie Altucher, Danny O'Neil, Virginia Dunwell, Vanessa Campbell, Joe Harris, Renée Gillis, Hazel Hankin, Rhea Ruggiero, Melanie Wellner, Leigh Wood and, as always, my sister Carolyn.

about the author

Joanna Torrey's short fiction collection, *Hungry,* consisting of a novella and six stories, was published by Crown in 1998. Her stories have appeared in anthologies published by The Crossing Press and Serpent's Tail. She lives in Brooklyn, New York, where she teaches in the creative writing program at Brooklyn College.